MW01287395

THE LAST MAN IN PARADISE

Also by Syed M. Masood:

The Bad Muslim Discount
More Than Just a Pretty Face
Sway With Me

THE LAST MAN IN PARADISE

SYED M. MASOOD

This book is a work of fiction. Names, characters, places, and incidents are the product of the author's imagination or are used fictitiously. Any resemblance to actual events, locales, or persons, living or dead, is coincidental.

Published by 8th Note Press
Text Copyright © 2024 by Syed M. Masood
First paperback edition published 2025
All rights reserved.

ISBN: 978-1-961795-42-6

No part of this book may be reproduced, scanned, or distributed in any printed or electronic form without permission from the publisher.

Cover design by Lindy Kasler

THE LAST MAN IN PARADISE

Chapter One

2011

The taste of forbidden apples changed my life.

No, I am not Adam and I am not Eve. None of this happened at the dawn of time, and I was not then—nor am I ever likely to be—in the Garden.

The scene was a dark car park behind a dilapidated office building in Redding, California, which is not at all my idea of Paradise, though at that moment it did feel a little like heaven must.

Because I wasn't alone there, in that deepening night, a few feet away from where my father—Imam Saqlain Saifi—was holding an interfaith outreach event. The town didn't have a mosque, so he was forced to rent a unit in a business complex to fill that role, always hoping to one day raise the funds necessary to build a proper place of worship for his flock.

But I wasn't thinking about him or his religion just then. Perhaps I should've been. It might have made me more prudent, and maybe the course of my life would've been different.

Well, it's no use talking about roads not taken.

Let's talk instead about what form my dreaming always takes.

Let's talk about them apples.

I was with Madison Porter, which wasn't unusual. We spent most of our days in each other's company. We had since we'd been thrown together by our school's drama class in the ninth grade, four years ago, when she'd been cast as Juliet and I as Romeo.

We were rarely together at night. Her godparents—who'd unexpectedly become her foster parents last year—liked having her home before sunset.

The novelty of being with her in the moonlight was not what made that moment special.

It was special because of what we were doing.

We were kissing, sort of for the very first time, because all our kisses before had been fake, staged for the benefit of other people. These were just for us, and they were so real and surreal. They were also increasingly French and involved a sour lip gloss, the flavor and smell of which called to mind the cause of the Fall.

We'd snuck out of my father's event because it was unbearably, if predictably, boring. Leaning against her car, where we could barely hear the droning religious speeches being delivered inside, I'd asked her, "So what do you want to do?"

Madi had turned to face me, stood on her tiptoes, grabbed the front of my T-shirt, and pulled my mouth down to hers.

Just like that the die had been cast.

To those who would judge me for being simultaneously Muslim, in the shadow of a mosque, and in a frenzied make-out session with a girl, all I can say is that I was not the one who cast it.

That isn't to say I wouldn't have, if I'd dared risk our friendship. I had been in love with Mads for a while by then, and I knew she liked me too. I'd just always been scared to ask her how much because I'd been afraid she'd say not enough. In retrospect, it's possible I may have failed to pick up on a hint or two about the nature of our relationship.

When I finally broke away from her, she was pressed up against me and pinned against the passenger-side door, flushed, a little out of breath, one of my hands in her short, straight hair, somehow black and shining at the same time, the other at the small of her back. I could feel heat radiating through the soft, thin fabric of her top.

She was prettier, in my opinion, than everything and everyone, with these amazing blue-gray eyes that were like . . . like . . . well, I don't know. Like the sky prophesizing the coming of a mighty storm, maybe?

That sounds stupid.

That's what they were though, eyes that could make a man stupid, a condition to which I—being just a seventeen-year-old boy then—was naturally inclined.

Madison put a hand on my chest and looked up at me, biting her lower lip, a gesture that always drove me to distraction. In a quiet, uncertain voice she said, "Say something."

I cleared my throat. "This is . . . it's the best interfaith outreach I've ever been part of."

Madi laughed.

"As for kissing you, that was a lot fruitier than I imagined it'd be."

She raised her eyebrows. "So, kissing me is something you've thought about?"

"Yeah." I ran a thumb over her clavicle. "Kind of a lot."

"What were you waiting for?"

"You."

She smiled and looked away. "Sorry about the apple lip gloss. I'm, like, addicted to it or something."

"It's okay. I liked it."

"Yeah?"

"I mean, I think so. I'd have to try it again to be sure."

She shook her head but obliged, and our lips met again.

It was delicious.

Until it wasn't.

Until my name, in my father's deep, booming voice, echoed around us like a dangerous, shallow quake close to the surface of the earth.

"Azaan!"

I jumped away from Madison and spun around and saw my father storming toward us, and the look on his hard, lined, awfully familiar face made it clear that my existence was at an end.

He hit me.

I'm not sure when that started, the hitting, I mean. I realize not everything has a beginning that can be identified, that some things just are, like the sky and the sea. But in this case, there had to have been a first time. I don't remember it, which is strange. You'd think it was the kind of thing that'd leave a mark.

Mom told me once that the reason my father beat me was his father. I was just experiencing the aftershocks of something that had happened already, in another place, in other lives to which I happened to be connected.

It was a grand inheritance.

It seemed like a strange thing that this man whose name I didn't even know—everyone just called him Baba—could have such a profound effect on my life.

I'd met Baba only once, when I was nine and we visited Pakistan. Even back then, it had been clear that Dad had very little regard for him and vice versa. Their exchanges had been formal and cold—well, my father was always cold, but on that trip what freezings I felt, to borrow a phrase from the Bard.

Years later, my mother explained that Baba was someone who liked to break things. Growing up, my father had watched him break promises, hearts, contracts, vows, laws, and bones. The man was a grifter, a scoundrel, a hustler, a liar, a lecher, a cheat, and an alcoholic haunted by demons and, worse, by creditors.

He had driven Saqlain Saifi to religion by being the exact opposite of what a decent Muslim ought to be, and he'd seen his son's choice of profession as the personal rebuke that it absolutely was.

This was apparently why my father was so hard on me. He was determined to make sure no part of Baba would live on in my person. He would whip it out of me if he had to, and he'd decided, some time ago, that he did indeed have to.

It was, in my mom's opinion, proof that he loved me, in his way. He was doing it for my own good. He wouldn't bother if he did not care.

Besides, I gave him plenty of cause.

Life would have hurt less if I had prayed five times a day, eaten only halal food, kept my distance from Madison, and stayed away from drink and drugs—not anything serious, mind you. I'd tried pot a couple of times, which was really my parents' fault for raising me in California.

Islam shouldn't have been difficult. It didn't appear to be for other people. Some of the boys around my age were really into it. They fasted and shunned parties and averted their gazes when they saw women. Some of them had even sworn off music. They didn't seem to feel deprived or constrained or suffocated by any of it. Instead, they appeared happy and rather pleased with themselves.

If they could do it, there was no logical reason I couldn't.

And yet, inexplicably, I couldn't.

My father said that this was because the devil assigned to tempt my soul was strong and had to be broken. The fact that he hadn't managed it yet hadn't dented his determination to try, and on that night, I had for sure given him a reason to try again. By flouting the rules of his religion publicly and kissing Madi in sight, if only accidentally, of his congregants, I had crossed a line that I'd never crossed before.

As a result, he did something he hadn't ever done before either. Every action has an equal and opposite reaction, don't you know. It's a basic tenet of Newtonian parenting.

He struck me right there, in front of other people.

It shouldn't have been as bad as usual. There were no sticks or coat hangers or belts. It was just slap after slap after slap. But they were vicious blows, and it occurred to me that almost always, in the past, Saqlain Saifi had been holding back.

Madison shrieked. A couple of people shouted, protesting, and then finally, as I staggered back, Tiger Uncle, my father's best friend, ran to pull him away from me.

I shook my head and blinked tears away. My face stung, my ears were hot, my world unsteady. Instinctively, I wiped at my nose with the back of my hand, and it came away with streaks of blood on it.

There wasn't a lot. Nothing was broken. The skin around my nostrils had ruptured. I was fine. I would heal.

Mads started to step closer to me, but my father yelled out, "Stay away from him."

So she did.

I was glad. I didn't want her to see my face. I hated that she was witnessing my humiliation in the presence of all these people. Being punished in front of her was somehow worse than the worst I'd endured before.

My father looked like he was going to try to push past Tiger and strike me again. He didn't. He just spoke. "And you, Azaan, you will never see her again. Do you understand?"

That would have been a good time to say yes.

Unfortunately, I had a bad habit of speaking the truth.

"I'll see her whenever I want."

I saw my father's fists close, but Tiger whispered something to him, after which he snarled, stared me down, turned, and left.

Tiger Uncle started to follow him, then hesitated, looked back at me, and asked, "Are you okay?"

I nodded.

He considered this for a moment and seemed not to believe it. "Go inside. I will be there in a moment to take a look at you."

"I'm good," I protested.

"Just listen, Jaaneman? Let me talk to Saqi and call your mother."

"She won't care," I told him.

Tiger Uncle grimaced. "You're probably right about that."

Tiger Heart—who had been born Sher Dil and had, at some point, decided to translate his name into English—brought a glass of water to the so-called mosque's administrative office, where I was waiting for him.

It was a small space, little more than a supply closet my father had squeezed a desk and a couple of chairs into, and Tiger's presence in it was instantly overwhelming. His cologne was heavy on musk, and he'd put on a reckless amount of it. He was a lot visually too, with his trademark drooping mustache, garish yellow sateen shirt, tight-fitting pants, and mottled snakeskin shoes. All of it together would have been enough to give me a headache if I didn't already have one.

He watched me take a sip, then said, "I spoke to your mother."

"Yeah?"

"She wanted to know if you needed medical attention. I told her you didn't, so she's—"

"Staying at the hospital," I guessed.

"Both your parents are very dedicated to their professions."

"Yeah."

He folded his arms across his chest. "What are you dedicated to?"

I frowned. "Sorry?"

"Bhai, I'm asking, what are your goals? What are your plans? I heard from your father that you have some crazy dreams, that you want to become an actor. Hollywood. Bollywood. Lollywood. Tollywood. All these names tell you that it's a line in which there's a high chance of getting shafted, no?"

Not sure what to say or why he was suddenly playing at being a career counselor, I just shrugged.

Tiger studied me. "You're good looking enough. Almost as good looking as me. I could have been a star, you know."

"Uh . . . sure, I guess."

"I didn't want fame, though. Do you know what I wanted more than anything? Women. And you know what I got? Tell me, Sitamgar, do you know my story? You must know the legend."

I did.

Much of the local Muslim community, especially its female population, didn't like Tiger Heart much. They spoke disapprovingly about the failed lawyer turned entrepreneur who lived in their midst. They looked down upon his personal life.

Specifically, they didn't appreciate how many times he'd been married.

Muslim men are allowed four wives at a time, not four wives in total. In other words, it is theoretically possible for them to have as many weddings—and wedding nights—as they want, so long as they divorce one of their spouses before they acquire a new one.

This isn't usually practical. Convincing people to marry you isn't an easy task, even in the best of circumstances, and there is a pervasive stigma against the old, fading practice of polygamy.

American law poses a challenge as well. Not only does it forbid multiple marriages, it also demands expensive court proceedings. It's not like the Sharia. You can't just say, "I divorce you" three times and move on. Legal fees and spousal support make being a forever groom a financially crippling prospect.

Despite all this, Tiger Uncle had tied around twelve knots in his life and he'd undone them all. He'd managed this by being a good capitalist and seeking market efficiencies, which he'd found offshore.

Not only is divorce quicker and easier in some Muslim

countries, but women aren't entitled to alimony. Instead, they get mehr, a sum of money agreed to by both parties at the inception of a wedding contract. It is owed to the bride whether the relationship lasts or not. It's a system Tiger Uncle could exploit given the strength of the dollar.

Many thought that what he did was little more than greenwashed sex tourism. They felt he was making a mockery of a sacred institution and treating marriage as little more than prostitution as his nuptials often involved young women from poor, sometimes desperate, backgrounds who couldn't afford to turn down the mehr he offered.

Even so, Tiger Uncle remained a prominent figure in the community because of his wealth and his willingness to share it. The mosque, such as it was, ran primarily on his contributions.

"I got everything I wanted," he said, "but no one has ever seen me violate God's law."

"What does that have to do with me?"

"You should learn from my example, Shareek-e-Ghum. Do whatever you want but find a way to justify your actions. And if you can't, then at least hide them. Like tonight. You got your hooks into a beautiful girl. Very good. But why make a public show of kissing her? When it comes to sins, you should be like a cat. Because a cat, after taking a shit, buries it. It doesn't leave its business out in the open like a dog. Muslims, you know, many of us, we don't like dogs very much."

"You want me to—"

"Be cunning," Tiger Uncle urged. "Show a little discretion. You want to be an actor? Make your life a role you play. Pretend to be one of the pious. It'll make everyone happy. Then, when no one is looking, enjoy life."

I frowned. "You're saying I should lie?"

"What's wrong with that? Listen, your father says you have only one good quality. You don't speak false. Why is that? Don't you realize that honesty is the worst virtue? Let me give you an example. Tell me, what happens when your father asks you if you prayed?"

"I tell him I didn't," I said.

"And then he yells and screams and punishes you. What are you really paying the price for? For not doing what you're supposed to do or for not pretending that you might? Telling the truth is the hardest thing in the world. You keep doing it and you keep wondering why your life is difficult. Just stop. Deception makes living easier. Try it. You'll see."

"It just . . . doesn't feel right."

"How does getting beat feel?" Tiger Uncle countered. "Do you know what your father said to me as he was leaving? He said he's done with you. You're out of the house."

"What?!"

"Yes. You're on your own. You can sleep on the street as far as he's concerned. That's what being honest has gotten you. You're homeless and, to be frank, you have no viable plan to make money. Okay. Calm down, calm down. Breathe. I have come up with a scheme. It requires a few . . . misdirections, but it will work. I'll fix everything for you. Trust me. Put your life in my hands and nothing will go wrong."

Chapter Two

2022

"I really don't want to be a terrorist," I said, giving voice to what ought to have been an entirely unobjectionable thought but which somehow wasn't. It's impossible to get people to agree on anything these days.

"Come on, Azaan. It's a great opportunity. This could be your chance to blow up. Look, I know you have moral objections, but if you don't do it, someone else will. There's no shortage of willing and able Muslim lads around, is there?"

All of that was true. However, being just another brown guy with a bomb strapped to his chest wasn't the career I'd imagined for myself when I'd dreamt of becoming an actor. If I auditioned for this role, as my friend, landlord, and agent, Brayden Hall, was trying to convince me to, I'd be walking a path I'd never wanted to tread.

On the other hand, I was already almost thirty and hadn't landed any significant work in film. This was a chance to try out for a big budget action flick with glitzy, hot stars. It'd capture eyes. It was possible that some of those would land on me, even if I were just a mindless henchman with only a few lines and limited screen time.

Maybe I was past the age when I got to choose what road I took. Maybe all that was left was doing what I had to do, serving the dictates of necessity, which may or may not be the mother of invention but is most definitely a bitch.

"The iron's hot," Brayden said. "Everyone's talking about how bloody brilliant you were as Mercutio at Regent's Park. You can't afford to pass on this."

There was no need for him to tell me that. I knew my financial situation was grim. We were, at that moment, in my "room," which was just the living area of the small, run-down apartment I shared with five other people, all fellow thespians with Brayden's talent agency. It was the opposite of luxury and yet, in typical London fashion, it still wasn't cheap.

Brayden wasn't exactly set himself. He'd left his draconian father's big-time talent agency to strike out on his own, taking some low-level, neglected clients like me with him. The results, so far, had been mostly terrible.

"And honestly," he went on, following me into the kitchen as I went to get my morning coffee, "I don't get why it bothers you so much. So the script makes Islam look . . . not great. But why do you care? You don't even practice."

"It doesn't offend me as a Muslim. It offends me as an artist. It's just so . . . cliché, you know?"

"Are you an artist if no one ever sees your work?"

I paused in the act of reaching for a mug, trying to think of a good response to that, but I couldn't come up with one.

Brayden leapt on my hesitation. "Aha. I win. You're going. Sonya will go with you."

"Really?" Sonya, one of my flatmates, was a sweet girl, always willing to inconvenience herself to help people. Even so, having her chaperone me to make sure I did what I was told seemed like a colossal waste of her time. "She doesn't have anything better to do?"

"She's trying out too. It took a lot less convincing to get her on board, by the way."

"I thought the call was for male actors."

"I had words with the casting director and told them they needed to be more inclusive. There is no reason Muslim women can't be terrorists too, is there?"

I took out my French press and put water on to boil. "I guess not."

"Don't be a wet blanket for Sonya, okay? She's very excited to do this. Wouldn't shut up about the importance of representation and all that."

"Really?" I asked.

"It was something about how little brown girls need to see themselves on screen more so they'll know they can be anything they want to be when they grow up. I kind of tuned her out, to be honest. Just hold your tongue, will you?"

"Fine."

"What are you doing, by the way?"

I blinked. "Talking to you."

"No. I mean, your breakfast. Don't drink coffee on an empty stomach. It's not good for you."

"I do this every day."

Brayden frowned. "That's worse. Is this part of that whole one-meal-a-day thing? I can't believe you're still doing that. It's been . . . what? Like two years? It's not healthy."

"Of course it isn't healthy. It's show business."

"Look, mate, I get that you've got to stay fit, but you don't have to starve yourself. Don't shake your head at me. I'm saying this for your own good."

"Could you sound more like my parents?"

"As if you know what they sound like," he said.

I raised my eyebrows.

Brayden held up his hands. "Sorry. That's a yellow card for me. It's just . . . unfair that I have to have dinner with my family every week, while you haven't talked to yours in years."

That wasn't true. I called my mother every other month or so, and recently she'd started reaching out too.

As for my father . . . well, Imam Saifi and I did not speak often, though we did speak routinely.

Every year, I rang him on his birthday, and he sometimes remembered to wish me on mine. We also felt compelled to check in with each other on both Eids. I'm not sure why. It just seemed like the thing to do. Humanity appeared to have reached a consensus–regardless of religion, race, culture, or creed–that we were obligated to ruin at least some portion of our holidays by spending them with our families. Given that all of us agree on so little, it felt churlish not to honor this collective commitment our species had made to be miserable.

"When was the last time you even saw them?" Brayden asked.

"Eleven years ago."

"Lucky bastard."

I chuckled.

"I'm seeing mine tomorrow. It's going to be hours of my father taking shots at our agency and hinting that I'd be better off just giving up."

"Sounds awful."

"Always is," Brayden told me. "It would be nice to be able to tell him either you or Sonya got a gig. So will you please, for the love of God, break a leg?"

Sonya Barelvi was cute, fond of pink, Ray-Bans, and loud music. She was the Energizer Bunny brought to life—happy, irrepressible, and inexhaustible. I liked her very much in tiny doses and had lived under the same roof as her for two years.

As a result, I often found myself seeking to escape her presence, mostly because of her inability to be still or silent for more than five minutes at a time.

Despite this, I'd gotten to know her pretty well. We were kindred spirits in that we were both Muslims in name only. We wouldn't have gotten along otherwise. My upbringing had left me with an aversion for devout people.

I was more than a little surprised, therefore, when she emerged from her room that day wearing a hijab. She blushed when I did a double take and looked everywhere but at me.

It seemed improbable that she'd found God overnight, so she was wearing the headscarf as a costume, her interpretation —or Brayden's—of the look that was most likely to land her this role, which was mildly awful.

I thought about what to say, then decided to let it go and asked, "Ready to go?"

"Yup. Not sure why I'm bothering, though. You're going to land this. You were born to do it."

"I was born to play a terrorist?"

"I was there when Brayden was talking to the casting director. He told them that you've got the background for it, that your dad is a crazy-strict fundamentalist imam who forced you to attend some jihadi madrassa and you ran away and made your way to freedom. Azaan, that's such a wild story. How come you never told me?"

"It wasn't as dramatic as all that," I said, which was true.

When I'd been kicked out of the house at seventeen, Tiger Uncle had intervened. He had brokered a deal between me and my parents. My father agreed not to throw me out immediately or cut me off financially. In exchange, I promised to clean up my act and dedicate myself to Islam. I pledged that I would abandon all dreams of being something as useless as a creative and, instead, apply to Al-Azhar University in Egypt to follow in my father's footsteps and become a holy man.

It was the perfect solution. My father could be sure I'd stay on the straight and narrow while still being rid of me. I, on the other hand, got the chance to escape him and live my life.

I had flown to Cairo, but I'd gotten on the next plane out to London without ever seeing the city. Tiger's plan was never for me to follow through on my oaths. It was to give my family the illusion that I was still under their control.

He'd been right. Lying does make life easier.

At least as easy as it could get for an aspiring young actor of limited means in one of the most expensive cities in the world. Luckily, I'd had the funds that were supposed to be my tuition to help me get started.

As far as my parents knew, I'd graduated from a prestigious institution that had been around since 975 CE and was employed now as an imam by a small mosque in Dover.

Tiger Uncle had made my world my stage.

"Whatever. I know you. You keep everything buried. I swear that if anything like that had happened to me, I wouldn't shut up about it."

"I know."

"Seriously. I'd tell everyone willing to listen. I'd, like, write a book about it."

I smiled. "Yeah, well, no one is writing a book about my life. Come on. We don't want to be late."

The room where the audition was being held—a brightly lit, slightly cold, generic office—was full of desi and Arab actors. Sonya and I knew some of them. We'd congregated like this before, in other places, crossing our fingers together, but only for ourselves.

No one seemed interested in exchanging pleasantries or engaging in small talk. Whether that was because the stakes were high, due to this being a big budget production, or because they also had reservations about portraying yet another Muslim villain on the silver screen was impossible to say.

Even Sonya went quiet for around ten minutes, which was probably a personal record for her. Eventually, however, she broke the silence by asking, "Do you have anything else lined up?"

"Maybe. Tim Atherton is trying to put a production of *Arms and the Man* together. He said he wants me to play Sergius."

"What is that?" Sonya asked. "A Bernard Shaw play?"

"Yeah."

"It's a comedy, right? You don't go in much for those, do you? Which is . . ."

She fell silent when my cell buzzed in my pocket. With a quick, murmured apology, I pulled it out, saw the caller ID, and said, "Shit."

"What is it?"

"Bad news," I told her.

My father was calling.

"I have to take this." I got to my feet. "If they ask for me, tell them I stepped out to deal with a family emergency."

"Is everything all right?"

"Probably not."

With that, I rose, hurried out of the waiting room, and answered the phone.

"What's going on, Dad?"

"Wa'alaykum salam."

I rolled my eyes, something I almost never did when I wasn't in contact with the people who had pushed me—kicking and screaming—into this darkening world. But I gave him what he wanted. "As-salamu alaykum."

"Better."

"So who died?"

It was meant to be a joke, of course, but my father's reply was serious. "Baba."

I winced.

"He is not gone yet. But his doctors say there isn't much time."

I didn't know what to say. In some ways, it was like hearing a stranger was about to pass. I'd never gotten to know my grandfather. At the same time, however, it seemed like a significant event, given how Baba's relationship with his son had shaped my relationship with my father.

"I'm . . ." I threw my free hand up, abandoning my search for the right words. "I'm sorry, Dad."

"It is Allah's will. Every soul has to taste death."

"Yeah."

There was a short silence, then my father said, "He wants you to come home."

"Baba wants me to go to Pakistan?"

"No. He's here. He says—"

"Wait. Baba is in California?" I asked.

"I flew him over a few years ago so I could take care of him."

"You didn't tell me."

"Did you need to know?" Imam Saifi asked.

"I guess not. But why? I mean, given . . . everything."

"Because he wouldn't do it for me."

I scratched the back of my head. Mercy motivated by spite. I hadn't known that existed.

"Anyway, I'm calling because he wanted me to. He says he wants to see you. It's his last wish."

"But—"

"I know it's silly," my father cut in.

"Right? I mean, he doesn't even know me."

"He is being emotional," Dad said. "The shadow of death makes people who aren't ready to face it lose their minds a little."

"Is anyone ever really ready to face it?"

"I hope to be."

"Okay. Well . . ." The door behind me opened and Sonya poked her head out, gesturing for me to make my way back in. "I've got to go. I'll think about it."

"He doesn't have long."

"I'll let you know," I promised.

"Azaan . . . you should come if you can. It would not be such a bad thing to see your face again."

That was the closest thing to a hug I had gotten from my father since I'd been seven.

I let out a deep breath. It limped out of me, struggling to escape my chest, like it was tripping over the Gordian knot there I hadn't ever attempted to untangle. "Yeah," I managed to say. "All right. I'll see what I can do."

I've never been able to properly explain that knot to anyone. It lives just below where my ribs meet. I know it isn't a real, tangible thing, but it feels like it sits inside me like a stone, like the black meteorite that is set into the wall of the Great Mosque in Mecca. I know others have it too. I've read about the tightening people have in their breast when they're experiencing grief or loss or shock.

But for me it's like it's always there, though sometimes it is so light that I almost forget about it. Other times it's incredibly heavy, a mass of roiling emotions seeking to break out of me.

I asked my mother about it once, and she had one of her colleagues, a cardiologist, run all kinds of tests on me. They came back negative. There is nothing wrong with my heart.

The problem lies elsewhere.

The brain stem, according to Mom, controls emotions, and there is something in it—the anterior cingulate cortex—that becomes active under stress. This agitates the vagus nerve, which is connected to the chest, causing a physical manifestation of what we are feeling there.

Her theory is that either this part of me is more sensitive and active than usual or that I'm imagining the whole thing. Either way, it's all in my head.

Every girlfriend I've ever had has complained about it. They say I'm closed off and stoic to a fault. They believe they never really get to know me because I can't express how I feel.

Sooner or later, they all want me to touch the knot.

That's when all of my relationships end.

I can't do it.

Well, that's not true.

I can. I just don't like to.

It's mostly made up of pain, I think, because when I probe it, my chest constricts and it becomes difficult to breathe and my eyes well up and I feel that I'll start crying. I'm afraid that if I start, I won't ever be able to stop. It is easier to leave it alone.

It's growing, though. It's getting more complex, more layered as I get older. I hope that will change, that it won't continue to accumulate power, but I fear that it will.

It was worse than ever then, standing in that hallway, after speaking to my dad.

I had to take a few moments to stay still, inhale, hold air within me, then exhale, like Atlas adjusting to the weight of the world after lifting it for the first time.

I was lucky I was about to act. That would help ease the knot a little. Because even if, according to all the reviews that were in, it made me a terrible romantic partner, it also made me a gifted dramatic actor. I could reach for the knot when I needed to channel anxiety, sorrow, grief, or pain. Doing so hurt less when I was pretending to be someone else. It never seemed like I would unravel on camera or on stage.

Ultimately, I don't really understand it myself. I do know that Sonya was right, though. I don't go in much for comedies.

"You're sure you're okay?" Sonya asked for what was, by my count, the third time. We were in the Tube, barreling through the belly of the earth, past Headstone Lane Station, and we hadn't been able to find seats next to each other. She was across from me and having to raise her voice a little to be heard.

The devil sat on her right, the recently deceased Queen Elizabeth on her left. Neither one of them seemed particularly interested in my well-being.

Did I mention it was Halloween?

I was next to a nurse—a real one—who looked like she hadn't slept in a long while and a distraught older gentleman in a business suit carrying a heavy, overstuffed legal file in his lap. They studied me a little warily, probably wondering whether Sonya's question was about my physical or mental health.

The world was recovering from a global pandemic. There was no such thing as a mild cold or a harmless cough anymore. Every minor ailment was regarded with caution and suspicion, and no one wanted to be anywhere near someone under the weather.

"I'm fine," I called back.

"Are you sure? You've been super quiet. Did the audition not go well?"

My neighbors both relaxed a little.

"It was great," I told her.

"I'm sure it was. You're brilliant."

"I hope you get it, though."

"No," Sonya said. "I hope you do."

She was lying and so was I, mostly, which was fine. It was the convention in these circumstances.

My cell rang again. I looked at it, hoping it wasn't my father.

It was Tiger Uncle instead. I got to my feet.

"What's going on?" Sonya asked.

"I'm going to get off."

"This isn't our stop," she pointed out.

"I've got something I have to do. I'll see you at home."

Her eyes found the phone in my hand. The incoming call was visible on the screen. "I hope things are okay."

"Yeah. Thanks."

"Brayden is going to want to know what happened. I'll tell him it went well, yeah?"

"Sure. Tell him I was the bomb."

"Hello? Azaan Beta? Can you hear me?" Tiger Uncle screamed over a clear line. I'd learned quickly after leaving the States that he had little faith in the remarkable technology that allowed people to communicate through the ether, over oceans and continents, and which we all now took for granted.

When making international calls, Tiger Heart thought he absolutely had to shout to be heard, as if his voice was what was doing the heavy lifting. I'd told him often that he could speak normally, but he kept yelling throughout our conversations. Apparently, this was something they'd had to do when he was young. It was a habit he could not shake.

"I hear you just fine."

"Good. Good. How are you, Gul-e-Chaman?"

"I'm fine, Uncle. What about—"

"Your father called you?" he asked.

"Yeah. I spoke to him earlier. He wants me to come home."

"You should. That's why I'm calling. To tell you that I think it's a good idea."

"To see my grandfather? I—"

"Forget about that Baba of yours. It would do Saqi good to have you around."

I snorted.

"I know you and your father have had your differences, but you are needed here now."

"Why?"

Instead of answering, Tiger asked questions of his own. "Haven't I always been on your side? I did what I could to help you, no?"

"Yeah. And I'm—"

"Do you remember what I asked you to do all those years ago when you had no place to go?"

"You said to trust you."

"I am saying the same thing again. Saqi is in a bad place. It will do him good to have you here. It will do you good too, I think. Look, I've already wired you money for a ticket. You might as well book a flight."

I frowned as the first droplets of a light drizzle started giving me cold kisses. "You didn't have to do that."

"It is only money," he said, giving voice to a sentiment I'd never had the luxury to have in my life. "Use it, don't use it, that is up to you."

"What's this about? Is Dad sick too?"

"Saqlain's health is fine. You don't worry about that. The issue is . . . other things are happening."

I looked around for shelter just in case the rain picked up. I didn't have an umbrella with me. It had been overcast when we'd left, but Sonya had said that the threat of rain wouldn't materialize. There was supposed to be sunlight later. The clouds were supposed to clear. That wasn't happening. One never knows with such things, even if everyone speaks of them with confidence, relaying information they've read on websites or heard on the news.

To Tiger, I said, "What things?"

It took a moment, but eventually he answered, "As you know, Saqi's dream mosque is nearing completion."

"That's a good thing, right?"

"Haan. But some problems are arising with it. There's been a bit of vandalism."

I blinked. "Really?"

"Minor things, nothing to worry about too much, but you know how worked up Saqi gets. It's just a few broken windows and lights, things like that. The newspaper here thinks it's skinheads, which makes sense."

"Yeah."

"The bigger issue is that the community has elected a board of directors to run the new facility. The treasurer who is in charge now says some of the money donated to the project is missing. He wants answers. Saqi is under a lot of stress."

"What do you mean there are funds missing? Where'd they go?"

"I am sure it is just an accounting error, beta," he told me. "The investigation is in its early stages still—"

Spotting a bus stop nearby, I made my way toward it. "There's an investigation? As in, they're accusing Dad of doing something wrong? He would never—"

"Relax. So far it is only one guy with a splinter in his bum. We don't even know how much is unaccounted for yet. It is probably not much. But, again, you know your father. He is worried about what people will say if this gets out, how it will impact his image and that of the mosque. Making one headline is quite enough for him."

"Right."

"So come make it easy, okay?" he said. "He is proud of his mosque. He would like it if you were there when it opens. More important, he is proud of you."

I laughed, ducking under the plastic ceiling of the bus stop just as the heavens began to open up in earnest.

"He is. Saqi always tells people about how he snatched you away from the devil's grip. He'll enjoy parading you around. It will be a nice distraction for him."

"I've got better things to do with my time than be his show pony, Uncle."

"Acha. Fine. Listen, I don't want to argue anymore, Pardesiya. Don't come back for him. Come back as a favor to me. You owe me."

I sighed. I did. That was undeniable.

Tiger didn't wait for me to respond, or maybe he just took my silence for assent. "Then I will see you soon, okay? Have a good flight."

Chapter Three

2005

My father laughed as we ran through the rain. He was carrying a cardboard box with a few umbrellas in it, and I had a backpack in my arms. I was grinning too. At eleven years old, I couldn't define irony, but I could sometimes spot it when I saw it.

It was a big day. My parents—well, my mom, mostly—had bought a home and it was our first day there. She'd wanted to hire movers, but Saqlain Saifi hated paying others to do things he could do himself. That was, in his opinion, something only lazy people did.

As a result, our move was being handled with the help of a couple of men from the community and a U-Haul truck. They were all soaked and wondering if my father had checked the forecast. He claimed he had, but that it had been, as it was prone to be, inaccurate.

The box with the umbrellas he was carrying had been buried at the very back of our stuff and would have, in any case, been useless as we'd all needed our hands.

When we got inside, Dad dropped it next to the combination safe he usually kept in his closet and ruffled my wet hair. "Good job today. Why don't you go take a hot shower? It'll warm you up. After I make some tea for the others, I'll bring your suitcase up for you. Have you picked which room you want?"

"I'm taking the one with the poster," I told him.

"A poster of what?"

"Some guy with long hair," I said. "Come see."

Whoever had lived there before had left behind a picture of a man in a leather jacket with a cap on his head on one of the walls. He was sitting on a motorcycle, and below him a caption in bold, white letters declared: Image is Everything.

"That's Andre Agassi," Dad said. "He is a tennis player. A legend."

"Oh."

"Do you want me to take it down for you?"

"No," I said. "I like it."

My father looked confused. "But if you don't know him—"

"Doesn't matter. It's cool. Also, it just seems . . . true."

He frowned at me, then seemed to register the words I was talking about. "'Image is Everything'? That's a very anti-Sufi message."

I didn't really understand what that meant. I wasn't familiar with the tradition of religious asceticism he was referring to, why it was controversial, or even why it was important. I did know that I'd only ever heard my father use that word in a negative context. Whoever these Sufis were, my father did not approve of them. He thought they were deviants. I suppose I'd grow up to have that in common with them.

"You're very anti-Sufi too," I countered.

He smiled. "Not always. It is undeniable that purifying one's heart is a part of Islam. It is just that some of them reject outward expressions of religion and focus only on their inward states, which is not right. That makes them dangerous."

"But I can keep the poster, right?"

My father regarded the slogan again, then looked down at my hopeful face, and sighed. "Yes, fine, if you want. Just remember, Azaan, that things are not always what they seem. Mr. Andre is wrong. If you are searching for the truth, you need to look beyond appearances. That is the Sufi way. They try to look at the nature of things, at ultimate causes, instead of what is on the surface. They focus on intent rather than ritual. There is some merit in what they say, but you don't understand or care about any of that, do you?"

I shook my head.

"When you are older, inshallah, I am sure you will."

It's hard to properly value money when you're a child. Ten dollars seems like a fortune, a hundred bucks the kind of wealth only Qaroon or Mansa Musa or Elon Musk could realistically have. Every forgotten quarter rescued from between couch cushions or spotted on the ground in the wild is a blessing.

The adults around you smile when you tell them about the forty or so dollars you've managed to save up in your piggy bank, and they act like what you've accomplished is an impressive feat. But they're liars. Because they know that what you have is basically nothing and, most probably, even after a lifetime of work and toil, what you manage to accumulate will never feel like enough.

I learned this truth earlier than most people because my father was obsessed with acquiring wealth.

Don't get me wrong. I'm not saying Imam Saqlain Saifi, with his long, mustacheless beard and his habit of wearing thobes in the largely White city of Redding was a fraud. He was only interested in the material world for the sake of God.

Part of his job was to ensure the day-to-day running of the mosque he was in charge of. This required funds. The space we prayed in may have just been a small unit in an old business park previously occupied by a succession of failed startup companies, but possession of it still required the payment of rent and bills. The board of directors, of which Tiger Heart was the only other member, covered some of this, but my dad still had to get up in front of his congregation every Friday to ask for their generosity.

He was also working on a side project for which he needed several million dollars.

I didn't know my father well. We spent a lot of time apart, even when we were living in the same place. I'm sure he, like everyone else, had many hopes and aspirations, but he only spoke to me about one of his dreams, which was to build a proper place of worship for his flock.

The problem was that he didn't have the means to construct it, and the Muslim community in town didn't either, given that they were a small, if growing, number.

In order to answer what he felt was his calling, Imam Saifi needed cash. To get it, he'd go on fundraising trips across the country, visiting mosques in major cities, hat in hand, begging in the name of the Almighty.

A while before we moved into the home I'd eventually be kicked out of, Tiger Uncle decided that my father ought to take his tour international, so the two of them started traveling to Muslim countries in Africa, the Middle East, and Asia, where they'd try to get help for Dad's cause.

Over the years, these trips became longer and longer, lasting weeks and then months. I asked Mom once if she missed him while he was gone.

I remember Dr. Iqra Saifi looking up from the romance novel she was reading, raising her eyebrows, and saying, "Of course not, dear. No one likes having reminders of their mistakes around."

With my dad gone for long periods of time and Mom busy at work, I was often in the care of my babysitter. This was Clarissa Pavlides, a woman of around forty, a model turned actress, who claimed to have performed on Broadway, which was technically true. She simply failed to mention that she meant Broadway Sacramento, formerly known as the California Musical Theatre.

When Claire, as she liked to be called, got cast in a production of Chekhov's *The Seagull*, I had no choice but to accompany her to her troupe's rehearsals of the play.

I was certain I was going to be bored out of my mind. After all, I had no interest in birds.

But I was wrong.

It was incredible.

The transformation the actors underwent when they took the stage was almost magical. The way they spoke and the things they did all changed, and they became entirely different people.

Claire, as the casually callous Arkadina, was amazing. The cold inflection of her tone, the mild, self-absorbed disdain with which she looked at the other characters, the haughty way she carried herself—so completely opposite to her usual sweet manner—was a sight to behold.

What really got me was her son, Treplev, who felt that his mother didn't like him. She didn't want him around. She wanted to live a different life than she could because he existed. He wished she were an ordinary woman and knew that this was selfish. I didn't get all of what he said. The knot in my chest tightened, however, and made me want to cry because I felt, for the first time, I think, that someone understood me and was speaking a truth I never could.

"Oh my God," Claire said the first time she came to check on me. "You're literally bored to tears."

I shook my head. "No. It was nice."

She tilted her head a little. "Really? What'd you enjoy about it?"

I shrugged, not sure how to articulate what I was feeling and not wanting to do so either. A heart has rooms and it has basements, and some emotions that are shoved below are hard to bring up.

"It's just . . . ," I managed to say, "I liked that it seemed . . . real."

She smiled. "Chekhov would be thrilled to hear that, I'm sure."

"Who's that?"

"The man who wrote the play."

"Oh. Is he here?"

She chuckled. "No. He died over a hundred years ago."

"That's so cool."

Claire raised her eyebrows.

"Not that he's dead. Just that . . ." I gestured vaguely at the stage she'd been on moments ago. "It doesn't matter. I mean, it does, but—"

"No, you're right. There is some measure of immortality in art."

"My dad says everyone dies, that people only live forever in heaven or in hell."

"Well, there is a bit of those in art too. It's the closest some people will ever get to feeling connected to something greater than themselves."

I frowned at that, not because I disagreed with her, but because I was trying to understand what she meant.

"We're all looking for more than ourselves, right? We want to belong to a place, to a person, to . . ." She waved her arms around, to encompass the theater we were in. "Well, to whatever we love, I suppose."

I think now that what she said was profound.

I know now that she was right.

But back then I was still young, and like my dad once said, some things you just have to be older to understand.

"I'm not looking for anything."

"Just wait," Claire told me. "Someday you will."

Chapter Four

2022

"So you blew everyone away at the audition?" Brayden asked as he joined me at the dining table, where I was reading as I had dinner. His eyes, covetous, drifted to my plate. When he saw that it was a salad with a small, admittedly over-cooked piece of salmon on the side, however, they moved away, uninterested and despairing. He reached, instead, for a bowl of fruit nearby.

"I thought it went really well," I told him. "Have you heard from the casting director?"

"No. She's not answering my calls."

"Well, that's a good sign."

Brayden snorted, picked up a green apple, bit into it, and grimaced. "I forgot these are always sour here. Why is that?"

"I'm the one who buys them."

My agent frowned. "How is that an explanation?"

"It's my favorite flavor."

"You're a freak."

"There's no accounting for taste."

Brayden grunted in a way that told me he agreed. "I guess you've always been a few sandwiches short of a picnic. By the way, do you ever wonder what the apple Adam ate was like?"

"What?"

"In the Bible. Can you imagine how he would've felt if he disobeyed God and what he got for it was as awful as this?"

I put my fork down and sat back. "Maybe he was like me. Maybe he would have appreciated it."

"Probably not, though."

"Anyway, we don't know what he ate. It might have been a pear."

He blinked. "What?"

"The Old Testament doesn't tell us. The Quran doesn't either. It could've been anything. A fig. A grape. I've even heard some Muslims say it was wheat."

"Then gluten really is evil."

"Good and evil," I corrected him.

"Where'd the apple come from then?"

"Milton. *Paradise Lost*."

Brayden frowned. "That sounds like something I was supposed to get to in uni."

"You were."

Unlike him, I wasn't a college graduate. I had, however, devoured everything in his syllabi even when he hadn't. As a result, he had a degree and I had trivia.

"What're you reading?" he asked as I turned my attention back to my food.

"*The Seagull*."

"I see it's time for us to go out and get pissed."

I raised my eyebrows. "What are you talking about?"

"You always read Russkies when you need to get shitfaced."

"Sonya told you about the family emergency."

"She did."

I sighed. "I'm fine."

"That's what you always say. Come on then. What is it, mate?"

We had been friends long enough for me to know he wouldn't let it go, so I told him about the calls from my dad and Tiger Uncle.

He whistled. "That's a lot of drama."

"My life is basically professional training," I said.

"So when are you going?"

"Am I going?"

"You have to."

"I really don't."

"I know you, Azaan. You'll regret it if you don't. I mean, I know for a fact that there are people you'd like another shot with. Like that girl you were in love with. What was her name?"

"Madison Porter."

"You talk about her all the time. It's obvious you're carrying a huge torch. If you—"

"When have I ever talked about Madi?"

He shrugged. "You bring her up every single time that you're properly mortal."

"This is why the Prophet told us not to drink."

"I'm just saying, everyone deserves a second chance. Seems mean to deny a dying man that."

I sighed.

"I'm right about this."

I took a bite of my now lukewarm fish. It was dry, chewy, and unpleasant. If religion were true and God was merciful, it would've been the kind of thing that was bad for you. We would live in a world where nutritionists recommended burgers and biryani and kebabs. Instead, we had to plumb the depths of the ocean for omega-3s and eat kale if we wanted to live long and, more importantly, look good.

"I'm just saying, I'd go if it were my granddad."

"Yeah, but you're expecting an inheritance."

He grinned. "True. You're not?"

"I think I already got mine."

"What'd you get?"

Pain was the accurate answer, but there was no call for histrionics.

"Nothing good," I said.

There is something special about Russian writers. At least, there is something special about the masters I have read. I don't know what it is precisely. I mean, they're excellent, but every culture has produced great artists, even if some in the West try to start and end the list with Shakespeare.

The literature they produce up there is just different. It's unflinching, like someone who isn't indifferent to the world, exactly, but used to it and tired of it and a little numb despite possessing a poetic and sensitive soul.

Done with *The Seagull*, I slid it under the sofa on which I slept. There was a small library there, inconvenient and dusty, but necessary and close. Most of it consisted of plays, which were short enough that I was allowed a larger collection than you'd think in the small space that was mine in the world.

Well, not mine, really. It belonged to Brayden. I was renting it from him, which was not at all the same thing. It is customary, however, to pretend ownership when we talk about things that look like they belong to us, even if they really belong to banks or the faceless, nameless shareholders of multinational corporations.

I turned off the lights, closed my eyes, and resolved to sleep.

Unfortunately, it doesn't work that way. You can't dream on demand.

I lay there, in the dark, disturbed by the bathroom habits and snoring of my flatmates, waiting for an end to the day.

It would not come.

With a sigh, I sat up and reached for my phone.

There was an email waiting. It was from my father. The subject line read: *Baba wants to know if you are coming*. The body of the message said, *He wants me to remind you he has very little time.*

"Damn it," I muttered.

No one does guilt like family.

In that moment, I wished I were the protagonist of a Russian novel—a sadistic desire, if there ever was one—because then I would have been immune to this entreaty or at least capable of ignoring it. I would've regretted it, like Brayden predicted, and the remaining pages would have dwelled upon that guilt, how it changed me, and the consequences of my decision to stay where I was, safe from the bonds of blood.

But this wasn't a Russian novel.

So, despite my better judgment, I began looking for tickets "home."

In life, as in the theater, if you're going to play a part, you have to dress for it. That is why before I got on a plane heading to Sacramento International from Heathrow—via Frankfurt and Seattle to save money—I bought myself a few new outfits. Nothing I owned spoke of a life spent pouring over the Quran, collections of Hadith, or weighty tomes containing the laws of Islamic jurisprudence.

I got a couple of long flowing thobes, a set of thick prayer beads to carry around, leather sandals, a kufi—basically a skull cap that has converted to Islam—and a pair of large wire-framed glasses. I didn't need those, but the optics they created were excellent. They made me look studious and earnest.

I even reached out to a few makeup artists I'd worked with and managed to score a pretty realistic fake beard. It also wasn't strictly necessary. There was no hard and fast rule, to the best of my knowledge, requiring that Muslim men, even if they were imams, sport facial hair. It felt, however, like something my character—that is to say, the person I would have been if my soul had been saved—would have definitely had.

"Do you really need all this?" Brayden asked as he watched me pack.

"There's no other choice."

"You could try being a man," he suggested, reaching for my toiletry kit, which was stuffed full of South Korean beauty products.

I grabbed it before he could. "Masculinity is toxic now. Haven't you heard?"

"I'm serious. I don't get why you can't tell your family the truth. You did what you did to get out of there. You were a teenager then. You're almost thirty now. What are they going to do to you?"

"It's too much."

I meant that the conversation that kind of coming out—for lack of a better phrase—would require was too hard. The confession, the reaction, the recrimination, the sheer tonnage of shame and anger that would follow . . . I couldn't deal with it. The words I'd need to even start such a conversation would be impossible to push past the knot in my chest.

And there was another, deeper reason.

I'd been a disappointment to my father all my life. This was something I'd done—well, pretended to have done, anyway—that he was proud of. I didn't want that to go away. I couldn't have the one thing he liked about me be false.

"Okay. You do what you have to. Just know that what you're doing—impersonating a holy man—I'm pretty sure that road leads to hell."

"I'm already on my way there," I said, closing the lid on my suitcase. "Besides, I've got no use for heaven. It sounds awful. I'm pretty sure my family's going to be there."

Well, except for Baba, probably. Based on everything I'd heard about him, he was going to roast for all eternity too. God would make sure we were well done in the afterlife because we hadn't done well in this world.

If my grandfather was interested in building a relationship with me, it was too bad he hadn't chosen to do so before now, just as the curtain on his life was about to fall. Given that we seemed to be in the same boat, spiritually speaking, it was possible that we might not have found each other entirely insufferable.

"Well, I'm glad you're going. I'll keep chasing leads here. If anything comes up—"

“Let me know. I’ll head back right away.”

“All right, mate. Have a boring-ass flight.”

“I will.”

Whether or not the flight would be uneventful was, of course, not really up to me. That was the responsibility of the hundreds of people I didn’t know who had touched my plane at some point in its life, making sure the pressurized metal tube I was getting on was fit to hurtle through the sky. Still, I did what I could to follow Brayden’s admonition.

For one, I decided not to wear my imam costume for the whole seventeen-hour trip. I’d never been profiled at an airport or pulled aside for a special search before, but I also hadn’t ever tried boarding a plane while cosplaying as a practicing Muslim. I didn’t think it was likely to improve my traveling experience.

I also downloaded a couple of books about the finer points of the Sharia and spent most of my time at high altitude pouring over them. They were exactly the kind of texts I would’ve had to read if I’d actually attended Al-Azhar, containing the same information for which I’d previously had no use, in the same elaborate, effusive, purple prose I found suffocating.

It was essential, however, that I become at least a little familiar with these topics, so I could sound like I knew what I was talking about in case they came up in conversation. It was the only way to convincingly play the character I was claiming to be, and I was determined, as always, to be excellent in the role I’d taken on.

I mean, religion is one thing, but acting . . . well, that is a serious business.

Chapter Five

After landing in Sacramento, I wandered around the airport looking for a restroom that was more or less empty. There I pulled off my regular clothes and got into costume. I put on the new long, flowing thobe I'd bought to play the part of the pious and applied the fake beard to my face using cold glue.

Having watched makeup artists do this kind of work many times over the years, I'd assumed it'd be easy for me to mimic. It wasn't.

Art was always this way. It was why I'd heard people call poetry and acting and writing and painting and composing music "the easy impossible," because when you see someone else do it or you only have access to the completed work, it appears effortless.

What you can't see are the hours of toil and struggle and practice and heartbreak that resulted in the mastery you're witnessing. You think to yourself that you could easily do it too, if you wanted and if you had time. So maybe you try it, and what you manage to finish, if you manage to finish at all, sucks.

Because not everyone is willing to give art what it demands. It requires sacrifice. It's like God that way.

It took a long time, but eventually I was able to get results that seemed sort of passable. I then put on my glasses, redid my hair into a side part, and walked out looking like an entirely different person than I'd been going in.

When I finally got to the airport exit, I saw my father there waiting to pick me up, and I realized all of a sudden that he had gotten old.

The gravity of that thought held me in place as I looked at him for the first time in a decade. Saqlain Saifi had never been a large man, but he was beyond slim now. He looked positively gaunt. His back was bent, the black of his hair flooded with gray, and his gait was slow and shuffling.

There were many new lines on his face, and the old ones, marks left by his frequent grim expressions, had deepened. They made him look terribly severe, like a man who was displeased with everything and who rarely experienced joy.

He was struck by my appearance too, I think, because I saw the long shadow of some emotion pass over his face before his features returned to their natural set.

A moment followed in which neither one of us moved. We didn't know what to do next. Other people would probably have thrown their arms around each other and embraced. But we were not, as was perhaps the great tragedy of our lives, other people. Just like everyone else, we were cursed with being ourselves.

Eventually, he came up to me and with solemn formality offered me a cool hand to shake, and I stepped forward to take it and this was our family business.

Then, after not having seen me for a good third of my life—really, the best third of my life—he said his first in-person words to me, his voice a little more raw, a little more gruff, than it sounded on the phone.

"I have been waiting a while. What took so long?"

That was a reasonable question, but one I hadn't anticipated. I scrambled to find a believable answer. "Uh . . . well, they had some questions for me at immigration."

"But you are a born citizen."

"Yeah. They know that. Still."

"Still?" He snarled. "What does that mean? Still? What were they going to do? Were they not going to let you into your own country? How can they do that? Do they think we don't see what this is really about?"

And just like that, he was in clergy mode.

Imam Sucky, as the kids at his mosque used to call him—a name I may have had some hand in crafting—didn't give great sermons. This was unfortunate because delivering those was a significant part of the job he'd held for around twenty-five years.

I'd been around preachers who were too dry and preachers who tried but failed to be funny. I'd been around men of God who lacked passion and others who didn't have the common touch, which meant that their cerebral musings about the intricate, intellectual problems of dogma went over the heads of their congregants. A few wrestled with the English language, others with the inability to come up with any original takes on a religion that had, in all fairness, been around for fourteen hundred years.

My father had none of these issues.

His flaw was that he believed, for reasons I'd never quite understood, that there was no difference between persuading someone of a position and asking them an endless stream of pointed, leading questions. It was as if he were utterly convinced that no one could ever arrive at any answers different from the ones he'd come up with. Having me for a son ought to have cured him of that particular delusion, but it somehow hadn't.

He was still going on, his volume rising, and we were starting to attract attention.

I love an audience, but only when they are looking at me. When their eyes are on my father . . . well, that's almost always mortifying. It didn't help that his building fury was directed at something that hadn't even really happened.

"Will they admit that they delayed you and asked you questions because you're Muslim and look like it? They imagine we are powerless, don't they? Do they not fear the voice of the people? Is it their belief that we will not raise that voice? Do they think we will be timid like mice? Are we not the spiritual descendants of men who tore through the hearts of deserts and shook the thrones of every worldly king? Is—"

"Dad."

"What?" he snapped.

"Can we go? Your tirade might end up being longer than Baba's life."

"It's an American disease," he grumbled, more subdued as we turned to leave, "this hatred, this fear of the sacred. The fact that we have faith eats away at these people, Azaan, like a worm in their hearts."

I ran a hand over my face.

Two minutes into my visit, I already missed the lengthy silences between us.

"It wasn't that big a deal. Can we drop it, please?"

He nodded but continued to rage under his breath for a

while before finally running out of steam. "I am just going to say one more thing."

"Of course you are."

"Don't change the way you look just because this happened. You look like a righteous man now, a man following the footsteps of Prophet Muhammad, Peace Be Upon Him. Don't be bullied into looking like every other Mark, Matthew, Luke, and John."

"Okay," I said.

"I mean it. You look good. There is a light, a noor, about your face now that wasn't there before. Such beauty is a blessing from Allah, and I am sure he has given it to you because you have devoted your life to the study of his Word. I especially like the beard. It suits you."

[#]

It was an excruciating three-hour drive from Sacramento to Redding, where I'd been reluctantly raised. People called it the "Jewel of Northern California," but the name given to the area during the gold rush—the "Poverty Flats"—was equally apt.

As with everything in life, the places you go are either for you or not, depending on who you are and what you want.

I would have enjoyed Redding more if I could have made myself care about the outdoors, if the glory of Mount Shasta, the flow of the Sacramento River, and the overabundance of sunshine there had ever held any charm for me. One of Wilde's characters once said they were glad they had lost the faculty of enjoying nature. I never possessed it.

I loved being in London, which was . . . well, it was the center of the world, a hub of culture, art, and industry. Yes, it could be gloomy and cold and the daylight hours could grow short, but that just meant I could happily be indoors looking at paintings of lakes instead of fending off friendly and wretched invitations to actually go visit them.

My hometown—where the largest employers are the government, a hospital, and Walmart—was like the place I'd chosen to live only in that it was also called a city. It appealed to people who liked sitting on horses, walking over trails, going to rodeos, and floating on pieces of wood for hours while waiting for fish to get peckish. They would look at my modest apartment, overstuffed with roommates, with the same horror with which I regarded their suburban lives.

As was tradition, I pretended to fall asleep in the car. It was the only way to survive significant periods of time around my father with one's sanity intact. I ended up actually dozing off, and when I woke, the sky, which had been bright blue in Sacramento, was a deep gray, and it looked like it was snowing.

I shook my head and sat up straighter, looking around at the once-familiar fields that lined the sides of the freeway. We were almost there, but something about this scene didn't make sense, and then I realized that it was November, and way too early here for any signs of winter to show themselves.

Squinting at the stuff falling from the sky, I asked, "What is that?"

"Ash," my father told me. "It's fire season."

"They're calling it a season now?"

"That is new." He smiled a little. It was the equivalent of a full-on grin from another man. "When I was young, we only had four of those. We also had nine planets."

"I remember that."

"And they used to say that the sun never moved."

"There's been progress."

"Has there?" He waved a hand vaguely at the grim horizon

around us. "Or have we just discovered that no one should be trusted, not even ourselves, because so much of what we believed to be true about the world, about us, has turned out to be a lie?"

There was something unusual in his tone, something sad and melancholic, that drew my attention away from the flecks falling onto the windshield. Where was that coming from? From the fact that he was being investigated by the treasurer of his own mosque, probably. That had to be weighing on him. "You okay?"

"Have I ever told you I am not?"

"No."

"Then why bother asking?"

"Whatever," I muttered, staring straight ahead.

We drove in silence for a while, then he looked over at me, exhaled, and said, "Speaking of changes that have happened, I have to admit not all of them are bad. Some are very good. The new mosque is almost complete. You might even be here for the ribbon-cutting ceremony unless it is delayed."

"Why would it be delayed?" I asked.

"There's been some vandalism of the property here and there."

"Tiger said it wasn't anything to worry about, that it wasn't serious."

"It has not been yet. It is just . . . I don't know if it will stay that way. You never know what some people will do."

I nodded. "Do the police have any leads?"

"No, and I do not think they are looking very hard. It feels like that school friend of yours from the newspaper has asked more questions than the cops."

"What friend?"

He gave a dismissive wave of his hand. "That doesn't

matter. What matters is that, inshallah, everything will be fine, and you'll get to see the mosque open. That would be good. It's the best thing I've done in my life."

"Thanks."

He smiled, clearly taking that one word to mean we were fine. "Don't get me wrong. You have turned out okay. I'm glad you are walking the path of God, but you started out as an accident and everything since then . . . well, it has been a difficult reclamation project. Don't you agree?"

"That it's been difficult? Yeah."

"But this mosque I've built, I wanted it. It is my dream."

"I know."

"I am glad you will get to see it. At least some good will come of your trip, even if you are only here because Baba is being ridiculous. Making a man fly halfway across the world just because he's dying. It makes no sense to me. When I die, I don't want you at the funeral."

"Really?"

"You should be there if you are here, in Redding or nearby, but why should you come all the way from England just to put me in the ground? Anyone can do that. It makes no difference to the dead who buries them. They've got bigger concerns."

"What if I want to be there?"

"Why? What good does it do, all this rushing and scrambling around the earth that people do these days for weddings and endings? Company is for the living. Mourning is for the living. Only prayers can help the dead. Just remember me when you speak to your Lord. Tell him I was a good father—"

"You want me to lie to Him?"

If that remark stung, he didn't show it. "Tell him, at least, that you thought I was a good man. What you would spend on your flight over, give it to charity in my name, so that it may make a difference to someone. Don't come looking for me, Azaan, after I am gone. It would be a waste, and God loves not the wasteful."

[#]

I don't like hospitals. The lack of silence in them bothers me. Every hush is interrupted by the beeping and chirping of machines. It makes me think of a restless audience, watching uninterested as the actors on stage stumble through the last of their script, waiting for the end.

Like a bored crowd, a hospital doesn't care about or remember much of what it has seen. It even smells of disinfectant, the chemical of forgetting, of moving on.

It's a place of impermanence, where souls are churned in and churned out, leaving nothing behind but medical records. I've never been comfortable with it. When I was a kid, my mother would sometimes bring me here, hoping that seeing her practice, seeing her help people, would inspire me to aspire to a career like hers.

This was her temple as much as the mosque was my father's, and like him she would have loved me more if I had wanted to worship what she worshipped. Unlike him, at least she hadn't tried to force her religion onto me.

I found Baba in his room, its door open, headphones in his ears and his eyes fixed on a tablet that he was holding over his rather large stomach.

It took him a moment to realize I was there.

I'd heard, years ago, that because he'd developed cancer in his larynx, surgeons had removed it. Now there was a hole in his throat, surrounded by plastic with a short tube in the middle through which he was breathing.

The cancer had returned—or perhaps a new one had developed—to target his liver. A part of that had been cut away and he'd survived.

It was back again. Now it had come for his lungs, and according to my father, doctors had thought they could remove a segment of them to keep him alive, but Baba had decided that if his body was this determined to kill him, it was time to stop saving it.

He'd changed his mind a few months later, but by then the cancer had spread everywhere, and there was nothing more anyone could do.

Baba eventually felt my presence, looked up and smiled. Covering his stoma, he wheezed, "You are very different from your pictures from before Saqi tossed you into the land of the pharaohs. You hardly seem like the same young man who convinced a girl to give him a blowjob in the mosque."

"What? Who told you that happened?"

"Where there are many tongues, there are many tales, hmm?"

"Well, it's not true. I kissed a girl outside the mosque once, behind the building. It was an indiscretion, not a desecration."

"I see. Well, here's a tip. To be a legend, you need to let people exaggerate your deeds and misdeeds. I recommend it. Notoriety opens some interesting doors. Walking around dressed up like a fundu closes them."

I looked down at my thobe and scowled. "I'm not a fundamentalist."

"Everyone says that, hmm? No one thinks they're an extremist. Well, I will admit freely that I was an extremist." He positively chortled. "Extreme drinking. Extreme smoking. Extreme eating. Extreme fucking. Extreme joy. Extreme sorrow. I always went for the maximum."

Baba waited to see how I'd respond to what he'd said. When I didn't react, he went on.

"It was a very fun life. At least, it was for a long while. The end . . . well, this could be better. I thought I was ready for it, you know, but I'm not."

"I'm sorry."

"What difference is it to you? I'm just a shooting star you're seeing fall. You don't think of me as your grandfather. Not really. No, don't bother denying it. It's my fault, not yours."

"Well, that's all right. We have a chance to get to know each other a little now."

"Oh," he said. "No. I'm not wasting what little time I have left on you." He held up the device that had been occupying his attention. An actress wearing very little was paused in the middle of a Bollywood dance routine. "Look at her waist. It's incredible. Perfection. I'm going to leave this world imagining the taste of this masala on my lips. You're not taking that away from me."

"But . . . Dad said you wanted to see me."

"I do. Not to build bridges with you, though. Life is not a sitcom, hmm? There is no happily ever after to be had. No. I brought you here as a gift for my son, so he won't be by himself after I am gone."

"I'm here for Dad?" First Tiger, now Baba. What was with these old men assuming that my father needed help and that he would accept it from me of all people. "You don't know anything about us, do you?"

Baba raised his bushy eyebrows, cast a longing glance at the video stream suspended on the screen before him, then put it aside. "I know enough. He made up strict rules for you. He tried to control you, to make you what he wanted. You rebelled. He beat the shit out of you. It's not so complicated."

I looked away from him.

"Now you lovingly hate each other from a distance. I understand. There is no hurt that way. There is no healing either."

"I am fine with the way things are."

"Well, this is not about you, boy. It's about me. It's about the fact that I can't be here for Saqi, who is in trouble. I know you'll say I was never there for him before, so what's different now? What's different is that this time I want to be there. However, since I cannot, you'll have to do."

I frowned. Did Baba know about the investigation at the mosque? My father wouldn't have told him, and it seemed unlikely that Tiger Uncle would have done so. Maybe it was something widely known in the community. Still, I decided to make sure we were on the same page before I started blabbing about something that might very well be a secret. "What do you mean Dad's in trouble?"

"I don't know. Something's wrong. He's gotten quiet. He's not sleeping well. He doesn't eat. He's up at all hours, crying as he prays. I've seen him outside at night, talking to people in the dark. I've also seen his mail. He's behind on his bills. Now he says he's considering stepping back, retiring from being an imam. How can he do that if he can't pay for electricity?"

"Retiring? He was just telling me about the new mosque and he didn't mention—"

"Strange, hmm? You know that is Saqi's baby. After twenty years of planning, getting permits, and raising money, he is moving his congregation out of that office park to their own space. But right at the moment of climax, he's thinking of pulling out. Tell me. Does it make sense?"

"It is odd," I conceded, not liking how this information

appeared to fit in with the donations that had gone missing from the mosque.

Someone who didn't know Imam Saifi would likely suggest two theories based on what I knew so far. The first being that my father was experiencing some kind of unexpected and urgent financial emergency and had stolen money in order to deal with it.

Or they'd say he was going to abscond with the cash to finance his retirement on some tropical beach.. With his departure imminent, maybe he'd decided there was no point in honoring his current financial obligations.

In either case, it'd have to be a pretty big sum.

Tiger had made it sound like a rounding error.

Anyway, this was all baseless speculation. Dad wasn't like that. He wasn't the sort of man who'd steal from God.

Plus, he'd never go to a beach. There were too many women in swimwear there, showing what was forbidden for him to see.

"Well," I told Baba, "whatever is going on, I'm not sure what you want me to do about it."

"Fix it. And if you can't, at least make sure he's not all alone."

"I—"

"You don't think you owe him that?"

"I don't think I owe anyone anything."

The dying man stared at me for a long while. "I see. In that case, I'm sorry for the trouble. You can go."

"Baba—"

"We're done talking now."

My primary thought, just then, was how astonishingly infuriating my family was.

My second thought . . .

"What do you mean I should make sure he's not all alone? He's got Mom."

"Hmm? Oh. Her. No, Iqra is no use. They don't talk much since the divorce."

"What?!"

[#]

An hour later, I was sitting in Iqra Saifi's private practice office, watching her make tea. At least, that was the name by which I'd known her all my life. Maybe she'd changed it after she had left Dad. I had three living family members and, just then, I couldn't have introduced two of them to a stranger with any confidence.

"You've always been a sensationalist, jaan. There is no reason for you to be upset right now. I feel like you're over-reacting."

"You got divorced and didn't tell me."

"That was three years ago. Let's stop living in the past, shall we?"

Struggling to keep my voice even, I said, "I just found out today."

My mother shrugged. It was her favorite gesture. It was also a perfect encapsulation of her philosophy, which was to care for nothing too much, and to deal with whatever happened in stride.

I wondered sometimes if this cavalier attitude was some weird remnant of the whole British stiff-upper-lip thing, because she was still almost comically attached to the island of her birth, as evidenced by the china tea set she'd always kept in her office, the perpetual presence of a miniature union jack on her desk, and the pixie haircut she'd borrowed from Princess

Diana in the nineties and never returned. She may have married my father and left England, but England had never left her.

"That just serves to underscore my point," she insisted. "Has our splitting up impacted your life in any way? Not even a little, right? Therefore, it follows that your reaction is not warranted and you are, as has long been your habit, wasting my time."

"It's nice to see you too."

"Oh, come on. I didn't mean it like that. I am glad you are visiting, but we should be talking about more productive things. Recriminations are boring, my dear. They're why there is nothing interesting about your generation. You don't understand that whining about how things are is not the same thing as having a personality or a purpose."

I started to respond, but what was the point?

"Tell me about yourself. Have you met any nice, challenging women?"

"No."

She studied my appearance critically, and I was reminded again of the devout Muslim costume I was wearing. "Unsurprising. Thanks to Saqi's influence, you are probably going to need to be married off the old-fashioned way. It won't be easy. You made yourself infamous around these parts with the way you behaved when you were young."

I frowned. This was new territory for my mom, in which she was not at all welcome. She hadn't ever shown any interest in my romantic life, or any part of my life really, before. Strange that she'd start now. "I don't need your help."

"Nonsense. Your being here, even if it is at the behest of that disgusting old man . . . did you know, by the way, that Baba of yours has been begging his nurses—people I work with, mind you—to get him Viagra so he can gratify himself? How embarrassing. And in his condition. Can you believe it?"

"Yes, actually."

"I suppose we are lucky his last wish was to see you and not a prostitute." She tilted her head to one side, then asked, "What did he have to say to you?"

"He thinks there is something wrong with Dad."

"Well, there are many things wrong with Saqi. That is common knowledge. Regardless, the fact of the matter is that your grand pervert has given us an opportunity to arrange your future."

"Why are you bringing this up, Mom? I can't imagine you want grandchildren."

"Of course not. You know I have no patience for babies. They're just germy little time sinks with an excellent and deceptive marketing campaign."

"Then?" I asked.

She drummed her fingers lightly on the cup she was holding and took her time answering. "Over the last few years, I've had occasion to realize that even obnoxious company is . . ." Iqra formerly Saifi but maybe now Rahman glanced up at the ceiling, cleared her throat, then fixed me with eyes brighter than they had been a moment ago. "It's important to have people in your life, dear, even if you don't always enjoy them. I didn't understand that when I let your father send you into the desert by yourself. I see now that it must have been difficult for you to be forced into the desolation of solitude."

"You really don't have to feel bad. Millions of people live in Cairo."

"Yes," she agreed quietly, "but how many of them knew you? Still, you must have friends now. You're in your motherland. There can hardly be room to be lonely."

"There really is very little room."

"I'm glad to hear it. Very well. I'll happily wash my hands of your personal life." Then, changing tracks suddenly, she asked, "How long are you staying?"

"I mean, I came because Dad kind of—"

"Guilted you into it? Oh, don't try to defend him. I don't doubt he did. He's remarkably skillful at the art of manipulation." Her tone was drenched in disdain. "He's made a profession out of it after all."

I had no real experience being the child of a broken home—well, maybe it'd be more accurate to say that I had no experience being a child of a split household—but it seemed obvious that indulging either one of my parents in taking shots at the other was likely unwise.

"Okay," I said. "Well, anyway, I thought Baba wanted me to spend time with him before the end, but after talking to him . . . honestly, I'm not sure what I'm doing here. Even if Dad needs to be cheered up or something, I'm not going to be any help. You know how it is."

My mother raised just one of her shoulders this time and let it drop.

"So, I don't know when I'm heading out. Probably soon. But don't worry," I added with a grin. "I'll leave you alone unless it's absolutely necessary."

"I know you will," she said, not returning my smile. "That is precisely what I raised you to do."

[#]

Instead of calling Dad to pick me up like he'd instructed, I decided to make my way to my parents' house—where now only my father lived—on foot. It wasn't smart. I was tired, the way was long, and the day wasn't exactly nice. Ash was still drifting down from the sky like a light, lazy flurry and accumulating on the ground. It definitely looked like snow, but it was a poor imitation of winter, because the air was hot and smelled charred and felt heavy somehow, as if burdened by the memory of all the life being extinguished by California's latest wildfire.

Still, I chose to walk because that usually helped clear my mind. I'd wandered this city's streets on many nights—though I had never ventured quite this far from home—when I was young and being around my parents, with their arguing and bickering, got to be too much to bear.

I needed time to process what I'd learned that day. Maybe it was time I should have already taken. It would have been wiser to sit with the information regarding my parents' decision to dissolve their marriage instead of racing off to see Mom at work. But I'd never managed to make good decisions around these people.

Truth be told, their divorce wasn't surprising. In fact, it should have happened sooner. They were a well-intentioned match, I'm sure, but a poor one. It didn't make sense to be upset they had called it off.

They should have told me, though. It was the kind of thing other families talked about and shared with each other, families whose close bonds, embroidered by love and affection, seemed easy and effortless. For us, however, in the shadow of the Sierra Nevada, such simple things had always seemed to lie on the other side of an impassable mountain.

I drew in a deep breath. It made me cough, and I thought of a word that I'd never thought of before.

Acrid.

I'd come across it in books. Though I knew its definition, I had never really understood what it was, because it was one of those words that no one ever used, except writers flailing about in a thesaurus for adjectives. So, in effect, it had no meaning anymore. It had no resonance for me.

Until then.

Then, I got it.

Acrid was a burning tree. It was inhaling the remains of a hummingbird, a hawk, a finch, a mountain lion, a black bear, and all the things around you that creep and crawl, and knowing that they had died in a panic, screaming, with no escape.

Acrid was the possibility that the winds might change and the places where people had long lived, even if only unhappily, could burn.

Acrid was knowing that there were men out there fighting to put a stop to the fire, to save everyone, having to face the kind of fierce thing holy men had for untold centuries begged us all to fear.

Acrid was the ability to know all this and still feel sorry for yourself and to give up on walking and call an Uber, because it was all too much, entirely too much, and not something that one ought to have to endure.

[#]

My phone rang almost as soon as I got into the car. It was Brayden.

"How was your flight?"

"Fine." I decided not to mention that everything since then had been kind of bonkers.

"You sound tired."

"I'm going home now."

"Get some rest," he said. "I'm just calling because I heard back about your audition."

"The one where I was a terrorist?" I asked.

The Uber driver turned around to look at me.

I waved at him a little to indicate he had nothing to worry about. He didn't seem all that reassured.

Brayden said, "Yes, obviously. What other—"

"I tried out for a play too, remember? The . . . citrus one."

"*Lemons Lemons Lemons*—?"

I nodded. "—*Lemons Lemons*. Yeah."

"Haven't heard from them. No, Azaan, listen, these guys thought you were great."

"Really?"

"Why are you surprised? You're a talent, mate. They really liked your take on the part. You perfectly captured how emotionally distraught someone would be right before taking on a suicide mission."

"Well, I do what I can."

"Now, they haven't made up their minds yet, so I don't want you to get your hopes up, all right?" Brayden warned. "They've called Sonya back. They hadn't considered a woman for the role. They think it might be an interesting angle."

"Nice," I said.

"Looks like it's down to you two. I win either way."

"Congratulations."

"Don't be like that," Brayden protested. "You didn't even want it."

"I wasn't being sarcastic. I mean it. Good for you, dude."

"A few hours in California and you're already talking like a native."

I snorted. "Yeah. I guess it brings some stuff back."

"Good stuff?"

"Not necessarily."

"Well, you'll be back in the civilized world before you know it. Hang in there."

"Yeah."

"I have to run. Give me a ring if you need to talk."

Putting my cell away, I looked out the window at the city passing by.

As the car I'd hired got closer to my childhood home, the streets gradually became more and more familiar until they began triggering memories.

We went past the park where my father had tried to teach me how to throw a spiral, though he did not understand American football and was of the opinion that all athletic pursuits ought to be abandoned in favor of cricket, the kind played with a red ball, not the white one. The shorter, more colorful, modern variants of the sport were not for him. He was very much old-school, not just in that regard but in all things.

I saw the building that used to house my preschool, a place where I'd thought I would always be happy. It was now a Krispy Kreme.

My high school, a place where I'd thought I'd never be happy again, looked very much the same.

It struck me that—doughnuts aside—very little about the area had changed while I was gone.

I was no longer the teenager I'd been when I was here last, chasing after the disapproval of everyone around me. It seemed incomprehensible that I was fundamentally altered, but this place to which I'd been linked remained almost entirely the same.

The Shakespearean characters I sometimes inhabited got the benefit of pathetic fallacy and were able to see their inner realities reflected in what happened around them. I was used to

Macbeth's unruly nights and the most unnatural omens of which Caesar had heard tell.

The truth was that the physical world itself—that most ancient of whirling dervishes—had been entirely unconcerned with William and his creations and was most definitely unbothered by what I had gone through and was feeling. We were small and it was vast. It aged differently than we did.

There was a silver lining, though.

If most things remained the same, that meant the popular saying was untrue. Perhaps you *could* go home again.

We pulled up in front of my father's house. The first thing my eyes fixed on—by design—was a real estate agent's giant sign on the front yard, loudly proclaiming that the property was for sale.

Chapter Six

"What the hell, Dad?"

I found him in the kitchen, kneeling by an open box of massive steel pots—the kind of things you could cook in for a small village—and wrestling with a roll of tape, trying unsuccessfully to find the edge again because he'd let it get stuck to itself. Unlabeled U-Haul boxes surrounded him on all sides, stacked up high, some stable, some precarious, their cardboard sides bulging with all the stuff he'd forced into them.

A familiar flicker of anger flashed in his dark gaze as he looked up, likely upset with both my tone and my words. He glared at me a moment, then turned his attention back to his packing without speaking.

"You're selling the house? Why?"

"It's not your business. It does not belong to you."

"Is that why you didn't tell me that Mom left you? Because it wasn't my marriage?"

"Exactly right."

"You're all fucking unbelievable."

Saqlain Saifi flung the tape he was holding aside. It crashed into the box nearest to him, made a muffled thump, and then dropped onto the tiled floor. He started to lunge to his feet, with that old menace that used to make me run, a snarl etched onto his face.

This time was different though. This time he didn't manage to rise.

Either his legs had fallen asleep beneath him or one of his knees buckled and he stumbled on his way up. He reached out for support, trying to lean against one of the cartons he'd piled up, but it gave way under his weight, and the tower he'd created collapsed. He fell with it and with the sharp, musical, cutting sound of glass breaking.

"Dad!"

I rushed forward to help him, but he slapped my hand away with as much force as he could manage. Very slowly, he got to his knees, then he forced himself to stand. His lips were pressed together hard in a pained grimace.

"Are you okay?"

He didn't respond for a while, didn't look up at me, didn't move at all. Just before I could ask again though, he nodded once.

"You're sure you didn't hurt yourself?"

Now he did glance up. Our eyes locked. Then he inexplicably barked out a laugh, a bitter, twisted, mocking thing. "Yes, of course I did. You've hurt yourself too."

I frowned. "What?"

"Rabbana zalamna anfusana . . ."

He'd taught me more than enough of both Arabic and the Quran for me to recognize the verse he'd started reciting. It was the prayer Adam and Eve had used to beg God for forgiveness after they had been cast out of heaven.

"Our Lord, we have wronged our souls: if You do not forgive us and have mercy, we shall be lost."

"No, that's not . . . I meant physically—"

"I am not a fool. I know what you meant," he snapped. Then, more coolly, he added, "I am fine."

"Okay. Good. Listen, I'm sorry, I shouldn't have said what I did. It's just . . . can we talk please? Let's just sit down and—"

"What is there to talk about? Nothing happened. I broke some things. It's not a big deal. We have other bowls and plates."

"We're really going to leave it like this?"

He considered my question. "You are right. We shouldn't. You go ahead and pick up the boxes, open them, and throw away what's shattered. Go on. Handle it. See if anything survived in there, if there's anything worth saving. Just be sure not to cut yourself."

That hadn't been what I'd meant, but I suspected he knew that. He was clearly not up for climbing the restless volcano simmering between us just then.

We had gone to nearby Mount Shasta once on a family trip and when I'd seen it, I'd wondered out loud what would happen to Redding if it erupted. He'd told me not to worry, that this only occurred, at most, once a millennium and sometimes not for three thousand years or more, and it was likely we'd all be gone before that happened.

Our family was apparently built on this same . . . optimism.

The thing about Shasta, however, was that it had been boiling a little. Lava had been rising up periodically and almost reaching the surface. Where it touched groundwater, there were small explosions. It hadn't properly blown in thirty-two hundred years.

So maybe we were due.

"Actually," he said, "you know what? Forget about all this. You must be tired. Such a long journey you've had. Go to your old room and lie down. I'm going to take care of some things and will be back soon to pick you up. I'll deal with all this later."

"You're sure?"

"I didn't call you here to have you help me, Azaan. I was going to do all this on my own. Now that you are here, that doesn't have to change."

"I don't mind—"

"You go rest. I will get everything under control."

[#]

Home alone, I decided to look around a bit. The recent mail was in the same drawer as always. I found the delinquent bills Baba had mentioned easily enough, obnoxious, red, stamped warnings of last chances and overdue fines bright on their pages. From water to electricity to credit card payments, my father was behind on everything.

The community paid him for his services as the imam, of course, and Mom was probably having to pay him some kind of spousal support, given that she out-earned him by a ton. There ought to have been plenty of money coming in for what should have been modest expenses. The fact that he was having financial trouble didn't make sense.

It did explain why he was selling this paid-off place though. Even assuming that Mom would get half of the proceeds, his share would be in the hundreds of thousands. It seemed like he could use the cash.

Just how urgently did he need it, though?

After picking up the stuff that had fallen over in the

kitchen, I indulged in a little nostalgia and walked through the house, my eyes seeking things I'd known growing up—items of decoration on coffee tables, art on the walls, old photographs of smiling faces—and found very little. Almost everything had been carted off somewhere. The home had been stripped naked and, so exposed, felt like little more than a wooden box.

My room was empty too, except for my old Agassi poster, a comforter, and some pillows on the floor that had been fashioned into something approximating a "bed" and, next to it, a small pile of books. Among them I saw a few texts by Al-Ghazali, the *Guantánamo Diary* of Mohamedou Ould Slahi, and a history called *Destiny Disrupted* by Tamim Ansary. It was an unsurprising collection for Dad, who had no use for literature or any nonfiction that might challenge, instead of confirm, his worldview.

I was about to lie down on the ground when the doorbell rang.

It was a hijabi woman, maybe around a decade or so younger than me, with strikingly thick eyebrows and a small, thin mouth. Her eyes were so unnaturally dark that it seemed like she didn't have any pupils. They were unsettling more than pretty.

Even though there was something familiar about her, I didn't recognize her.

Her voice was soft when she spoke, barely rising above a whisper, and was pretty heavily accented. She'd spent a lot of time in Pakistan and recently at that. "You . . . you are his . . . his son? Imam Saqlain's son?"

"The one and only," I said.

Instead of replying, she stared at me with those unnerving eyes of hers, almost unblinking.

"My dad's not here," I volunteered.

"Where do you live? Not in this place. I haven't seen you before."

"No, I'm from the UK."

She offered a guarded smile. "Is that what you tell them?"

"Who?" I asked.

"When you're there and people ask you where you are from."

"Uh . . . no, I tell them I'm from here."

"Isn't that interesting?" she asked.

"I'm sorry. Do I know you?"

"I am called Kashaf."

"Azaan," I said.

"Are you truthful?"

"What?"

"I was supposed to meet the imam here. Is he really not inside?"

"I'm sorry. He's not."

She sighed.

"Is there something I can help you with?"

The woman seemed to notice my getup for the first time. "Are you also an imam?"

"I don't have as much experience at the job as my dad does," I told her, which was entirely true. "If it's a religious question, you should probably just ask him."

"I will."

"I'll let him know you missed him," I added helpfully.

"He knows that."

I frowned. "What?"

She ignored the question. "I'll find him later."

"Okay, well—"

"It was good to meet you," she said.

"Yeah. You too. Kashaf, right? I'll see you around."

"Yes. You will."

[#]

I frowned as I closed the door on the Kashaf woman. When did my father start taking house calls from his congregants? He definitely wouldn't have let her into his home if she were by herself. He'd always taught me that a man and woman who were unrelated could never be alone together, because in those situations the devil always appeared.

He hadn't bothered to tell me that the devil could be a lot of fun. I'd figured that part out on my own.

But this Kashaf person seemed to have been here before. When she had said I didn't live here, it had been a statement, not a question.

Maybe her problems were serious and private enough that Dad figured they needed to speak where no one could overhear. Well, except for Baba, whose presence in the home—now that I thought about it—probably served to keep my father's interactions with Kashaf above reproach.

I hadn't gotten very far when the bell rang again.

I hoped Kashaf hadn't changed her mind about seeking my advice. I really didn't want to start giving out spiritual guidance to people, especially if they were in real trouble. That seemed like crossing a line. Even actors have some morals.

It wasn't her.

"Wow," I said.

"Damn," I said.

"Mads," I said.

She stared back at me, her lips parted a little, her stunned expression probably a mirror of my own. Then she shook her head, either in disbelief or in astonishment or both. "Azaan? My God."

Madison Porter had changed. Her straight hair, which she used to keep short and sometimes streak with various loud colors, had been allowed to grow long and return to its natural shade of deep black. Her eyes somehow seemed bluer and brighter than usual, which may have been a trick of the light. They were better defined too, just like her jawline, her lips, and her nose. They were small alterations, probably the result of the passage of time and her increasing skill in the use of makeup.

The spring of her life—our lives—had passed, but this summer was glorious. She would be lovely in autumn too, I imagined, and in the winter, each season the advent of new cares and new marvels, a sequence of transformations, some inevitable, some wished for and some dreaded, but all beautiful in their own right, like daybreaks and moon rises and noons and witching hours and twilights, all different, all majestic.

Madi laughed, clasped her hands together, and stepped forward to give me a hug. At the last second, she hesitated and drew back. "Oh. Sorry. I guess I can't touch you anymore."

"What do you mean?" I asked, part of me trying to decipher her question, part of me remembering the last time I'd seen her, that secret night, that best and worst of goodbyes.

"You're Muslim."

"I've always been."

She waved her hands in my general direction, at my appearance. "Now you look like it. Like you're . . . reborn. You look—"

"You look amazing."

Madi smiled and bit her lower lip.

Good Lord.

"You can touch me," I said.

"You sure?"

I nodded.

She moved closer and wrapped her arms around me, and I did the same to her, and she was soft and warm and I couldn't help but think of sour apples. She no longer smelled of them, though. Her scent was more sophisticated now, a subtle overlay of Earl Grey and vanilla and jasmine. She was dressed differently too, in a light pink floral-pattern dress with three-quarter sleeves and a hem that fell just above her knees.

We held each other just a little too long, I think, because when we pulled ourselves apart, neither one of us knew what to say. I cleared my throat. She looked down and away.

"So," she finally said, "hi."

"You look amazing."

Madi chuckled and ran a hand through her hair. "You said that already."

"It's just . . . so good to see you."

"It's been forever."

"Yeah, it has. What're you doing here? And don't just stand there. Come in."

"Oh, no. I can't. Julie's got a game night. Tali and Dan were watching her. I was about to go pick her up and I thought I saw . . . I thought I saw you talking to that woman. And I told myself I was imagining it, that it was impossible, but . . . here you are."

Tali and Dan were the Altmans, Madison's godparents.

"Julie?" I asked.

Madi grinned. "My daughter."

"Whoa."

"Right? It's crazy. She just turned eight."

I couldn't help but start doing some math in my head.

Mads spared me the trouble. "She's not yours, you idiot."

"That's not what I was thinking."

She raised her eyebrows.

I ignored her skepticism. "You're sure you don't have time?"

"I'm sorry," Madi said. "I have to go. But . . . what about you?"

"I don't have any kids."

"I meant, what are you doing here? Are you back?"

"Oh," I said. "Baba wanted to see me. He's in the hospital."

"Your grandfather, right?" she asked, her tone gentle. "I met him a couple of times. He's such a sweet man. Dan tells me he's always asking after me."

That sounded about right.

"How's your father taking it?"

I shrugged. "It's impossible to tell."

"Well, it's good you're here. You'll be able help him with the move."

"Yeah. I can't believe he's selling this place."

"The average American family moves every eight or ten years. Your dad is actually behind schedule."

"You just happen to know that?"

"I was married to a real estate agent," she told me with a wry smile, "so I heard a lot of stuff like that. Some of it stuck. If you ever need to know anything about countertops, I'm your girl."

"Sounds . . . exciting."

"We don't all grow up to be preachers."

"I didn't."

She frowned. "But I heard—"

"It's a long story, Mads. I'll tell you when you have more time."

"Sounds good," she said. "Let's grab a coffee sometime."

"Absolutely," I said.

"Give me your number. I'll call you."

[#]

I stood in the doorway and watched Madi walk over to the Altmans'.

Before leaving California, I'd made several oaths to my father. They were terms, really, of a peace treaty negotiated between Imam Saifi and myself by Tiger Uncle. I had never intended to abide by any of them, and, over the years, I'd kept none.

The deal was that I would give up acting and never see Madison Porter again. I would break off contact with all my friends, who were apparently bad influences, and dedicate myself to the study of religion and God. The latter I would do at Al-Azhar. In exchange, my parents would pay for room, board, tuition, and any unavoidable expenses.

This last clause, Tiger Uncle had pointed out, was vague and could give rise to conflict. Just so there would be no arguments between me and my father as to which of my expenses were necessary, Tiger Uncle had suggested that the money be managed by him, a proposition to which everyone agreed.

My mother had offered me an alternative. She'd support me if I decided to pick a different path, so long as that path led to my becoming a physician. I showed her my transcript and that was the end of that.

The promise about Madi was the first one I'd broken.

Before I left, Madison and I had snuck into our school's auditorium, which was just a gym with a raised stage built in it. I had wanted a last moment on there with her, because we'd had so many of those and it seemed like we'd never have one again. I had decided to do what was then my favorite soliloquy from Shakespeare for her. The one that starts: "But soft, what light through yonder window breaks?"

Things hadn't gone at all like I'd imagined. She'd started crying when I explained that I was leaving. She thought she was in love with me. I thought the same except, of course, vice versa. She kissed me and I kissed her, and we kept on kissing each other until we lost our breath and our reason and our words and all barriers between us and we learned, together for the first time, that poetry and eloquence are not the most profound, most powerful, most beautiful languages of love.

The first and best language of love is love. It is sufficient unto itself. It is all.

Holy men would be offended by that thought, I'm sure, once they were done being appalled that our virtue had been lost—no, not lost, but surrendered, perhaps, or maybe gifted to each other, on that night—because that is how they describe God, as needing no one but Himself.

They are, however, not the same thing. God, as they conceive Him, is eternal and not contingent upon circumstances or even belief, while love is mortal and can only survive if faith with it is kept. It lives and dies in the world just like we do and is buried too, not within the earth but within our hearts.

It is more than human and less than divine.

On their porch, before she walked into the home of the people who had finished raising her, Madi paused and glanced back in my direction, I think with the expectation that she would find me where she'd left me. She waved. I nodded and retreated inside, a mess of thoughts and hopes and memories.

[#]

My heart wanted to pause and take some time to process

the turmoil seeing Madison again had unleashed on it. My stomach had other ideas. It growled, insisting that it be served first, which was fair. I hadn't eaten in a long time.

Unfortunately, there wasn't much in the house. The pantry was empty and the fridge had nothing promising in it. There was a gallon of two-percent milk that smelled expired, a nearly empty bowl of fried okra, and a few stale chapatis, now as hard as crackers, folded up in aluminum foil.

I had no idea what Mom's life was like these days, but based on what I'd seen so far, she was most likely winning the divorce.

I thought about ordering in from a restaurant, but then I realized that if I went to Tiger Uncle's grocery store, I might find more than food there. I might find answers. He might be able to shed some light on Dad's inexplicable financial problems.

It was possible, of course, that he wouldn't be there. The store had been his first venture. Tiger had subsequently made a fortune by buying and renting out properties in Redding and the adjoining town of Anderson. He'd built a modest real estate empire for himself over the decades and, I suspected, no longer had any need for his first small business.

He'd been rich even when I was young, though, and yet I'd seen him manning the cash register often. Maybe that hadn't changed. Maybe he still cared about the place where his story had begun

I didn't see him when I got there, but I did see someone I now recognized.

"Azaan," Kashaf, the woman who had just shown up at my father's place, greeted me from behind the counter, "I told you that you would see me around."

"Looks like you were right. Is Tiger Uncle around?"

"In the back."

"Could you get him, please?"

"Are you looking for something? Maybe I can—"

"No," I said. "It's personal."

She didn't move.

"I just want to talk to him about my dad," I added, hoping to prod her into action.

"What's wrong with Imam Saifi?"

I sighed. "Could you just—"

"Let's hang out," she said.

"What?"

"I want to talk to you."

I blinked. "Uh . . . look, you seem like a nice girl and everything, but I'm not interested in—"

She scoffed. "I did not mean that. It's just that you seem interesting, and my brother, Ilham, and I recently moved here. We don't really know anyone. It would be useful to make a friend."

"Ah. Well, I'm not going to be here very long. I'm going back to London soon." I grimaced when I realized I'd slipped. "I mean, um . . . Dover. I'll be back there soon. My point is that I won't be able to be much of a friend to you guys."

Kashaf thought about this, then nodded, "Fine."

"So, could you go get—"

"You don't look like him," she said.

"My dad?"

"He has weak genes."

"Well, thank God for that."

She chuckled. "Yes."

A door across from us, near a line of refrigerators offering all manner of caffeinated and non-caffeinated beverages, flung open and Kashaf jumped. Then, with a quick nod in my direction, she moved away and started rearranging, entirely unnecessarily, a stack of tabloids next to the register.

Tiger Uncle marched in. He had aged well, and I had no doubt there was a complex skin care regimen behind this preservation of his . . . well, not his youth, exactly, but his very late middle age. I'd have to ask him about it someday.

He was wearing a bright pink sateen shirt, the top three buttons of which had been left open, revealing a dense patch of salt-and-pepper hair on his chest.

His sharp eyes locked on me, and I waved a little to greet him. He didn't respond. He turned quickly to look at his cashier and, seeing that she was occupied with a task, seemed to relax. When his attention returned to me, there was something not quite right with the grin he tossed in my direction. "Azaan? You're back."

Before I could respond, he came over and engulfed me in a bear hug, which, along with the cloud of cologne that surrounded him, was suffocating. Then he reached out and grabbed my hand, holding it in his rather than shaking it. He was wearing rings with orange gemstones of various shades on all his fingers.

"Welcome home, meri jaan. You seem to have returned in good condition. Fit. Broad shoulders. Tall. Nice. But your dressing, that's too much like your father. Learn from me, not from him. Pretty peacocks get to wet their beaks."

"What?"

"I'm saying that God has blessed you in your looks. Do not be miserly. Share with the world His generosity. If you dressed like me, women would faint when they saw you. They'd be falling over themselves before you in the streets. That's how it was when I was young."

"Sounds inconvenient."

"Appearances are important, I'm saying."

I gave him a pointed look. "Exactly. I look like an imam."

"Bhai, where is it written that imams have to walk around in their work clothes? Doctors don't always carry their . . . those things they put in their ears to check your heart. Do lawyers in London wear their black coats and silly, curly wigs everywhere?"

"No."

"What some of these preachers do, going everywhere in their thobes and kufi caps, it's like a basketball player living in his uniform. It's not necessary, right?"

I nodded.

"Wear what you want, and if Saqi has a problem with it, say to him what I said to you. Just don't go around looking like you're prowling for converts. Women don't like that. Well, most of them don't, and the ones that do, they won't climb your minaret."

A few feet away, Kashaf made a sound. It sounded like disgust.

Tiger Uncle shot her a dangerous look, then grabbed me by the arm and started pulling me toward the door. "Let us talk outside."

"It's awful out there."

"It's awful everywhere. This world is an abode of suffering. Everything is and has always been terrible. That is why they say what they say in Algeria."

"What do they say there?"

"C'est la vie."

I bowed my head a little to concede his point.

Tiger Uncle grew serious and stern as soon as the door closed behind us. "Did she say anything to you?"

"Kashaf? No. Not really. Why?"

"She's trouble, that one."

I blinked. "She is?"

"I want you to stay away from her. She is not . . . no good will come from you getting to know her."

"I don't—"

"Trust me, Azaan," he said, with a lot more intensity and earnestness than was usual for him. "All your life I have guided you, no? Have I ever led you astray?"

I shook my head.

"Then believe me when I tell you that you should not go anywhere near this person. Promise me you—"

"Who is she?"

Tiger Uncle hesitated, then said, "She is my daughter."

"I didn't know you had children."

"I didn't either. It turns out that it is hard to keep track of these things. Just leave her be, okay? Promise me you'll stay away."

"But why?"

"After everything I've done for you," he said, "you ask me why? Is that right, Dil Shikan?"

"Okay, Uncle," I said. "You don't have to tell me."

He studied me intently, as if he could figure out just by looking at me if I were sincere. He would've had an easier time of it if he hadn't taught me how to lie. After a moment, however, he seemed satisfied and his easygoing manner returned. He clapped me on the shoulder. "Good. There is plenty of other fruit for you to eat, yes?"

"Uh . . . what?"

"Women, meri jaan. Women. Have you made any of them halal for yourself?"

"You're asking me if I'm married?" I asked, genuinely confused. "No, of course not. I would've told you."

"Would you? Sometimes I don't tell people. Less questions that way. But what are you waiting for, Sheikh Stud? It is not Ramadan. Why are you fasting? Follow my example. Marry but don't tarry, and your life will be extraordinary."

"You're a poet."

Tiger Uncle smiled. "You make fun if you want, but the truth is that I really am an artist. So many backs I have painted."

"That's . . . really gross."

He giggled like a schoolboy who'd just told his first dirty joke. "The stories I could tell . . ."

"That's why I'm here, actually. A story. I need to know what is going on with Dad."

He turned serious again. "What do you mean?"

"Baba told me that Dad is behind on his bills."

"I wouldn't pay attention to your grandfather. He's a useless man."

"I thought you'd like him," I said.

"Why?"

"You two seem to have a lot in common."

For the first time in my life, I saw Tiger Uncle look truly offended. "What are you saying? Me? Like that . . . animal? No, beta, no. You have not grasped the fullness of me."

"There has to be a less weird way to say that," I muttered.

"I am a goldsmith. Your Baba is a blacksmith. You see? People like him, they think you cannot follow a religion and still have fun at the same time, which is something I have made happen. I have never violated the letter of the law. I've just had my way with its spirit. I am a sharp tool. He is a blunt tool."

"But you admit that you're both tools?"

He went on, undeterred by my interjection. "I understand

what he doesn't, that God is a technician. So, I look for ways to get what I want in little details. I don't disregard them."

"God is a technician?" I asked.

"Of course. What is the Quran but a user's manual?"

"I must have missed that sermon. Anyway, no matter what you think of Baba, he isn't wrong. I've seen Dad's overdue bills myself. He's in financial trouble."

Tiger Uncle's brow furrowed. "Really? I didn't know. I would have helped him if I did."

That rang true. Whatever his other faults, Tiger was famously generous.

"It doesn't look good, does it?" I asked. "With the cash missing from the mosque."

My father's best friend gave me a disappointed look. "What a thing to say. You are talking about Saqlain Saifi. He should be above your suspicion."

"I meant it wouldn't look good to other people," I explained.

That seemed to pacify him.

"If he needs money," I continued, "at least that explains why he is selling the house."

"Oh, that's not related," Tiger said. "He told me it is too much space for him. You know the new mosque we've built? There's a lot of land attached to it, so we also made a few small apartments on the grounds. We can lease them out and that way the community has an ongoing stream of income."

"Smart."

"Thank you. Anyway, your father is living in one of those now. He's closer to the community this way too. It helps him serve us better."

"And he's not behind on rent?"

"Well, he's the imam, Azaan. The board of directors is not

charging him anything. We aren't charging you anything either."

"Me?"

"You are staying in the unit next to Saqi's. He didn't tell you?"

I shook my head. "I figured I'd be at the house."

"No, his realtor wants it empty for showings. You will be our guest. I'm speaking now as a member of the board. We're happy to have you."

"Thanks. Let's go back to what we were talking about, though. If he isn't paying rent, Dad should have plenty for his expenses, right? He's still working, and Mom is probably still giving him some support—"

"No, no, that door, like Iqra's legs, is permanently closed. He wouldn't accept any alimony from her in the settlement. He didn't think it was manly."

"Smart," I said again, in a different tone this time though.

"Your point is still valid. Even if he only has his own income, why he's having issues is difficult to understand. Knowing Saqi, he probably gave too much to charity and is stretched a little thin right now." He patted my back. "You don't worry about this, beta. I'll take care of it."

"You're sure?"

"This is what I do. I solve problems. You leave it to me. Now come. I'll take you where you're supposed to be."

"Can I get something to eat first? I'm starving."

"Of course. Tell me. What is your pleasure?"

[#]

I couldn't help but be impressed when I caught sight of the new mosque. It wasn't grand by any means, especially by the standards of the rest of the world. It had no imperious domes, soaring minarets, or elaborate tiles with pretty patterns anywhere.

It was, instead, a plain rectangular structure—twenty thousand square feet, boasted Tiger Uncle—painted the color of sand, with some scaffolding still attached to its left side. For some reason, there were two large Romanesque columns at the entrance. They framed what looked like a solid wood door, which was the most beautiful part of a building that seemed like it had a lot of functionality and, perhaps ironically, very little soul.

It was the perfect spot from which to practice what I'd heard British Muslims, who tended to be a lot more conservative than their American counterparts, call McIslam—the more, shall we say, user-friendly version of the faith, which they thought was practiced in California. It was not, in the minds of some, the true path.

Of course, that was not at all the flavor of religion my father would teach here. His interpretation of Islam's doctrine and dogma would be viewed as strict, even by some across the pond. He was very much what one might call a Salafi.

Around the mosque was a massive parking lot, at the edge of which, to one side, stood a small three-story apartment complex. There were nine units in total, though at the moment only one had its lights on.

"Not bad, right?" Tiger Uncle asked, his tone shining with pride.

"Amazing," I said.

That was true in a way. Unlike the glamorous places of worship, sparkling with splendor in Turkey, Malaysia, Saudi, or Iran, this wasn't a gift granted by some sultan or a command decreed by a king. This mosque, humble though it was, had been built by the uncommon efforts of common men. It was the result of grassroots funding solicited by my father and Tiger Uncle all over the world.

It had taken them almost two decades to raise the millions needed. That was where the time had gone in this particular project, not in the making of it, but in the gathering of resources to make it possible.

In that sense, the squat building was a towering achievement.

"You should be proud of Saqi," Tiger told me.

"I am."

"Are you going to tell him that?"

"Probably not."

He shook his head. "You like that Shakespeare fellow, right?"

"He's all right."

"Do you know what he wrote? He wrote that having a kid hurts more than when a serpent bites you or when your tooth rots."

I smiled. "Are you sure that's what he said?"

"Definitely. I had to read his stuff in school, and my memory, you know, it's like a steel cage. A tiger never forgets."

"I'll take your word for it."

"Anyway, that's why I decided not to have little ones. It's the most natural relationship in the world, I think, but also the most difficult one. Besides, they always seemed like a lot of work. Freedom is better than children."

"Except you do have a child now."

Tiger Uncle frowned, and it seemed like he had no earthly idea what I was talking about. Then his brow cleared and he smiled. "Right. Kashaf. You're correct, of course. Sorry. That still slips my mind. Old cat, new tricks, you know? Chalo, let's go see what is going on with your father."

He led me inside the mosque and past a series of offices built for the staff. It was a major step up from the utility closet out of which my father had been working for most of his professional life.

Quite a few light fixtures still had to be installed, there was some sawdust on the ground, and none of the doors had handles yet. This was still a work in progress. These were all finishing touches, though. The heavy lifting had already been done.

I stopped by a message that had been poorly spray-painted in furious, uneven, jet-black paint on one of the walls. It read: "You know what you did." There was no context to it, except for the fact that this was a mosque in America, and this was the work of vandals, which led me to deduce this was an oblique reference to 9/11.

"What do you think?" Tiger asked.

"It's no 'Redrum.'"

Tiger didn't look like he got the reference, but he didn't ask me to explain, indicating that he didn't care, which was fair.

"How are you guys going to put a stop to this, Uncle? Are you going to hire guards?"

"Your father says he'll take care of it."

"How is Dad going to do that?"

"Well, he lives nearby now. If he sees anything amiss, he'll tell us. Come this way."

The conference room Tiger took me to was small and unassuming and contained a modest variety of junk food, a large water dispenser, a coffee maker, an old projector, and a picnic table around which sat the board of directors of the Nameless Mosque.

It was tradition to name masjids after famous historical figures, usually companions and sometimes sultans or kings. This particular institution hadn't yet been so honored. There was a committee, according to Tiger, which was currently deadlocked. There was no hope of a quick resolution to the issue.

The board, in addition to my father and Tiger, was made up of three other men. Two of them I didn't know. The third, the youngest by far, got to his feet and walked over to us when we came in. It took me a moment to place him, and he used that time to embrace me, which was an excessive amount of affection from someone I'd barely known.

Jibreel Jameel had been that kid in the community no one under the age of forty liked. The adults in our lives had adored him. They constantly talked about his accomplishments. We had to hear all about how he was a wunderkind who got the best grades in school, who'd memorized large portions of the Quran, who stayed up late every night in Ramadan to pray, and who was universally known to be well behaved.

Jibreel had known they admired him, and he'd walked around with his nose in the air, thinking he was the bee's knees. Because he was held up as an example to the rest of us, as someone who ought to be emulated, we naturally hated him a little. He grew up with no friends.

I was lucky. No one ever said nice things about me. In fact, my father routinely told people about my faults, which were many. Some of these he shared with the community from the pulpit. "Don't be like Azaan" was a sentiment voiced by many families in the area. It made me very popular.

As a result, Jibreel and I hadn't been at all close when we were young.

You wouldn't have known that, though, from the warm way

he greeted me just then. He hugged me longer than Madi had and kept squeezing me long after I'd let go of him, my arms flopping uselessly at my sides.

When he finally released me, he looked at me with small, watery eyes that a thick set of spectacles magnified a little, and said, "Wow. Look at you, man. What a transformation. I can't believe it. Who would've thought you, of all people, would end up being an imam? Nobody. Truly, Allah could even guide Shaitan if He wanted."

That seemed like a shot at the person I'd been . . . well, the person I was, really, even if it was delivered in a ridiculously friendly manner. Not that I cared. He wasn't wrong. If anything, he was the one who ought to have grown up to become a peddler of piety.

As a teenager, he walked around with a small notebook in which he wrote everything he did.

You see, Islam works off a system of merits and demerits called hasanat—beautiful actions we are supposed to accumulate—and gunah, which are sins we are to avoid. Everything we do in our lives is written down by angels, and the record that results will be used as evidence for or against us on the Day of Judgment.

If the righteous stuff someone has done outnumbers their bad actions, they go to the Good Place. If not, the fiery depths of hell await.

Some actions are worth more than others. When you are reciting the Quran, for example, you earn hasanat at the rate of ten per letter, which means—according to Jibreel—that a complete reading of the holy text is worth around 33,200,000 points, redeemable at a later, as yet unannounced date.

The exact value of every possible good thing people can do as participants in this rewards program isn't known. Muslims don't usually obsess about the score. They just live decent, upright lives and trust that their account is growing in the afterlife.

Jibreel, however, had come up with his own system to encourage righteousness. He'd put together a chart listing every action he could think of and had assigned it a value. His plan was to record all his actions every day and then, right before going to bed, figure out how good or bad he'd been in numerical terms. It was the only way, he believed, to keep his soul in check and to track his progress toward heaven.

I knew all this because he'd explained it at Sunday school, where he'd tried to get our instructor to make us all adopt this method of reckoning. Our teacher had tried it, but it hadn't caught on. It was way too onerous for everyone except Jibreel, who, being the holy little trooper that he was, had persisted with it.

"Don't just stand there," he said. "Come in, come in. You already know the imam, of course, and the president, Tiger Uncle. I am the treasurer here—"

"You're the treasurer?" I asked. "You're the one who is—"

Tiger nudged me in the ribs rather hard.

"—the one who handles all the finances?" I finished after taking a sharp turn in the middle of my sentence.

"Yes, that is what a treasurer does," Jibreel said.

I shook my head. This fastidious, preening little cockatoo was the one creating all the fuss about missing funds at the mosque? In that case, it could be much ado about nothing. Unless he'd changed a great deal, Jibreel was the kind of guy who'd throw a fit over a quarter he couldn't account for. This whole thing was probably just him overreacting to the mismanagement of some petty sum.

Jibreel was still talking. "That over there is Uncle Nadeem, who handles public relations and interfaith outreach."

"I've found that can be a lot of fun," I said, shaking the man's proffered hand.

"And this here is Uncle Karar. He's in charge of HR and of supervising what construction remains, though that will be done soon. Have you seen—"

"Thank you," my father broke in. "That's enough. Azaan is obviously very tired. You can see from his eyes that he's exhausted. There is no need to bore him with our business."

"Brothers," Tiger Uncle said, throwing his arms out in a grand gesture, "it is late for all of us. Whatever issues you are discussing will still be here tomorrow. Why don't you wrap up and go home. I need to talk to the imam."

Jibreel frowned. "But he and I were supposed to go over the accounts to—"

"Yes, yes, Mr. Newly Minted Treasurer, we will deal with it. Your work is important, not urgent. You have to learn to tell the difference."

It seemed to me that Jibreel disagreed and was about to say so when Uncle Karar got to his feet. "My wife will be waiting for me to eat dinner, I'm sure, and I have to tell you, Imam Saifi, she won't be happy to hear you won't let our daughter hold her class here. Not happy at all."

"Yoga is haram," my father said with utmost certainty. "We admire your daughter's desire to help the community, but—"

I was so sure that I must have misheard him that I actually leaned forward. "I'm sorry. Did you just say yoga is forbidden in Islam?"

All eyes turned to me.

"Isn't it?" My father asked, his voice laden with authority, irritation, and hints that he would brook no disagreement.

"Why would it be?"

"Because it is based on non-Muslim practices," he snapped, slipping into preacher mode. "Like saluting the sun. Why do people need to salute the sun? What possible sense does that make? They should be saluting God."

"And the poses are not decent enough to be taught in a holy place," the other board member, whose name I had already forgotten, pointed out. "Brother Karar's daughter practices at home for fitness. That is one thing. Having the women of the community come here to learn doggy style and how to open their lotuses, it is not right."

"Not to mention the pants," Jibreel added.

"Mmm. Yes. Those delicious, tight, clingy, stretchy pants," Tiger Uncle murmured, not at all helpfully.

Dad pointed at his old friend. "You see? This is why it is not permitted."

I shook my head. These guys were unbelievable.

"There is some dispute on the matter among scholars, but the strongest written opinions on this are on my side," my father declared. "I'll send you—"

"Wait. People have spent actual time writing legal opinions about this?"

Jibreel nodded. "It is a hot button issue."

"You're kidding," I said.

"Well, ever since the attack on that event in the Maldives—"

"What attack?"

Jibreel seemed to think this was something I—or at least my character—should already know about. "Some Muslim protesters got . . . zealous at a Yoga Day event there and disrupted it. Did you not hear about it? It was all over the news."

"I don't know." I tried to mask my ignorance with indignation, a trick everyone who'd grown up in the era of social media knew well. "I must have missed it. Maybe it was a day when I was distracted by less pressing news from the Muslim world. Maybe something had happened in Syria or Afghanistan or Palestine or Myanmar or—"

The rest of them had the decency to look chastised, but my father cut me off. "Okay, okay. We will deal with this. You go rest. Here is the key to unit two. Your things are already in there."

"Actually, Dad," I said, "since it sounds like you're almost done here, Tiger Uncle and I wanted to—"

Tiger put an arm around my shoulder. "You relax. I'll talk to him about it. Go on."

"I am pretty beat," I conceded.

"Then go. We'll catch up some other time," Jibreel promised. "I'll come find you soon. After all, I know where you're staying."

"Awesome," I said. "Something to look forward to."

My father stopped me just as I was about to leave. "One more thing."

"Yeah?"

"Do you want me to hold your passport?" he asked. "I can put it in my safe."

"No, it's fine."

"Are you sure?"

"Absolutely," I told him. "After all, it's a mosque. Who'd steal something here?"

[#]

The apartment was a studio, and a small one at that, but it

was still grand when compared to the sofa I was sleeping on in London. My luggage, as promised, was waiting for me, and next to it was a rolled-up sleeping bag.

I made my way to the bathroom. The mirror there showed me a stranger, with his tragic side-part hairstyle, useless glasses, and glued-on beard. The sight of him—of me in this role—made the knot in my chest grow a little heavier. I didn't understand why. I'd seen him before, at the airport, but the long day had shifted the burden of my emotions somehow, and it was now upsetting to see what my father wanted me to be.

I swear I'll never understand myself.

Taking a deep breath, I slowly started to peel the—well, I guess you could call it a wig—off my cheeks. I winced as the adhesive gave way to my persistent pulling, leaving behind splotches of a thin white film on my face. These were difficult and painful to scrub off. When I finally managed to rid myself of them, they left behind irritated, itchy red skin, almost like I was having a reaction to the chemicals I'd had on all day. Hopefully, that would subside by the morning.

I took off the spectacles I was wearing and ran my hands repeatedly through my hair, but I still couldn't manage to get me to look like me.

I heard raised voices from the unit next door. It sounded like my father was yelling at Tiger Uncle and Tiger was screaming back, and all I could make out were the words "and look what happened." It was so typical, this being alone in my room, listening to my father fight with someone. In this case, it wasn't Mom, but that didn't make it different enough for it to feel unfamiliar.

I shook my head at my reflection, then pulled off my thobe and threw it aside. I stepped into the shower knowing that it would drown out the argument. I'd ask Tiger Heart what was said later. There was no way I was going to intervene now. I'd learned long ago not to be around Imam Saifi when he was angry.

I ran the water as hot as it would go, even though it stung a little. It wasn't until I stepped out that I realized there was no towel around, so I stood there, naked, growing cold despite the steam lingering around me, drenched and fully myself.

I went over to my suitcase leaving wet footprints on the floor. The muffled argument next door was still going, but the voices of the two old friends were more subdued now.

I used a cotton T-shirt to dry myself, then pulled a second one on, along with joggers, and rolled out the sleeping bag. I lay down on it with no idea of what time it was and, briefly, I slept.

Chapter Seven

2008

The school rarely served bacon cheeseburgers for lunch, and I almost never ate them. I'd learned through painful experience that if I did, other Muslim students would tell their parents that Imam Saifi's son had been eating pork, and I'd have to pay for lunch a second time when I got home.

In addition to getting walloped by my father—eating swine was majorly prohibited, after all—I got yelled at by Mom too. According to what she'd read, the "beef" patties involved in this meal somehow had twenty-six or so ingredients, and she didn't approve of me putting food that processed into my body. She was concerned it wasn't good for me.

In Ramadan, however, I was free to do what I wanted. Anyone inclined to tattle on me would be fasting and so wouldn't be around the cafeteria in the first place. It was the perfect opportunity to sin.

Still, out of an abundance of caution, I found a spot in a quiet corner and decided to eat by myself. I did it fast too. It wasn't about pleasure. The food wasn't any good. I only wanted it because I wasn't supposed to be having it.

"Hey, Romeo," someone behind me said just as I took my first bite.

I jumped, knocked my knee against a table, groaned, choked, sputtered, let go of my burger, then lunged for it as it fell toward the ground, grasping and gasping. It slipped through my fingers and rolled away to land close to the black, white, and light pink Air Jordan 1s Madison Porter was wearing.

"Oh my God," she said, kneeling down to pick up my now-wasted meal. "I'm so sorry. I didn't mean to startle you."

I held up a hand so she'd wait a minute. Once I finished coughing, I took a swig of water from a bottle, and trying to look as awesome as possible under the circumstances, using a deeper voice than usual, said, "Madison. Hi."

"Are you okay?"

"Yeah. Of course."

"Let me buy you another one," she said, handing me the pink slime concoction I'd been about to consume. "Wait. Is that bacon?"

I dropped my unfortunate lunch down on my tray and veiled it with napkins. "It's fine. Really. You don't have to."

"I feel bad."

"Don't."

"Okay," she said uncertainly. Then she looked down, cleared her throat, and ran a hand through her dark hair and asked, "So, um . . . can I talk to you for a second?"

I rubbed my knee and got to my feet. "Sure."

"We don't have to go anywhere. I can just join you."

"Oh. No, you're right, it's just . . . I should have gotten up when you first came over. It's . . . uh, you're a lady, so . . . my dad says it's a sign of respect."

"Aw. He sounds sweet."

"He's . . . really something."

I tried not to stare as Madison took a seat across from me. She was the only prayer of mine that God had, so far as I could remember, answered. I wasn't much for speaking to Him, but since I was forced to do it, I'd asked for her. Not for her to be my girlfriend or anything. That would've required a miracle, and though Allah could perform those, I didn't think I had any right to ask for them.

Yes, Moses had been allowed to part the Red Sea and Jonah had survived being swallowed whole by a whale, but those were great men with great purpose. I was a teenager with an ardent crush on a girl I'd only spoken to a couple of times. We were not the same and, therefore, it wasn't right to demand or expect the same treatment.

I'd made a more modest request. I had asked that Madison win the part of Juliet in the play I was cast in as Romeo and—whether because of her own talents or because of divine grace or some combination of both—it had happened. I was pretty sure no one had seen my fist pump when the announcement had been made.

"I looked everywhere for you. I thought you'd be fasting."

"Everything all right?"

"Uh-huh," she said. Then she looked away and bit her bottom lip, a habit of hers that was going to send me back to Mom's cardiologist friend one day, I swear. "Well, no, actually. I . . . so you know, obviously, that we're going to be together. Acting together, I mean. In the play."

"It's going to be fun."

"Right. Listen, Azaan, the thing is, I'm really nervous and I don't know who to talk to about it. And since you've done this before . . ."

"A little stage fright is normal."

"It's not that." Her blue-gray eyes were locked on her delicate hands, which were intertwined and resting on the table between us, and she was blushing hard. "It's about the kissing scenes. I haven't done that before. With anyone. And the idea of doing it in front of an audience is freaking me out."

"We're not really going to kiss."

"We're not?"

"I've heard some actors do, and that would be . . ." I paused to clear my throat. "What I'm saying is that I'm sure Ms. Aceves expects us to just fake it."

Madison frowned. "Fake it?"

"It's a stage kiss. You put your hands on my face. Then you cover my mouth with your thumbs and your lips touch those."

"Oh." She exhaled and sat back in her chair. "Okay. Well, now I feel silly."

"Don't. It's cool. You didn't know."

She smiled, then after a moment, asked, "What were you about to say before?"

"When?"

"You said that some actors really—"

"Yeah?" I prompted.

"And then you said 'that'd be.' That would be what?"

I hesitated, then admitted the truth. "Awesome."

She raised her eyebrows. "Awesome?"

"More convincing, is what I meant. For the play. I'd be willing to make the sacrifice."

Madison grinned. "Well, points for being selfless, I guess. I couldn't do it. I mean, having your first kiss in front of your parents. Can you imagine? That'd be so embarrassing."

"I wish I could kiss you . . . uh, anyone, I mean, in front of my parents."

"Why?"

"It'd be hilarious. My father is super religious. It'd piss him off."

She frowned. "And that's something you want to do?"

"It's what I'm good at, Madison."

"My friends call me Madi," she said, "or Mads."

"There's no consensus?"

She laughed. "No. You can pick either one."

"Okay," I said. "I'll think about it."

"It's not that serious. I mean, 'what's in a name,' right?"

"Quoting Shakespeare. A girl after my own heart."

Madi chuckled. "Come on. I'll walk with you. We've got history together, don't we?"

We did.

And we would.

Chapter Eight

2009

(530) 555-7866:

Why is Madison Porter sleeping with you?

THE TEXT MESSAGE TOOK ME BY SURPRISE FOR SEVERAL reasons.

For one, it wasn't true.

Well, okay, so technically it was true. It just wasn't accurate.

Madi and I were together, leaning on the school wall that faced the football field. We'd been studying biology—theoretically, not practically—and Mads had fallen asleep. She'd pulled an all-nighter to write a paper and was beat. Her head was resting on my shoulder, and she was holding on to my left arm.

In other words, yes, she was with me and, yes, she was

sleeping, but to say that she was sleeping with me was overstating the matter quite a bit, and in a manner that was sure to cause trouble. So even though I didn't know who the message was from, I was pretty sure it had been written by a social vulture, a scavenger looking to make gossip out of nothing much at all.

I'd figured we were alone. Classes had ended a while ago. We—along with a few other drama students—had stayed behind to rehearse for our upcoming play, but our teacher had been forced to leave to deal with some kind of personal issue. The others had all left soon afterward.

I glanced around. It was a bright, beautiful, warm day, which was good for everyone but me. It wasn't the kind of weather one wore a black leather jacket in. However, I was wearing mine. It's what I did back then. It was my thing. It told people I was cool. I was a brand before social media made everybody one. As a result, I'd wanted to stay inside, where there was air conditioning, but Madi had wanted to get some fresh air. There's no accounting for taste.

Not seeing anyone, I struggled to type out a response with just one hand.

AZAAN:

Who is this?

(530) 555-7866:

Jibreel Jameel.

AZAAN:

How'd you get my number?

JIBREEL:

From Haroon.

AZAAN:

What'd you say to him?

JIBREEL:

I didn't tell him you were sinning, if that's what you mean.

AZAAN:

Where are you?

JIBREEL:

On your left, behind the big tree.

AZAAN:

What are you doing there?

JIBREEL:

Watching you sin.

I rolled my eyes.

AZAAN:

Come here and talk to me.

JIBREEL:

I don't like looking at her.

AZAAN:

Why?

JIBREEL:

She's very pretty. She's one of those girls. The kind of girl that makes you think things. Things I don't want to write about in my journal.

AZAAN:

Your Ledger of Good and Evil?

JIBREEL:

I think my parents are reading it.

AZAAN:

Duh.

JIBREEL:

I'd marry her if she were Muslim.

AZAAN:

Sure.

JIBREEL:

I'd marry her hard. So hard. But she's Jewish. Did you know she's Jewish?

AZAAN:

Yeah.

JIBREEL:

I suppose I could still marry her. They're People of the Book.

AZAAN:

Good luck with that.

JIBREEL:

What do you guys do?

AZAAN:

What?

JIBREEL:

When you're alone together. What kinds of things have you done?

JIBREEL:

You have to tell me.

JIBREEL:

Or I'll let your father know what I saw. You'll get in trouble.

AZAAN:

Go ahead. I don't care.

JIBREEL:

Liar.

JIBREEL:

Come on. You're making things worse for yourself.

JIBREEL:

Are you mad?

JIBREEL:

I was kidding. I won't tell.

JIBREEL:

Azaan?

JIBREEL:

Let's be friends.

Shaking my head, I put my phone away without bothering to respond. Whatever. He could go running to rat me out to my father if he wanted. I wasn't afraid.

I mean, I was, obviously, but . . . I wasn't at the same time.

Sure, getting beat would hurt, and I didn't want to suffer through it, but being around Mads was worth that and more.

Clearing my throat, I straightened up a little, enough to cause Madi's head to move a bit. She groaned softly, blinked when the sunlight hit her eyes, and sat up.

"Ugh. So bright."

"You're the one who wanted to sit out here," I reminded her.

"How long was I out?"

"A few minutes," I said. "You all right?"

"Mm-hmm."

"You shouldn't stay up all night. It's not good for you."

Madison chuckled. "Right. Says the guy who's getting cigarettes—which are actual poison—from Daeshim."

"How'd you know?"

"He's the only senior who sells them," she said. "And you stink a little."

"I don't."

"I kind of hate it," she said. "I wish you'd stop." Then she yawned, rubbed her eyes, and sat up. "Anyway, where were we?"

"You were about to tell me you're going home."

"No. I meant in bio."

"We'll pick it up later. The assignment isn't due for, like, four days."

"I know. But Papa wants to take his plane out again this weekend. We're going to Santa Rosa, I think. I swear, ever since he got that thing, it's taken over our lives."

"I can't believe you guys have a private plane."

"It's not so glamorous when you see it. It's from, like, the seventies, and it's not at all nice. Papa said you could come check it out. He'll be happy to take you up."

"Well, I mean, since you make it sound so great . . ."

She laughed.

"Why don't you tell them you need to study? That you'll go on the next trip? If you say it's for school, he'll understand, right? And maybe I could come over and we could do biology."

"It'd be nice to stay home and chill," she admitted. "Plus,

we just got that new online streaming service from Netflix. We could watch a movie."

"Sounds like fun."

"Okay," Madi said, her eyes suddenly shining. "Let's do it. Saturday then? They'll be back Sunday and you're training with that acting coach of yours anyway, right?"

"Claire, yeah."

"So . . . ?" she asked. "It's a date?"

"Absolutely."

I decided it was a good idea to avoid going home for as long as possible. No doubt Jibreel would hurry over to his beloved Imam Sucky and report everything he'd seen. My father's temper would be up right now. His wrath was always worse when it was fresh. It sometimes cooled slightly with the passage of time.

Unfortunately, I had nowhere to go and nothing to do.

I called Daeshim—my source of tobacco and, once or twice, marijuana—who said he had a couple of people over and I could come too.

His friends didn't know me, but they were cool. No one asked how old I was. Not that it was important, at least not initially. They were just watching a Giants game.

That changed when we discovered that Daeshim had stolen two bottles of Devil's Springs Sunset Rum from his step-mom's stash. We all got plastered real fast after that. My age probably should have mattered at that point.

I vaguely remember someone driving me home and having to pretty much carry me to the front porch. Whoever it was rang the bell, dropped me, and ran, which for some reason seemed hilarious. I remember laughing and laughing and laughing.

I remember my father dragging me inside, making me take off my shirt, put my hands behind my head, and kneel.

The punishment for drinking alcohol in Islam is eighty lashes.

I didn't count how many times my father whipped me with his belt. He probably got to forty or fifty but stopped when his arm got tired and his shoulder started aching.

I remember the sound of hard leather cracking against the exposed flesh of my back and tearing it away, leaving it raw.

I remember my spine arching, my muscles spasming, crying out . . . no, wait, that was me. I was screaming and rolling around on the ground as he rained blows down on me.

He left me there, curled up with my knees against my chest, weeping, by the entrance.

My mother found me when she came home.

She took me to my room, put some ointment on my back, and said something about how pills would have to wait until I was sober.

The sound of them yelling at each other was much louder than usual.

There was a bottle of prescription painkillers on my side table when I woke the next morning. My head was pounding. It seemed like I had a fever. My back felt like it had been shredded. I tried to get up to go to school. I didn't want to say home, not with Imam Saifi, but moving hurt too much. I gave up and just lay where I was, wondering what would happen next.

Around noon, during what had to be her lunch break, Mom came home and checked on me. She gave me a peanut butter and jelly sandwich to eat and watched as I finished it.

"You crossed a red line, darling," she said. "You simply

cannot behave this way. For better or worse, you are Muslim and you are Saqi's son. Your father wants you to act like it. Now, I do think that what he did was a little excessive—"

I laughed. It came out twisted and unpleasant.

"I've had words with him and—"

The knot in my chest was making it hard to breathe. I thought maybe if I said a little about how I was feeling, it'd relieve some pressure. The effort of forcing words up past it broke my voice and made tears well up in my eyes. "I hate him."

"I am sure you feel that way now, and I certainly understand—"

"I hate you too."

She went quiet for a while, then got to her feet, gathered my plate, and said, "There is no reason to be melodramatic. My brothers used to get this and more from my father, let me tell you. I was very glad to leave that house, even if it meant marrying Saqi. Just remember, Azaan, it could be worse."

"It could be better too, though, right?"

"Yes, well . . . you can take more Vicodin in around four hours. Get some rest."

As she was leaving, I asked, "How long do I have to be here?"

"In our home? Around three years, no?"

"In my room."

"You're not grounded, not that your father and I discussed. So, I suppose that depends entirely on how much pain you are able to tolerate. I imagine it'll be more than a few days. I told your school you were sick. Don't worry about that. Just get some rest."

"You sound terrible," Madi said over the phone.

This was true. My voice was hoarse, but not from a cold like she'd assumed. I'd told her I didn't feel well, which was true.

"I wish I could see you," she added.

"Yeah." There was a pleasant haze around everything, making the world seem dull and distant, urging me to close my eyes and drift away. I was a little high because of the medication I'd been given, but I staved off sleep because it was important to talk to her and cancel our plans. "I don't think tomorrow is happening."

"Oh," she said, not sounding as devastated as I felt, "that's okay. Take care of yourself. We'll do it some other time."

"I'm sorry."

"It's fine. Really. I don't want what you have."

"You really don't," I agreed.

"Honestly, my folks will be relieved. They were trying to be cool with the idea of me having a boy here when they weren't around, but I think they were struggling with it a little."

"You told them our plan?"

"Of course."

I shook my head.

Madison's relationship with her parents made no sense to me. She actually talked to them and told them things, like they were her friends or something. It was so bizarre.

I mean, I knew my family was more messed up than most. There were guys at the mosque who had closer-knit homes than I did, where there was more love and kindness and a lot less . . . violence, I guess. Even so, I couldn't imagine any of them asking permission to have a girl come over while their parents weren't in the house. Or even while they were. It just wasn't a done thing.

It felt, sometimes, that Mads lived in another world with different rules and laws, though I could have—and had—biked over to her place in, like, ten minutes. It was as if we were living in the same place, but not in the same civilization.

I didn't know what to make of that.

This was good, right? This was tolerance. This was America. People were free to be who they were, live how they wanted, believe whatever they identified as true. No one had to dissolve into the melting pot.

Except I couldn't move much just then and my life felt like nothing more than an amalgam of constraints, commands, prohibitions, edicts, and directives, some made up by the people I'd been born to, some by the tribe I'd been birthed in, some by the religion I'd inherited. I didn't feel free, even though it was said, in a kind of important song, that this was the land of people who were.

"Azaan?"

"I missed what you said," I admitted.

"I said I don't think my parents would've even pretended to be okay with anyone else coming over. They really like you."

"They're the only ones."

There was a pause. "No. They're not."

And just like that, despite everything, somehow, my heart managed to dance a whole ballet in about a second.

"Mads—"

"You should rest," she added quickly. "I'll let you go."

"No. Don't."

We both fell silent.

"I'm sorry I can't make it," I told her.

"You said that already."

"I'm not apologizing this time. I'm letting you know I feel bad. For me."

"Don't be stupid. It's not that big a deal."

"It is to me," I said. "Because you are . . ."

"I am . . . ?"

"You're the one I choose first."

"What?"

"I don't always get to make choices. Stuff happens. Life and its awfulness. I was just thinking that I'm not at . . . what's the word? Liberty. I don't have that all the time. But when I do, when I get a chance to choose, you're the one I choose first."

I listened to her breathing for a while.

Then I said, "You're a big deal, Madison. So is not getting to see you."

"Azaan."

"Yeah?"

"How much cough syrup have you had exactly?"

I laughed.

"You're a huge deal too, you idiot. Just . . . feel better, okay? I'll see you in school Monday."

She was wrong.

I didn't see her in school Monday. I didn't see her there for a long while after that.

We also never really had our first date, not because of the disaster that was my life, but because of the one that was about to happen in hers.

On Sunday morning, the sound of my phone vibrating on my nightstand woke me. I had missed calls from Madi. Several of them. There were also texts from pretty much everyone I knew at school. I was about to read the first one when another call came in. It was Jibreel Jameel.

"What do you want?" I asked, more curtly than was polite. I should have been nice to him. It seemed like he hadn't told my father about me and Madi, though I couldn't know for sure. Dad and I hadn't spoken since my flogging, but I suspected that if Imam Saifi had that piece of intelligence, I would have been confronted with it.

"As-salamu alaykum. I am just calling to see how Madison Porter is."

"What's your problem, dude?"

"What do you mean?" Jibreel asked.

"I'm supposed to know how she is first thing in the morning because she is 'sleeping with me'? Get the hell away from me, all right? Leave me alone. And leave Madi—"

"Azaan, I just thought you'd be with her right now."

I growled. "Jibreel, I swear to God—"

"Haven't you heard? Her family died."

Chapter Nine

2022

WHEN THE BUZZING OF MY PHONE WOKE ME THIS TIME, IT was late, around midnight. I groaned and shook my head, pushing away the memory of the day the Porters had passed.

Their 1975 Cessna T310R, a six-seater plane with three people onboard—Madi's father, mother, and sister—had crashed into a mountain peak. It wasn't clear what had happened. The weather hadn't been ideal, so maybe their demise was due to a sudden squall or human error. The authorities tried their best to figure it out, but never could.

I wasn't sure it mattered.

That day I had called Claire and asked her to take me to Madison's house. When I'd explained what was happening, she hadn't asked why I couldn't just go over myself even though it wasn't far. She did note that I was sitting awkwardly in her bright orange Mustang, perched uncomfortably at the edge of the seat.

I'd told her that my back hurt, and Claire had laughed and said I was too young for that.

When Madi saw me, she'd rushed up and thrown her arms around me. It was agony, but I'd let her hold me, despite the pain, because she was hurting more, and it was what she needed then.

I wasn't sure what she needed now, though I knew she needed something, because she had been the one who'd called. She was the one who had pulled me out of my dreams.

I sat up, cleared my throat so my voice wouldn't give away that she'd woken me, and dialed her back.

"I'm sorry I called so late," she said as soon as she answered. "Did I wake you?"

"Is everything okay?" I asked.

"Yes, it's . . . I couldn't . . . what are you doing?"

I looked around the virtually empty apartment. My imam disguise was lying in a heap in a corner, the darkness around me and the darkness outside visible through the window. "I honestly don't know."

Madi didn't have anything to say to that, which seemed reasonable. After a moment, she spoke again. "I did wake you, didn't I?"

"Don't worry about it."

"I'm so sorry."

"You said that already. Mads, what's wrong?"

"Nothing. Honestly. I . . . I couldn't sleep. I thought I'd see if maybe you were awake."

"I am."

"Now you are. I don't know what I was thinking. I shouldn't have—"

"I'm glad you called."

"Really?"

I nodded. "I've missed your voice."

She didn't respond.

"I would have stayed in touch, you know," I went on. "I wanted to. But you said—"

"I know."

I let out a deep breath.

"How's your trip been so far?" Madison asked.

"Hellish."

"'Tis the season."

"I don't remember the fires being this bad before," I said.

"Everything is worse."

"Now you sound like my dad."

She chuckled. "Well, he's not wrong. Things were better when we were young."

"I don't know about that. We had pretty terrible childhoods."

"They weren't all bad."

"No," I agreed.

Another pause. "Azaan?"

"Yeah?"

"How long are you in town?"

"I honestly don't know. A week? Two weeks?"

"Then there isn't a lot of time. We should really get that coffee."

"Now?"

She laughed. "No. I mean soon. I've got Julie. I can't just leave her alone in the middle of the night."

"Oh. That's right. What's that like?"

"Parenthood? Amazing. Exasperating. Everything in between. You said you didn't have kids, right?"

"I don't."

"Do you want them?"

I snorted. "I'm renting a sofa in a flat with five roommates right now. I haven't given it much thought."

"So you're not married?"

"Not even a little bit."

"Girlfriend?" she asked.

"No."

"What was that earlier, by the way? That long story you didn't tell me about how you're not a preacher? That's what you went to school for, right?"

"You're not going to believe this," I said before telling her the truth.

There was silence on the other end after I was done.

"Madi? Are you still there?"

"I am. It's . . . so you're impersonating an imam right now is what you're telling me."

"Yeah."

"You see how that's crazy, right?" she asked.

"I do."

"Wow," she said. "It's . . . unbelievable."

"I warned you."

"You did," Mads agreed. Then she asked, "So you're not seeing anyone and you're not any more religious than you were before?"

"Less probably," I joked. "Though I'm not sure that's possible."

"What are you doing tomorrow? Maybe we can meet up?"

"I should be free all day. I mean, you know, unless Baba dies. That would totally ruin any plans we make."

"That's not funny," Madi said.

"I guess it isn't. I don't have a car, by the way. All these

Uber rides are doing a number on my credit card. Can you pick me up?"

"Sure. Where?"

"I'll meet you in the mosque's parking lot."

"You're kidding."

"What?" I asked.

"The last time we were in one of those—"

"You kissed me."

"More important, you got deported."

"I was exiled, actually, and that wasn't more important."

I could hear the smile in her voice. "More devastating then."

"No. Not more devastating either."

"It was for me," Madi insisted. "I felt so bad about it. I mean, that night changed your life. I didn't mean for it to—"

"Not entirely for the worse. I got to be free of my parents and move to one of the best cities in the world."

"But I lost you."

"Yeah," I said. "That must have sucked."

Madi laughed again.

I had taught myself to forget to miss that sound.

"Anyway," I told her, "it's not the same place. My dad built a new—"

"I know all about it. I've been covering it for the paper."

"What paper?"

"The *Redding Voice*," she said. "I write for it."

I blinked. That wasn't exactly a prestigious publication, and my first thought was that Madi was much too good for it, but I wasn't stupid enough to say that out loud. "You're a journalist?"

"Sort of. I mostly do entertainment and media, but it isn't a big staff, so I get to do other stories sometimes. I've done a few pieces on the vandalism that's been happening to your dad's mosque."

"I heard about that. Skinheads, right?"

"That's what everyone seems to think."

"You don't agree?"

"I don't know. I mean, sure, it's a possibility. It's just that . . . well, I don't mean to worry you, but a lot of what's happened has been directed at only a couple of the board members there."

"Which ones?" I asked.

"This guy who calls himself Tiger and your father. The tires on Tiger's car were slashed. The windows of Imam Saifi's office were broken. Another time, they actually went in there and set fire to some of his books, leaving a pile of ash on his desk. None of it has been directed at the Muslim community as a whole, you know?"

I told her about the graffiti I'd seen earlier, which had read: "You know what you did."

"You assumed that was about September eleventh ," Madi pointed out, "but it might not be, right? It could be something else, something personal."

"If anyone has a personal vendetta against my father, it's me, and I'm not responsible for any of this, so—"

"I'm serious, Azaan. There's more going on in that mosque than meets the eye."

"What do you mean?"

She hesitated. "Why don't we talk about it when we meet up? It's late. Let me talk to Tali and see if and when I can drop Julie off tomorrow. I'll let you know what time I'll be by."

"Sure," I said. "Can't wait."

What felt like a few minutes later, though it was actually several hours, a loud sound roused me. Someone was slapping the door of the apartment and shouting my name along with the Arabic phrase "as-salatu khayrun min an-nawm."

Maybe that statement was true and maybe prayer really was better than sleep, but my body did not believe it. My head was heavy, my eyes desperate for more rest, but the caller was persistent and didn't stop until I answered.

I found Jibreel outside and, behind him on the horizon, just starting to rise, the first rays of the sun. His look of wide-eyed surprise kept me from greeting him. Instead, I mumbled, "What?"

"Your beard, man. Where did it go?"

Shit. I'd forgotten I wasn't wearing my costume. "Uh . . ."

"You look like a lion who has lost his mane."

There was only one thing to say. "I shaved it."

"Why?"

An excellent question. I grabbed at the first answer that popped into my head. "Tiger Uncle said I should. He said imams walking around looking . . . imammy is like an athlete refusing to take off his uniform."

"First of all, brother, you should know it's not right to stop doing something you started to do to honor the Prophet."

I ran a hand over my face. It was way too early in the morning for this.

"Second, you are a trained scholar. You should set an example and not be swayed by the opinion of lay people. Tiger Uncle is not . . . he is a good man, don't get me wrong. He does a lot for us, for the community, but you cannot take his advice on matters of religion."

"You're right." Having grown up around a preacher, I knew that the thing to do in the face of righteous indignation, if you wanted to avoid a lecture, was to capitulate immediately and entirely.

Religious people don't typically argue with you in the spirit of discovery. They don't believe a debate will enlighten them and they'll learn something new. They think—they know—that their position is already correct. All they want is for you to acknowledge that. They want your surrender and the sense of moral superiority that comes with it. If you're willing to pretend to bow to them, they'll leave you in peace.

The fact that I made no attempt to defend my lack of facial hair or Tiger Uncle's advice seemed to disarm Jibreel, who probably had a lot to say on the subject but, unexpectedly, had no need to do so. "Well, I guess it'll grow back. Now come. Your father sent me to get you. It is time for Fajr. You should be at the mosque."

"I forgot to set my alarm."

"Why would you need an alarm? The prayer app on your phone should have adjusted to the time zone change automatically. Which one do you have?"

"I . . . I don't use one."

"You don't?" Jibreel asked.

I tried to think of a way to explain that away, couldn't, and shrugged.

"Why?" he pressed.

Because I haven't prayed since . . . well, I don't know exactly when.

I couldn't very well say that, though.

I racked my brain for what I knew about the programs that prompted people to offer their five daily prayers. My only exposure to them was through my flatmate, Sonya, who installed them on her devices during Ramadan, the one month when she felt obligated to practice.

Every year, she forgot to mute the adhan—or azaan, for those who prefer Persian influences to Arabic ones—and the sonorous call to prayer echoed through our little apartment at max volume.

I remembered her showing me outraged tweets, which I suppose are the most common kind, about the companies that made some of these apps selling data to governments, allowing the surveillance arms of nation states access to the locations of their Muslim users, along with other information.

She'd been properly worked up, even though as far as the developers were concerned, her data had to be little more than a blip, appearing and disappearing after thirty days every year.

"I got rid of them," I told Jibreel, "when I found out they were spying on us."

This seemed to make sense to him. "So you used to use Muslim Grow? A lot of their users got paranoid and deleted it once news of their betrayal got out. But, man, Uncle Sam already knows everything there is to know about you, and if he doesn't, then Apple does, Facebook does, Microsoft does. You're not going off the grid when you get rid of your prayer app. You're just making your religion harder on yourself."

"That's a good point."

"Privacy, in our time, is an illusion. True Muslims don't need it anyway. It's just a harbor for people doing shameful and illegal things. You remember my journals, the ones in which I kept track of my deeds? What did you call them? The Ledgers of Good and Evil."

"It's hard to forget," I said.

"I found out my parents were reading them. At first, I was very mad. Then I thought, why not? I don't have anything to hide. Let the world see. I made a blog and put everything in them online. My life is an open book."

"Must be nice."

"Tech, you know, is going to be the next big thing in religion."

"Really?" I asked.

"Most definitely, man. You'll see. I know because it's my field. I'm going to change Islam."

"Well, things can't get worse."

"They won't. Trust me. Anyway, as far as your prayer app situation is concerned, I know some developers who can be trusted. I'll show you after Fajr is done."

Under other circumstances, I would have told him that it was all right, that I could just Google them. Being around Jibreel was not my idea of a good time. However, he was the one investigating the mosque's missing money and, by extension, my dad. If I could get him talking, I might be able to find out what the size and scope of the problem was, what had caused it, and if any real concern was warranted.

Maybe, if the missing sum was minor enough, I could even talk him into dropping the whole thing. That would lift the dark clouds over my father's head. Not all of them, of course. He'd apparently been born with some, but a few at least.

"That sounds good," I told him.

"Now quickly go do your ablutions. You don't have much time."

Tiger Uncle put his arms up in the air and raised the roof—or maybe he was attempting a quick bhangra—when he saw me enter the prayer hall. There weren't a lot of people around. There never were at the early prayer, if the decades-long grousing of my father was any indication, though I supposed the sparse attendance might also be attributable to the fact that the mosque was, technically, not yet open for business.

The hall itself was a vast space with a high ceiling and brand-new maroon carpets, along with a simple minbar—a space carved into the wall for the imam to stand in and deliver sermons. I was still looking around when Tiger Uncle got to me and, without warning, pinched my cheeks as if I were a significantly younger person.

"You look good."

"Thanks," I said.

"Excellent change to the hair too, beta, and losing the glasses is also a solid decision. This is the way. Except your clothes are still very understated. There's no shine, no gloss. You know what they say. No bling, no fling, no fun for your thing. You can borrow some of my outfits if you—"

"What is going on here?" My father demanded, marching over. "Azaan? What have you done? All signs of holiness have fled from you."

"Nonsense, Saqi," Tiger said. "His heart is unchanged. Only his appearance is different. There's no reason for him to put his piety on display, to show on the outside what is on the inside and reveal his secrets like a . . . like a—"

"Codpiece," I suggested.

"What do fish have to do with this?" Dad asked.

Tiger shook his head. "Never mind. It was my idea, Saqi. Your son is a youth. Those Egyptians you sent him to turned him into an old man. He has to attract modern women raised in America or England, and fundamentalists are not in fashion with them. In fact, you should be grateful. It is your job to set him up with someone, to arrange his marriage, and this makes it easier."

My father gave me an appraising look. "Maybe it is time."

"No," I began, "you really don't—"

"As far as God is concerned," Tiger persisted, "he isn't any less religious than he was yesterday. Are you, Azaan?"

I could answer that honestly. "Absolutely not."

"See?" Tiger Uncle said brightly. "No harm done."

Dad, obviously unconvinced, continued to study me for a moment, then said, "That is a lot of stubble."

"What?" I asked.

"You shaved last night, right?"

"Uh-huh."

"That is a heavy shadow for such a short period of time."

"A real man," Tiger Uncle interjected. "That is what he is. He is not a boy anymore. He is a ripe fruit full of testosterone ready to burst open. You really need to start thinking about getting him a juicer."

"Fine, fine," my father grumbled. "But this is still terrible. I was going to have you lead, Azaan."

I blinked. Leading the prayer wasn't an honor my father had ever thought me fit for. "You were?"

"Well, I can't now, can I? Because you have no beard. You can't lead if you have no beard."

"Well," Tiger Uncle said, "actually, he can. It's preferable, but—"

"It's fine," I said quickly. "I don't have to lead."

I really didn't. My father recited the holy book beautifully, and he had taught me well. At least as well as you can teach a completely disinterested student anything.

A decade of disuse had likely atrophied my pronunciation of Quranic Arabic, which would make no sense to Dad. He'd expect me to have gotten better, not worse, especially with the help of my elite education in Cairo.

Besides, I knew that there were some prayers in which the

imam recited verses out loud and some in which he didn't, and I didn't remember if Fajr was one of the silent ones or not.

I really would need to do more research. I was underprepared for this role.

"It's okay, I suppose," my father said after a moment. "You are here for a while. Your beard will come back. Then, instead of leading this small crowd, maybe you can lead a packed house on a Friday instead. Then everyone can see that my prodigal son has returned."

After the morning prayer, I watched my father and Tiger Uncle leave the mosque side by side, talking in the same amiable way they usually did. Their friendship seemed to have recovered entirely from their heated argument last night.

I'd been under the impression that my father was the kind of man who held on to grudges and resentments. After all, I'd had a front-row seat to his marriage. Seeing him get over this disagreement with Tiger so quickly, I realized maybe that wasn't true. Maybe he wasn't like that at all. Maybe he just didn't care for my mother. We tend to only give grace to people we like.

I was about to make my way over to speak with Jibreel when a kid who looked like he was still in high school came up to me. Before I could acknowledge him, he'd grabbed my hand and started shaking it frenetically. "You're Imam Saifi Junior."

"I can't say I'm not."

"I'm Javad. Sorry to bother you, but I've got a problem and I need your help, please, and I would talk to your dad, but it's a little embarrassing because he's so—"

I waited for him to find an unflattering adjective.

"Talkative."

I could call my father many things, but not that.

"I mean," the kid went on, "he makes, like, all these speeches, which is his job, but when he's doing that, he draws lessons for everyone based on the questions people ask him and the things happening in their lives. He doesn't say who he is speaking of, but—"

"You don't want to be the subject of a sermon." Having had that experience many, many times—without the benefit of anonymity in my case—I could sympathize.

The young man nodded with an inadvisable amount of vigor.

"I get it." Out of the corner of my eye, I saw Jibreel, who was lingering within earshot, check his watch. "But I promised my friend here that we'd—"

"How about I find you later?" Jibreel said, stepping back from us. "You're working. We can talk some other time."

I didn't point out that this wasn't my job or responsibility. It wasn't like I was employed here, but that was probably the wrong attitude for someone supposedly in the imamming business.

"Fine," I said, trying not to sound as irritated as I felt. The one time in my life I actually wanted to speak to Jibreel, I wasn't going to get the chance. As he left, I asked Javad, "What's up?"

"Well, I . . . uh—well, the thing is, and don't tell anyone, okay, it's just . . . I have a question about trimming my . . . hedges."

"This is a mosque. You're looking for Lowe's or Home Depot."

"No, no, that's not what I meant. I meant . . ." He waved his hands in an agitated fashion over his groin. "My thicket."

Oh. He was talking about his pubic hair. "You meant to say bush."

Javad frowned. "I don't think it's called that when it's on a man."

"You know, I actually don't know if it is."

"Let's just call it the Bermuda Triangle."

"Why?"

He shrugged. "It sounds cool."

"It sounds like the site of many tragedies."

"Whatever. The thing is that my older brother told me that I have to start shaving down there and under my armpits and that my prayer isn't valid if I don't."

"So?"

"Is that true?"

Yeah. I had no clue how to answer that question.

My father had given me the same directive Javad had gotten from his sibling. He'd said it was to promote hygiene. It was one of the Islamic practices I still engaged in because the benefits were tangible. For one, getting rid of the hair in that region made everything seem larger. For another, it seemed a small courtesy to extend to anyone kind enough to explore that area.

What the Sharia actually said about it and what, if any, consequences there were for not doing it, I couldn't tell him.

"Ah." I said. "Right. Um . . . well, you see . . ."

Javad continued to stare at me in expectation of an answer as I floundered.

I closed my eyes, thinking, trying to figure a way out of this.

"Imam Saifi?" The teenager pressed.

I sighed. "Okay. I'm going to be honest with you. I don't know."

His mouth fell open. Not a lot, but enough that I could

tell he was properly stunned. His shock was understandable. It seemed like a pretty basic question. Besides, he'd grown up in an age when everyone had an opinion on everything and they were constantly voicing it, or typing it, anyway, to share with the world. Admitting ignorance just wasn't in vogue anymore.

"You don't?"

"I can look it up for you," I offered. "But I can't remember just this second. I'm sorry."

"That's okay. People aren't Google, right?"

I gave myself a little mental kick. I could have just excused myself to go to the bathroom or something and done an internet search. That would've worked.

"You've heard of this, though?" Javad asked. "My brother isn't making it up? It's just that he likes playing practical jokes, so—"

"It's definitely a real thing. What I can't tell you is if it's an absolute obligation or not. I'm also not sure what the consequences are if you ignore it. But I do it myself." I gave him a conspiratorial grin. "Women seem to like it."

Javad's brow furrowed. "Women?" Then understanding dawned on his face. "Oh. You're married?"

I managed to get away from Javad without inventing a spouse for myself. I briefly considered telling him that I did, in fact, have a wife once, but that she'd died. That would've been difficult to explain to my family if it got around, however, and it meant I'd have to come up with a cause for her demise. It was a tangled web best avoided.

Instead, I told him that I was passing on information I'd

heard from friends who already had their life partners. This seemed to satisfy him.

I tried to go back to sleep but couldn't, and I was researching the answer to Javad's question, which I'd promised to email him, when Madi called.

"Hi," she said. "What's going on?"

"You wouldn't believe me if I told you," I muttered.

"This sounds good."

"Seriously, Mads, you don't want to know."

"Come on," she insisted.

"No, it's really not—"

"Please."

"Fine," I said. "Right now, I'm reading an article called 'The Desirability of Shaving One's Pubic Hair.' Happy?"

She took a moment to process that. "Someone's real optimistic about tonight."

"It's for the mosque actually."

Madi laughed. "What are you guys doing over there?"

"I'll let you know when I figure it out."

"Well, I'm sorry to interrupt your fun. I'm calling about dinner. Tali's busy, but Julie's father said he can start his on month early. He can take her at seven. Is that good for you?"

"His 'on' month?"

"It's a custody agreement thing. We alternate who has her every thirty days."

"That has to suck," I said.

"It does, but it kind of is what it is. Anyway, seven?"

"Sure," I said.

"See you then."

Around half an hour later, when I'd finished composing my email to Javad—the consensus among scholars being that shaving one's pubes was not imperative but highly encouraged, and if one didn't, there seemed to be no punishment attached—there was a knock on my door.

I grimaced, not just because I was fully expecting it to be my father, but also because I hadn't had a moment's peace since I'd gotten to California.

My guest, however, was someone else entirely.

"Who are you?"

The man standing at my door was short but bulky and muscular. He was young, probably a decade or so my junior, which meant he was maybe nineteen years old. He'd shaved his head, which made his dark, bold eyebrows all the more noticeable.

Instead of answering, he studied me intently, looking me up and down, a small smile on his face. This went on until I repeated myself. That was when he held out his hand. "My name is Ilham," he said, his English heavily accented. He spoke carefully, almost unsteadily, like a colt trying to find its feet for the first time.

"Azaan."

"I know. My sister told me about you. You met her the day before this one. Kashaf. She works at Tiger's—"

"I remember," I said.

"She sent me to invite you. Come eat with us tonight. Have dinner."

"I can't," I said. "I'm sorry. I have plans."

His face fell.

"Look, you guys seem nice, but like I told her—"

"You cannot be a good friend for us. You will not be here long."

"Right."

Ilham nodded. "Kashaf said to tell you that you do not have to be a good friend. We just want a friend. A bad one is fine."

I couldn't help but smile. "That's funny."

The young man shrugged, as if that didn't matter.

I didn't want any part of . . . whatever this was. The Kashaf girl had struck me as strange. I didn't know what to make of this guy either. Speaking to him, you got the sense that he wasn't . . . well, that he wasn't all that sharp, to be honest, but it was possible he was just struggling with the language.

Regardless, I didn't have any inclination to spend time with them. I just needed to come up with an excuse.

"I really do have plans."

"Tomorrow?"

"I . . . look, I don't mean to be a jerk—"

"Then don't," he said.

"How did you know where I was staying anyway?" I asked, more to buy time than out of any real curiosity.

"Kashaf overheard Tiger talking to someone."

Tiger. That was it. He'd told me to keep my distance from his newfound daughter.

"Your father told me," I said, "to stay away from you guys."

Ilham frowned. "Our father?"

"Tiger Uncle. I'm assuming, of course, that you guys aren't, like, stepsiblings or something—"

"We are twins."

"Well, okay then," I said. "You've got the same parents, obviously. So yeah, he—"

"We are not his children."

"But he told me—"

"Just because you heard it does not mean it is true."

"Why would Tiger Uncle lie to me?"

Ilham countered with a question of this own. "Why do you not like us?"

"I never said—"

"Did Kashaf say something that upset you? She does that sometimes."

"No," I assured him. "She was fine. I'm just—"

"Eat with us," Ilham repeated.

"Jesus Christ."

He gave me a curious look.

I regretted snapping instantly, and what I'd just said was unfortunate given who I was supposed to be. More tamely, I added, "Uh . . . I meant ya Allah madad."

"The Prophet said you shouldn't say no when someone asks you over."

Sometimes I really hate religion.

"We would like to know you better," Ilham told me.

"Why?"

"Because you are Azaan Saifi."

"What does that even mean?" I asked.

"Only you can answer that."

"Oh my God. All right. Tomorrow night. Do you want to meet here?"

Ilham shook his head. "No. I will give you the address. Do you have a pen?"

"I have a phone. That's better."

"It is not better," he said, still all seriousness, "but it will do."

Chapter Ten

Madi raised her eyebrows as I opened the door to her small hatchback, the kind of car marketing departments have convinced everyone to call a subcompact crossover, because it is a sexier label. And sex, as is a truth universally acknowledged, sells.

"Somebody got a makeover," she said.

"You look . . . pretty good too."

That was a massive understatement. She was wearing a sunny yellow dress that had ruffled cap sleeves. It came down to her ankles and seemed modest at first glance, before one noticed the strategically placed tie at the neckline and the side slit that came up to her midthigh.

"You're staring," she pointed out, when I stood where I was for a few moments longer than . . . well, not longer than necessary, really, because beauty needs time to be appreciated. One does not rush past *The Starry Night* or run through the Hagia Sophia. We pause, we linger, and in doing so offer as tribute a small portion of our lives.

"You never used to wear dresses," I said as I got in and closed the door behind me.

"Are you complaining?"

"Definitely not."

She smiled and started to drive.

"Where are we going?" I asked.

"You'll see."

"Is it a surprise?"

She shook her head. "Not really. I'm just punishing you a little for making me plan the date. Granted, I haven't been out with anyone for a long time, but that used to be the guy's job."

"This is a date? I thought we were just catching up."

Madi fixed her blue-gray eyes on me briefly before turning back to the road. "Let's not."

"What?"

"Play games. There's no time. You'll be gone again soon. Let's be honest about what we want."

A moment that seemed important passed, then I said, "In that case, I should tell you that you look better than pretty good."

She grinned. "So how come you ditched the imam outfit? Aren't you playing your role anymore?"

"I got caught without it, which is fine, to be honest. Wearing it just felt . . . wrong."

"That's probably because it is," she said.

"I know. But—"

My cell rang.

I ignored it.

"Aren't you going to get that?"

"There's no one else I want to talk to," I said.

"It could be an emergency."

"I don't care."

"What if it's about your grandfather?" she asked.

I shrugged. "'If he dies, he dies.'"

"Azaan. That's terrible."

"It's from a movie."

"I know, Drago. Answer the phone."

I did as she asked, groaned when I heard the request the caller was making, told them I'd see what I could do, and hung up.

"Well?" Madi asked.

"It was the hospital. Baba wants to see me. He says it's urgent."

"Then you have to go."

"I'm sorry, Mads."

"Do you think he'll mind if I come with?"

"Oh, he'd be happy to see you, I'm sure."

"It's sweet of you to come back for him," she said.

"That's another long story."

Madison chuckled. "Is anything in your life simple?"

"No. I think I'm cursed."

The drive over to the hospital was short, which is one of the perks of living in a small town. You were never all that far away from where you needed to be.

She told me a few things about her life on the way. Mostly, she spoke about her daughter, Julie, who was eight, bright, affectionate, a huge fan of board games, and currently a Pokémon card-collecting fanatic. I wondered if she'd been named for Shakespeare's Juliet, but it didn't feel right to ask.

At the hospital, we learned there was no emergency. In fact, Baba seemed to be in better health than when I had seen him before. When he saw Madison, he did a double take, covered his stoma, and as loudly as he could exclaimed, "Damn, girl!"

"Really?" I protested.

"What?" The old man wheezed, reaching over for his bed's controls so he could sit up and get a better look. "That is the etiquette of how one compliments a lady these days. I've seen it on television. You're also supposed to say, 'you are working that dress.' Tell me, dear, is that thing backless? It looks like it is."

Madi laughed and did a little twirl for him. He wasn't wrong.

"So gorgeous. Ah, even now, even here, Allah blesses me with visions of loveliness. It is almost difficult for me to believe He despises me for my sins. In her glow, Azaan, you look a little different too."

"That's because I changed my appearance entirely."

"There you go again, making things about yourself. It's a very bad habit. Very bad. Now, let's talk about me, hmm? I won't keep you long. I didn't realize you were actually doing something worthwhile. I thought you'd be at the mosque or something."

"You can see why he gets along with my dad so well," I told Madison with a wry smile.

"We may have to involve him in this too, Azaan," Baba told me. "You see, I have another last request."

"I'm pretty sure you only get one," I said.

Madi swatted at my arm.

"I need," Baba declared, "as soon as possible, a hundred thousand dollars."

When I asked the obvious question—which was, of course, why Baba needed such a large sum—he handed me his tablet. The screen showed an advertisement by a company called Abracadavera in Nevada, which specialized in the field of cryogenics.

They claimed they had perfected the science of preserving the human body at extremely low temperatures for long periods of time. Using this technology, they could freeze people suffering from terminal illnesses alive in the hopes that they could be defrosted someday in the future, when medical science had advanced enough to cure their condition.

At least, that was the case for clients willing to pay two hundred and thirty thousand dollars. Baba was focused on the cheaper option, the one in which only his brain would be saved.

"You don't want to hang on to your body?" I asked.

"Maybe if I had one like yours," the old man said, "and definitely if I had one like your friend's. As for my shell, I'm done with it. In the future, they'll figure out how to make cloned bodies for us and put our minds in them. That is what I read on a message board for this company's customers. That will be nice, hmm? I'll be able to go on without end, just living life over and over again."

Madi frowned. "How many people have signed up for this?"

"Around five hundred," Baba reported.

"Incredible," she said.

I went and sat down next to my grandfather, on the edge of his bed. "Baba, this is—"

"I have no other choices."

As gently as I could, I said, "Yeah. You do."

Baba looked away, blinking rapidly. "No. No, it is too soon for that. I can't just let go."

"We don't get to decide—"

"Your father believes," he said, "that a man got on something like a winged horse in the middle of the night, flew from

Mecca to Jerusalem, and then flew up to the heavens and back before the sun rose. Is this more impossible?"

"There is a difference between science and faith."

"No, there isn't," Baba countered. "They are the same thing. Faith is magic before it is explained and once it is explained, we call it science. Think about it. If you take a cell phone back in time to the dawn of man, you'd look like a wizard, hmm?"

"I mean, you'd have zero bars, so it'd be useless."

"My point," Baba snapped, "is that many things that once seemed impossible, that once seemed like miracles, happen all the time now. Speaking to people over long distances, even if they're on the other side of the world, for most of history people thought that couldn't be done. Now look. You carry the ability to do that around in your pocket and don't even think it is a marvel. This is a chance. I want to take it."

I sighed.

"I know it seems strange, but this program can't all be nonsense," the dying man insisted. "I read that Paris Hilton has signed up for something like it. Who are you to argue with her?"

I glanced over at Madison, who shrugged.

"I must have more time," Baba said.

"Why?" I asked.

"Because there is so much I should have done and didn't do. There is so much I did that I shouldn't have . . ." He let out a broken breath and his massive body shuddered. He was having difficulty speaking. I recognized this agitation. It was how the knot made me feel when it was acting up. "The world happened to me and kept happening, and somehow now it feels like I just went along for the ride. I tried to live as I wanted. I lived more than most men, children. I wanted to have no regrets. And yet . . ."

Mads stepped up and took one of his hands in her own.

It made the dying man smile.

I was grateful for her. It was more than I could do for him.

"It would be cheaper if I could believe I was going to Paradise," he joked. "Look, just read about it, okay? That doesn't do any harm. Please."

Even if the literature produced by this company could convince me, it wouldn't matter. I didn't have that kind of money. Dad didn't either . . . well, he would once the house sold, but he obviously wouldn't spend it on this quixotic quest, and Baba didn't have the right to ask him that, not after everything that had passed between them.

I looked at Madi, who gave a slight nod.

"Okay. I will," I told him.

He exhaled, clearly relieved. "Thank you, beta." Then he cleared his throat and said, "Now it is getting late, hmm? Off you go, you two. Have fun and then go to bed. Or, better yet, go to bed and then have fun."

"Baba," I said. "Come on."

"What?" he demanded. "Do you think you will always be young and beautiful? Or that you are guaranteed tomorrow? What if it never comes? What if tonight is all the time you two have together and there is nothing more?"

"Sorry about him," I told Madi as we walked out of the hospital. Something was wrong with the lights in the parking lot. Many of them had either gone out since we'd gotten there or, perhaps, they'd been out already and I hadn't noticed coming in. Others were flickering on and off, struggling to stay alive. A few continued to shine, as best they could, in the deep dark of the night.

The stars were there, along with the moon, somewhere beyond the smoke that still covered Redding, but we couldn't see them. This sad veil drawn over the heavens would have made me feel terribly alone, I think, if Mads weren't with me, her steps locked with mine.

"What?" she asked, looking as though she'd been pulled away from her own thoughts by my voice.

"I said I'm sorry about Baba. He's—"

"Kind of great."

"My father doesn't like him."

"He doesn't like you either, but I've always been a fan."

"Madi—"

"I don't feel like going out to eat anymore," she said.

"But you got all dressed up."

"Not for the restaurant's benefit. Can we just order in?"

"Sure," I said.

We drove in silence for a while, until at a stoplight I saw a few men in white T-shirts talking to someone lying on the ground. That person was clearly homeless, his modest possessions piled up next to him at the side of the road. The men were shouting. Through the windows of Madison's car, however, I couldn't hear what they were saying.

"What do you think is going on?" I asked.

She glanced over and made a disgusted sound. "Looks like 'The Exterminators.'"

"Who?"

"It's what they call themselves. They are these . . . vigilante homeowners."

I blinked. "Vigilante homeowners?"

"They go after what they call RATs. Redding Area Transients. They harass them and try to drive them out of the city. The concern is that having 'vagrants' around lowers property values."

"That's messed up."

"Welcome back to the States," Madi said as the light turned green.

"Trust me, England's got its own problems."

"I guess there's misery everywhere."

"This is a cheerful date. We should do it again soon."

She chuckled.

"I really am sorry tonight went off the rails. I've been wanting to go out with you for . . . God, fourteen years now."

"Another long story for your collection."

The neighborhood Madi took us to was new and wouldn't have been out of place in any suburb in any part of California and perhaps even the United States, a result of the same giant corporations developing the same plans and selling their giant wooden boxes to people all taught to dream the same dream.

She pulled into the driveway of a small, single-story home. The front yard was dead, but it was meant to be. It wasn't composed of carefully manicured green grass like the neighbors', but was entirely made up of tree bark and rocks. It looked nice enough.

We walked up the porch, and she opened the door to let us in.

I'd always been a little jealous of the comfortable, cozy home the Porters had, so different from the fastidiously clean, hyper organized, minimalist house that my father kept and my mother only occasionally pretended to care about. There had been a warmth at the Porter's place, a brightness, a sense of belonging.

Mads had recreated that here for her daughter. It was all on a smaller scale, and none of it was glamorous, but it was the kind of place you could see yourself being happy.

"This is incredible," I said.

She reached over and took my arm. "This way."

I let her guide me into the living room, which was across from the kitchen. I paused to look at a wall of pictures and she let me go.

The photographs featured Julie prominently. She had her mother's dark hair and even though her eyes were light brown instead of blue gray, there was something about them that reminded me of Madison.

Not as Mads was now or even as she had been when I'd left her, but before the day her parents had died, when there had been a happy innocence about her, when she hadn't known how cruel the world could be.

When I turned to face her, Madi walked up and put a hand on my chest, like she had the first night we'd kissed. She looked up at me and bit her lip.

My heart stumbled a bit, but managed after a second, somehow, to keep beating.

"No games," Madi whispered. "No strings. No promises. Just two weeks." She pulled her hand back and her long fingers went to the tie at her neckline and started fiddling with the knot there, and I couldn't help but wonder how much responsibility it bore for holding up her dress. "Or however long you're here. It's enough time, I think, to finally stop wondering."

"Wondering what?"

"What might have been. Whether we too could have been happy."

With that, Mads turned and walked away from me, down a

short corridor. I could see a doorway, which led, I was sure, to her bedroom.

She paused there, head bowed for a moment, then exhaled, and there was the sound of falling fabric and her dress pooled around her feet and she turned to look at me over her shoulder with eyes so smoldering that every thought, except for thoughts of her, melted away, and she asked, “Don’t you want to find out?”

Chapter Eleven

2010

The shouting was worse than usual that night. It was also unexpected. My parents fought often, but there was usually peace for a few days after my father returned home from one of his fundraising trips, especially the longer ones he took with Tiger Uncle.

This wasn't because his absence made their hearts grow fonder, really, but because it made them less weary of each other for a while, more capable of being patient with the annoyances that made up their marriage.

This trip was different. He'd been gone for a few months and had just returned that morning, and they were already screaming at each other with such vehemence that even my noise-canceling headphones couldn't keep their voices out. So I left.

It was a warm, cloudy night. The moon had faded and was distant and dim, the stars few. A few doors down, across the street, the Altmans had their porch light on, and I could see a slender figure sitting on the steps leading to their house, hugging herself and staring up at the sky intently, as if it were somehow important, as if it were more than the mere backdrop to the play of our lives.

I stuck my hands in my pockets and made my way over.

She smiled when she saw me. "Hi."

"Hey, Mads. What're you doing?"

She shrugged. "Nothing. You?"

"Fleeing a war zone."

Her remarkable eyes drifted over to my home. Instead of pressing the issue, she asked, "Ready for the chem quiz tomorrow?"

"No. I'm going to fail."

"You never fail, Azaan."

I wasn't sure what she meant by that. She knew for a fact that wasn't true. She knew my grades better than my parents did.

"You don't try. That's different."

"Okay, Master Yoda."

Madison Porter patted the step next to her. "Sit."

I did what I was told. "You?"

"Hmm?"

"Chem."

"No," she said. "Fuck it."

That wasn't something she would've said seven months ago, when she used to take school seriously, before the plane crash. I never talked to her about it. Everyone we knew brought it up all the time, especially at school, and it always made her tear up. She paid a price for the sympathies that were offered to her and the curiosity she was met with. I'd never seen the need to add to the toll.

She knew I was there if she wanted to talk about it. She apparently never did. We spoke, instead, of other things, trivial things, like homework.

At least she still talked to me. With almost all the rest of the world, Madi had gone quiet.

"Yeah," I agreed.

Madi took my arm and put her head on my shoulder. If my father had seen us, he'd have had a conniption. I wasn't supposed to touch girls and vice versa, but this had become a habit of hers now and, to be honest, a habit of mine as well.

To anyone who didn't know any better, we would have looked like a couple. We weren't. We had been close to being one, I think, before her parents had died, but she was too wounded just then for romantic love and she needed me too much as a friend for me to risk trying to be anything more.

"New jacket?" she asked.

"Oh. Yeah."

"It looks ridiculous."

I sighed. "You said the same thing about the last one."

"That was too. Leather? It's, like, ninety degrees out."

"It's cool."

She shook her head. "You're an idiot."

"Whatever. You love it."

"It does smell nice," she conceded. Then she sat up, "Wait. It really does. Why do you smell nice? Actually, you've smelled nice for a while now. I didn't notice. You smelled like cigarettes before, when—"

"I quit smoking."

Madison smirked. "Your dad caught you, huh?"

"No. I mean, okay, he did, but you know I don't care about that."

"Then?"

"You told me you didn't like it, remember? You said you wished I'd stop."

She frowned. "And?"

"I stopped."

Madi stared at me. "Just like that?"

"Just like that."

She continued looking at me, and then inexplicably and without warning, she started to cry. It took me a moment to figure out what was happening, so I sat there like a fool as sobs overtook her, racking her small frame, and she struggled to breathe through the emotions flooding over her. Then, belatedly, I wrapped my arms around her and she buried her face in my neck and continued to weep.

If the Altmans had walked out to check on her then, I'm not sure how I would've explained the state of their goddaughter. Not that they were technically her godparents. Madi had explained that appointing those was a Christian, not a Jewish, tradition. The Porters, however, had designated their friends legal guardians of their children, and she felt it was a nice, less formal thing to call them.

When she recovered a little and pulled away, I peered at her and asked, "You okay?"

Madi nodded.

"If you're this upset about it, I can always take up cigarettes again."

She wiped at her eyes with the back of her wrist. "Don't be stupid."

"It's not really a choice for me." Then, more seriously, I asked, "You're sure you're—"

"Yes."

"Do you want to talk about it?"

"I'm fine." She cleared her throat and got to her feet. "I'd better get inside. They worry about me."

"Why?" I asked.

That made her chuckle. "It's a mystery." She turned to leave but hesitated when she reached the door. "Azaan?"

"Yeah?"

"I . . . uh . . . thanks."

"Anything for you, Mads."

"Really?" she asked.

"Absolutely."

Chapter Twelve

2022

"You sound exhausted, mate," Brayden said when I answered his call, my voice heavy with a lack of sleep and the five thousand or so miles I'd recently traveled. "Did you not catch any Zs?"

"Not many, no."

"It's important to get your rest, Azaan."

"Yes, Mother."

"Sod off. I'm just taking a professional interest, aren't I? Can't have you looking run down by the time you get back. Though, I suppose it'd be all right for this role."

I sat up in Madi's bed and arched my back to stretch. I hadn't slept on a proper mattress in a while and this one was fancy. It had a box spring and everything. It was going to require more than a little bit of will to get out of. "This is about that action flick? I got it?"

"No. They called in Sonya again—"

"Yeah, you told me."

Brayden sighed. "Now they want you back in."

"What? Come on. This isn't a big part. What are they wasting time for?"

"It's not a nothing role anymore," my agent said. "Someone put a flea in the director's ear about how having yet another Muslim terrorist is tone deaf and insensitive or whatever. Therefore—"

"The character isn't Muslim anymore?"

"No, they haven't binned the whole script. You people are still the ones blowing things up, but they're going to give the character some depth, you know, like a motivation beyond just causing havoc."

"That's much better."

Brayden gave an annoyed huff in response to my sarcasm. "It is, actually. Change doesn't happen overnight. They're trying."

"If you say so."

"Anyway," he said, "when are you coming back? I'll give them dates."

"No."

Silence.

Then Brayden echoed, "No?"

"Yeah."

"What the fu—"

I glanced at the bathroom, where I could hear the shower running. "I'm not flying back for this. I already auditioned for them."

"Is there something you need to tell me?"

"What do you mean?" I asked.

"Did you become a star at some point and fail to mention it? Because so far as I can tell, you're in no position to be a diva."

"Tell them I'm in the States because of a family emergency, but I'll be happy to read for them on Skype or Zoom or whatever they use."

Brayden went quiet for a while, thinking, then he said, "They may be fine with that. Most people are over that remote stuff after the pandemic, but they'll probably make an exception in these circumstances."

"Let's see."

"I'll get back to you." He paused, then added, "How's your granddad then?"

"He's pretty upset that he's dying."

"Don't think I'd take it all that well myself, to be honest. The prospect of eternal oblivion scares the shit out of me."

"For some of us," I said, "oblivion is the best-case scenario."

"That's properly grim. Anyway, try to have some fun while you're out there at least."

"Redding isn't my kind of place."

"It does have your kind of people," Brayden pointed out. "You should look up that bird you never stopped fancying. What's her name? Madison, right? Catch up with her maybe."

I grinned. "You think that's a good idea?"

"The way you talk about her? You know what, maybe not."

"Really?"

"That seems like a deep wound, mate. It'll hurt like hell if it opens up again."

I didn't have anything to say to that.

"I'll circle back when I have an answer on the Zoom thing. Stay tuned."

"Thanks, Brayden."

"All part of the service," he said.

I sat there for a moment, staring at my phone after he'd hung up. That was a somber thought my friend had left me with. I doubted Brayden would've said what he did if he'd known about last night. In fact, I knew he wouldn't have. We temper the truths we speak with kindness for the people we care about.

He was right, though. Mads and I needed to be careful, and I figured she knew that. That was probably why she'd laid out ground rules that made it clear this was very temporary and casual. There'd be no complications.

Still, I couldn't help but think about what she'd told me last night, that she hadn't been with anyone since her divorce seven years ago. "I'm glad it's you," Madi had said.

She had been protecting herself. She obviously wasn't the kind of person who had casual flings, even if that was, in effect, exactly what we were doing now.

It made a certain kind of sense. I was someone she'd been with. There was an epoch of history between us. I cared about her deeply. I always had and I always would. In all those ways, I was the perfect cure for her loneliness.

No. Not a cure. A balm that could give only temporary relief, because I'd leave soon, as she well knew, and then . . .

I shook my head. It was pointless to worry. We were just two friends who were helping each other out. The fact that we'd been in love with each other once was immaterial. Everyone knows lightning doesn't strike the same place twice. Our hearts were, therefore, safe.

"It'll be fine," I muttered to myself as I heard a hair dryer go on.

I looked through my notifications. At some point last night,

I'd missed a call from Tiger Uncle. He was getting back to me, I knew, as I'd tried to reach him several times after the visit from Ilham, Kashaf's brother, who claimed they weren't Tiger's children. Why had Tiger lied to me? I'd find out today.

There was also a message from my father, who had noticed I wasn't in the studio I'd been given and, more important in his mind, wasn't at the dawn prayer. He wanted to know where I'd been. I grimaced. I hadn't considered that I'd have to come up with some kind of alibi for my whereabouts last night.

"Morning," Mads chirped. I got to my feet without thinking about it as she walked in. She was wearing a simple white tank top over a pair of gray yoga pants. Her long dark hair was still damp and, somehow, very alluring. "Holy shit, you look beat."

"Yeah, well, someone kept waking me up last night."

She grinned. "I'd say I was sorry, but I'm not."

"You're okay?"

Madi nodded. "Okay? I'm . . . that was . . ."

"Good?" I suggested.

"So good. I have to admit I was a little worried it'd be like our first time."

"Hey. What was wrong with the first time?"

Mads shrugged. "You had no idea what you were doing back then—"

"Ouch."

"We had no idea what we were doing," she amended. "And I was just so sad that you were leaving and I felt so guilty that I'd caused it . . . is this too much honesty?"

"Just a little. I kind of . . ."

She crossed her arms. "Go on."

"This is not going to be a macho moment for me."

Madi rolled her eyes. "Spit it out, Romeo."

"I loved that night," I admitted. "It's been my best memory forever."

"I loved it too. Doesn't mean the sex was great." She walked over, stood on tiptoe, and kissed me on the cheek. "But it was last night, even though I'd built it up in my head. Not just because it had been so long but because . . ." Madi looked away. "Because it was us. That's all I'm saying."

"Well, I'm glad you had fun."

"At the cost of you looking like the walking dead."

"I'll be fine," I said.

"You need coffee. Lots of it. Go freshen up. I'll put some on."

By the time I got out of the shower, Madi had made us sunny-side up eggs and toast. I hadn't had breakfast in ages. I'd been intermittent fasting for so long that I no longer even thought of food as something you had more than once in a day. Still, I joined her at the dining table, thanked her, and tucked in without saying that. It's nice to have people be nice to you, and it's nice to let them be nice sometimes.

As we ate, we talked about nothing in particular. She'd gotten up before me and had, apparently, spent some time on a few social media sites. As a result, she was brimming with the news of the day and the opinions of other people about it.

"Your Prince Harry," she said, "has a new book coming out and—"

"My prince?" I asked.

"You are British."

"Only because my mom is."

"And because of the fact that you choose to live in England."

I couldn't argue with that. I didn't have any use for the royal family, though. They didn't serve any purpose that I could see. Sure, there were people who were obsessed with them, and Sonya, my flatmate, was among their number. For my part, I couldn't think of anything more useless to do than read gossip about them or anyone else.

Human beings had created so much art. Libraries were full of literature. Streaming services were overflowing. Museums were stuffed with paintings and sculpture. Cities were adorned with architecture.

So many attempts at capturing beauty, at ordering the world, at making sense of our collective experience, had been made by the people who'd gone before me and the people who shared the world with me that I wouldn't be able to experience them all even if I devoted all the hours of my life to that pursuit.

Why would I take time away from that to gawk at the ugly, unfiltered chaos of someone else's life then? It made no sense.

"According to an excerpt," Madi told me, "he admitted to killing, like, twenty-five Afghans. People are pissed."

"Why did he do it?"

"It was when he was in the military."

I yawned. "It'll blow over then. No one's going to remember it in a week."

"You think so?" she asked.

"Yeah. Everyone knows that murder is okay if you're wearing the right outfit. That's Western Civilization 101."

"When did you get this cynical?"

"While I wasn't around you."

"Why, though?"

"Because there was no light in the world anymore."

Mads smiled, glanced away, then looked back at me again. "You think you're so smooth, but you're really just a giant cheeseball."

"Cheese is good," I countered.

"This is true."

I took a blessed sip of coffee. "How about we talk about something real?"

She reached for her phone. "Let's see what's trending. There's the war in—"

"How about us?"

Madi pulled her hand away from her device. "Well, I'm pretty sure there are no hashtags about us. We're not shiny, happy people."

I sat back in my chair. "Aren't you? Happy, I mean."

She gave me a frail smile. "I am right now."

"I meant generally."

"I got that," she said. "Wait. I know. You can help me with a story I want to write."

"Sure. What's it about?"

"The mosque. Remember when we were talking on the phone the night before last? I told you something weird was going on over there."

I nodded. "Is this about the vandalism?"

"It was." She took a deep breath, then plunged into her question. "This would potentially be a different piece. While I was interviewing people about the repeated property damage, a source told me there's some kind of problem with the mosque's finances."

I tried to make sure my expression remained neutral. I hadn't been expecting her to say that. I shifted in my seat as she waited for me to respond. I didn't, of course.

Eventually, she went on. "I know you just got back, but let me know if you hear anything. This could be a significant story. I keep doing follow-ups on the vandalism bit despite the threats to stop because I'm hoping to find out—"

I frowned. "What threats?"

"Oh. That's nothing to worry about. I—"

"Mads," I pressed. "Tell me."

"Relax. It's the kind of stuff I get all the time."

"You get threats all the time?"

Madi waved my concern away. "It's mostly harassment."

"And that makes it better?"

"It's the life of a female journalist in an online world," she said, "even when you're dealing with something that should be fun and harmless like movies. You hated the new *Star Wars*? You loved the latest Marvel movie? It doesn't matter what your opinion is, there's always going to be someone ready to . . . well, vociferously express their displeasure. A small minority of people do it by telling me in graphic detail what they'd do to me if they had me alone in a dark alley."

"Jeez."

"I'm not scared of DiscardedForeskin666 with an anime avatar on Twitter."

"That's a real username?" I asked.

"It's hyperbole. My point is that I've gotten used to this kind of thing, so don't freak out." She paused for a beat, then conceded, "Though I must admit I was surprised I got any hate on the mosque coverage. It's the very opposite of big news."

"Yeah, that's weird."

"Anyway, will you help me?" Madi asked.

I countered with a question of my own. "Who is your source?"

She made a face. "I can't tell you. He doesn't have any details, which is why I haven't published on it. We don't run with rumors, and my editor won't green-light it unless I bring him something concrete."

"I respect that." I took a moment to think. I didn't want to lie to Madison. At the same time, I couldn't tell her what I knew about the missing funds from the mosque. A headline saying he was under investigation would crush my father and destroy his reputation. Ultimately, I decided to tell her the truth. "You're on your own on this one."

Madi blinked. "Really?"

"If there is something going on—and we don't know if there is—I'd rather the board, whom the Muslim community here elected, deal with it as they see fit. It's our business, not the business of the readership of the *Voice*."

"I disagree," she said slowly, "but I understand how you feel. You're not going to be upset if I keep pitching it to my editor though, will you?"

"No," I said. "Of course not."

At Tiger Uncle's grocery store, I found him at the cash register, a couple of notebooks open before him, reading glasses perched on his nose. His brow was furrowed, his expression—for once in his life—serious. He looked up when the door closed behind me. A smile came to his face.

"Azaan, meri jaan. Good to see you."

"You too, Uncle."

"Where have you been? Your father said you were gone all night."

"I slept at Mom's place."

"You should have told Saqi that. He worried without reason. Anyway, you've been trying to reach me, haan?"

"Yeah. If you're busy, I can come back another time. Or maybe I can help?"

Tiger Uncle shook his head. "There are more zeros here

than you are used to seeing and, I hope for your sake, more red too."

"Red? That's bad, right?"

He nodded.

"Everything okay?"

"It has been . . . how do you say it? A few thin years—"

"Lean years?"

He pointed at me as a way of showing I'd gotten it. "The pandemic was not good for me."

"Well, it wasn't good for anyone," I said.

"Yes, yes. But I was very leveraged and when the government froze evictions and tenants stopped paying rent, I had to sell a few properties to meet the shortfall. Anyway, the real estate market was very good, you know, so I made profits, but the money was gone before the taxes came due . . . never mind all this. It is enough for you to know that it has not been a good time to be a millionaire."

"How bad is it?"

He waved dismissively. "I am not very liquid. That is really the only issue."

"I can pay you back for my ticket here," I offered.

Tiger Uncle laughed. "That would be a very small drop in a very big bucket, Chand-e-Ramzan. Don't worry about it. Tell me what you need."

I took a deep breath. I had to approach this carefully. For all his quirks, Tiger Uncle was pretty much the only adult who'd been there for me as a kid. He'd made my current life possible. I didn't want to offend him, and coming right out and asking him why he'd lied to me would certainly do that.

"Well, Uncle," I said. "There were a couple of things. First of all, about Dad's money troubles—"

"That was nothing. He just forgot to pay some bills, that's all."

"I heard him yelling at you."

He shrugged. "You know how Saqi is better than anyone. He was just angry about how I found out and mad that I was putting my nose in his business."

"Then all that screaming was really meant for me?"

"You've had your share in your life, no? Look, I calmed him down and everything is fine now. He was normal with you yesterday, right? So there is nothing to worry about."

"Still, I'm sorry you got the brunt of it. I was going to talk to Jibreel to see if he's made any progress with finding the missing money, but—"

"Who told you to do that?" Tiger asked, his voice sharp.

"You did. Sort of. You said you wanted Dad to feel better. The best way to make that happen is to resolve this issue as soon as possible, right?"

"Bhai, I brought you here to be shown off. Let Saqi strut you around so everyone can see that his son turned out to be religious after all. You've been a black mark on his record for a long time, you know."

"I live to serve."

"I wanted him to have a chance to brag about you. It's what he really wants to do. That is why he wanted you to lead the prayer the other day. That is why he's going to have you do a Friday sermon. Let him have that and do nothing else. There's no need to be a detective."

"Someone has to figure out what happened. Better me than the media."

Tiger sat up straighter. "What do you mean, 'the media'?"

"A journalist has heard there are problems with the mosque's finances. She's looking into it."

"Is it that Porter woman? It must be. She was the one covering the damage the hooligans have been causing. Damn it. Who told her? It must have been our esteemed treasurer, I think."

"I don't know if Jibreel was her source. I just know she has one. I don't think she has any details, though, so she isn't writing a story yet."

"That is something, at least. Magar bhai, this is not what we needed. It is what they call in Pakistan having all your flour get wet when you are broke. Don't look so confused. It means a bad situation on top of a bad situation. Have mercy on my stressed little life, please leave all this alone. Trust me. I will deal with it. Now you go."

"Actually, there's one more thing . . ."

He let out a deep sigh from the very core of his being.

"I wanted to clarify something. The other day, you said that Kashaf was your daughter. But I spoke to Ilham, her brother, and he said that they're not your kids. So, I was wondering—"

Tiger growled at me. "I told you to stay away from them. Can't you listen to one thing I ask you to do? So much risk I've taken for you. My closest friend I have deceived for you, but you—"

I kept my voice calm. "You asked me to stay away from Kashaf. I did that. Like I said, I spoke to her twin, and only because he sought me out."

This seemed to calm him down a little. "I see. Okay. That was my fault. I did not warn you that there were two of them."

"Who are they?" I asked.

"First of all, I think there is some confusion, beta. I did not say that Kashaf was my daughter. I said she was *like* my daughter. You misheard."

"I'm sure I didn't."

"Then I misspoke. What difference does it make? I don't have spawn. I always wrap my presents. Yet there are people I consider to be like my children. Such as yourself. And Kashaf. That is why I have given her a job in my shop. It's not so difficult to understand, is it?"

"So why tell me to stay away from them?"

Tiger Uncle wagged his finger at me. "We agreed you wouldn't ask me that."

"You had a reason, though?"

"I did."

I sighed. "All right. Back to my first question. Who are they?"

"They are people."

"Uncle."

He grimaced. "Look, Azaan, this is my sincere advice. Forget about them. Those two, they are not good news. There is something dark in them. You have felt it, haven't you? They are strange. Not quite right. I met their mother, you know, and she was a most unfortunate woman. Her husband had left her. Abandoned the family. I took pity on her and promised I would help her children, so that is what I am doing. You don't need to be involved in this at all."

I considered telling him that they wanted to befriend me for some reason, that I was supposed to meet them tonight, but I didn't.

His explanation seemed reasonable enough and, if I didn't know he was lying, I would have believed him. After he'd said Kashaf was his daughter, he'd taken me to the mosque, and there, he'd misquoted *King Lear* to me, completely butchering the line about the serpent's tooth. He had reaffirmed then that he had at least one child.

Something very weird was going on, and I was going to find out what it was.

On the way back to the mosque, I got a text from Madi.

MADISON:

I keep thinking about you.

I sent her one of those purple devil emojis in response.

MADISON:

I meant how you are pretending to be an imam.

AZAAN:

The emoji works either way.

MADISON:

It's just so ridiculous.

MADISON:

But about the other thing . . .

MADISON:

Come back tonight.

AZAAN:

I can't do dinner, Mads.

MADISON:

I don't want dinner.

MADISON:

I want you.

She sent the devil back to me.

AZAAN:

I'm all yours.

That earned me three fire emojis.

It also reminded me that I had to set up my alibi. I called my mother and left a message, letting her know that if she heard I was staying at her place, she shouldn't say that wasn't true.

It certainly looked like my parents weren't in contact, so there was little risk she'd give away that I was lying to Dad directly. However, they were still part of a very small community, and news within it got around rapidly. It's true that Einstein said it isn't possible to travel faster than the speed of light, but that's probably only because he never got to see how quickly desi aunties can move rumors around.

If one of them ran into Mom somewhere and made an innocent comment like "it must be nice to have your son back with you," and Mom said she'd only seen me once since I got back, it'd be all over Redding like . . . well, wildfire, I suppose.

I was pretty sure my mother would help cover my tracks. She'd be irritated that I was involving her in something she perceived as trivial, but she'd get a little joy out of denying the community a juicy piece of gossip about me all the same. Not out of any desire to protect me, mind you, but because she didn't like them.

Saqlain Saifi's flock had always disapproved of the choices Mom made, from her lack of a hijab to her refusal to attend most of the events the mosque hosted because of her thinly veiled indifference to religion. She was very much not a traditional imam's wife.

I got to my room and was about to start packing for another

overnight stay at Madi's when someone started slapping the door. It was Jibreel. How had no one ever taught the man to knock?

He seemed unhappy when I greeted him. "As-salamu alaykum. Uff. You look beat. Didn't you get any sleep?"

"I'm all right. What's up?"

"Have you seen your father? Or Tiger Uncle?"

"Tiger's working at his store. I was just there."

He sighed. "I've been trying to have an important meeting with them for a while. This is the third time they haven't shown. It's like they don't take me seriously as treasurer."

"That sucks."

Jibreel nodded. "Maybe they'll always see us as children. I don't think they liked it when I asked to have an election so the mosque could have a proper board. Before it was like a dictatorship with the two of them doing whatever they wanted. Not that I'm saying Imam Saifi was a tyrant or anything—"

"It's fine. Tell me more about how my father is a terror and rules with an iron fist."

Unfortunately, he seemed to think I was being sarcastic. "No, man. Obviously, those two are the foundation upon which our community has been built. Now that it has been built, however, they have to realize they won't be around to run it forever. It is time for our generation to take the wheel."

"Sure."

"As treasurer, I'm helping modernize how they track the mosque's finances," Jibreel went on. "You should see the state of the books. They were still hand writing everything, and there are things I can't make sense of. That's why I need to sit down with them and talk."

It seemed unlikely I'd ever get a better opening to ask him about his investigation into the mosque's disappeared funds, so

I took it. "This meeting you want to have with them, is it about the donations that went missing?"

Jibreel's eyes widened. "You know about that?"

"Tiger Uncle told me."

"He shouldn't have. That's irresponsible. The right thing to do is to find the truth first, before telling anyone. If this gets around, it'll ruin reputations and that isn't right. I'm surprised Tiger Uncle did that, especially because it might be his fault."

"Really? He told me you were looking into my dad."

"Either one of them could have made a mistake. Like I told you, they handled everything for the community together. Tiger basically had my job."

I frowned. "That's right. He was the treasurer, wasn't he?"

"He wore many hats. They both did. Anyway, you can't tell anyone, Azaan. It would be—"

"I won't. Someone has been talking, though. I spoke to a journalist who has heard about all of this. She thinks there is a story here."

"A reporter spoke to you? May Allah protect the innocent. That is terrible, man. It will crash all the confidence our people have in the board. And what will White people say when they find out?"

I couldn't help but smile at that. "You're not concerned about the opinions of Black people? Or other Asians?"

He waved a hand dismissively. "I'm including them with the White people."

"I'm not sure how they'd feel about that."

"Azaan, be serious. We have a big problem on our hands."

"It's not all that bad. She said she doesn't have any specific information, so she isn't writing a story about it yet."

That seemed to make him feel a little better. "Alhamdulillah. That is a blessing, at least. And if she doesn't have details, it means that either Uncle Nadeem or Uncle Karar are the ones with the loose lips. As board members, they know I've been looking into the matter, but they don't know anything more. I will speak to them."

"Good. Anyway, hopefully this is all much ado about nothing, right? I mean, from what I've heard so far it's possible that everything is fine. You said you can't figure out their books. It could just be an issue with a way they kept records."

Jibreel scratched the side of his forehead. "Could be."

"You don't think so, though?"

"I can't say yet. It's just that . . . man, I don't understand why they aren't meeting with me about it. This is a problem that needs attention. We're not talking about a small number here."

"What number are we talking about?"

Jibreel looked me over for a moment, weighing my worth. He must have found me wanting, because all he told me was "a significant one."

"It sounds bad."

He didn't respond directly to my comment and, instead, changed the topic. "I can't rule out that their messy record-keeping is the cause." In a lighter tone that indicated I wasn't going to get anything else out of him, he added, "Can you believe it? They were using a paper and pen. In this day and age. But you already know how I feel about technology."

"You're for it. I remember."

He smiled. "I have to be. Professionally, I'm in the field."

"I always thought you'd end up being an accountant."

"Why?"

"It was a joke," I said, realizing as I pointed this out that it hadn't actually been funny. "Because you had that habit of recording everything you did and then doing the math on your deeds everyday—"

"You guys always thought that was odd."

"Yeah. Sorry about that."

He didn't seem to need an apology. "Actually, I'm still sort of working on those journals."

"You are?"

"I am developing a Muslim AI. It's nowhere near ready, but—"

I frowned. "Can artificial intelligence have a religion?"

"God created us," Jibreel argued. "We're as 'artificial' as any computer code."

"I suppose."

His eyes lit up in a way that told me he'd suddenly had an idea. "You know, I didn't expect to, but suddenly I have time."

"Uh-huh," I said, instinctively feeling wary, though I couldn't say why.

"And you're here. Come to the mosque with me. I have a surprise. Trust me, you'll like it, and we can talk about my project on the way."

Figuring construction had ended on some new feature of the building or something, I stepped out of the apartment and started walking with him back across the parking lot.

"What is it?"

"You'll see," Jibreel told me. "Now what was I saying? Right. The Ledgers of Good and Evil. Like I told you the other day, I put them online for everyone to see years ago. Honestly, Azaan, knowing that anyone in the world could just go to my blog and see what I had done at any time was life changing."

"Seems like it would be."

"It made me a better Muslim. I started describing what was happening in my life in more detail and, even when I didn't do anything wrong, I would get cautionary comments from our brothers from different parts of the world pointing out where my choices could lead me astray in the future or what better courses of action had been available to me."

He meant "brothers" in the "brothers in religion" sort of way, of course, not literally.

"It's always a good idea to take advice from the internet," I said.

"Don't joke. This was a revelation for me. I don't know what wild things I would have done if I weren't connected to all these believers throughout my college days, but because of this project, I never fell into sin. I couldn't. I was constantly being judged. I mean, everyone knows that God is watching, but people hope for leniency from Him. The audience I had, they were not forgiving and they were not merciful."

"I can imagine."

"I was always so scared. Fear of Allah was in constant bloom in my heart."

It seemed to me that what he was describing was fear of other people, not God, but that would have been a harsh thing to point out. Islam is radically monotheistic. So much so, in fact, that doing things, even good things like worship, with the hope of pleasing anyone but Allah negates any spiritual benefit. It can, in fact, put one's soul in peril. Being preoccupied with the wrath of an online mob, unsurprisingly, isn't what the religion is about.

"My AI is going to harness this power I discovered. Everyone carries their phones with them everywhere, right?"

"Sure."

"And these devices," he said, "they're perfectly capable of listening to everything that is happening around them and transcribing it with some accuracy. I am working on a program that will constantly hear whatever is said in its vicinity, transcribe it, and upload it to the cloud. Then it will judge what was said or done, initially with the help of humans and based on Islamic values, of course—"

"Of course."

"—to be a good deed or a bad one. It will give you a score that will tell you what kind of Muslim you are being. We'll even have a leaderboard of people from all over the world, so everyone can see where they rank."

I shook my head. "This sounds like something out of *1984*."

"Don't be silly. They didn't have this kind of technology back then. No. Trust me. No one has done this before. Just think about the benefits of this system. Parents will know what their children are doing all the time. Using motion sensor data, they'd know if the kids offered the five prayers and, if not, which ones were missed. Just imagine what your life would have been like if your father had access to this kind of information about you when we were young."

"I can't," I admitted. "I guess it would have been like *A Quiet Place*."

"Yes. Exactly, man. It would have been calm and peaceful."

"That's not—"

"Honestly, the possibilities are endless. I am going to let users change the settings so their actual actions, not just the score, are accessible by anyone. We could link it with computers and tablets and get an alert whenever inappropriate sites are visited and porn is viewed. Could you masturbate to some pixels knowing that people would find out? I don't think so."

"I—"

Jibreel, too enraptured by his own plan to let me get a word in edgewise, pushed on. "They say that it takes a village to raise a child. I can make it so that our children will be raised by the whole world. At least, the whole Muslim world. It will be 'amr bil ma'roof wa nahi 'anil munkar' on steroids."

I sighed. That phrase, which signified the duty of a Muslim to encourage what was good and forbid what was evil, was the rallying cry of everyone in the community who made other people's business their business. Jibreel was right. If his idea took off, this concept was going to become supercharged.

"Do you really think people are going to volunteer for this?"

"If they want to be good Muslims," he said, "they will. I think early adopters will be parents. They'll want it to track their children. We'll make it so that in order to get any useful data, they'll need to sign up themselves. It'll spread from there. I've spoken to marketers, and they say that we need to create prestige levels. You know, the Diamond League, the Gold League, etcetera, so people can compete with each other and advance. Games do this to get people hooked. My hope is that people will become addicted to God."

"What are you calling it?" I asked. "Big Brother?"

He blinked. "Yes. Exactly. How did you know?"

"Just a lucky—" I realized then that Jibreel had led me to the back of the mosque, to an overflow parking area I hadn't known was there, and we were headed toward what looked, suspiciously, like a hearse. "What is that?"

"Your surprise."

"What's in the car, Jibreel?"

"My gift to you. A great deed."

"Seriously," I said. "What's in the car?"

"It's Uncle Tariq. Do you remember him?"

"I don't. Please tell me that this Tariq person is driving that thing."

Jibreel frowned. "No, of course not. He unexpectedly passed away. His sons are inside the building, waiting for your father to prepare the body—"

"Prepare the body?"

"Of course. The last rites have to be done. Your father has had to do all the ghusl rituals for everyone who dies in the community since he's been the only imam. That isn't the case anymore."

I stopped walking as I realized what was happening.

This guy wanted me to touch a dead body, and he was pitching it to me as if it were a prize.

"It will lessen your father's burden if we have Uncle Tariq washed and shrouded before he returns. What a blessing this is. And since my meeting got canceled, I can assist you and get some of the massive reward for performing this service."

Chapter Thirteen

I TOOK A DEEP BRACING BREATH AND, FOR THE SAKE OF Jibreel, who was looking at me expectantly, nodded gravely. "I can certainly do that for Uncle . . . what did you say his name was?"

"Tariq."

"Yeah. I can handle Uncle Tariq's last rites. No problem."

In my head, screaming had started and would not stop. There was no way I was doing this. I mean, I understood why Jibreel was all about it. This kind of thing was worth a ton of points in the divine calculus he was obsessed with. I didn't care about that, though, and even if I could set aside the horror of handling the deceased—which wasn't easy to do—the truth was that I had no idea how to do the ghusl ritual. I'd heard my father talk about it, of course, but if I were in the habit of paying attention to anything he said, my life would be very different.

"The thing is," I said, trying desperately to find a way out, "since the mosque isn't technically open yet, shouldn't this be done—"

"Everything in the ghusl room is operational and convenient. There is no reason not to use it. Don't worry, man. You will have everything you need. I stocked the place myself."

"Oh. Good."

I looked up at the sky and shook my head.

All I wanted was to pretend to be a religious leader for a fortnight so that I could fool my father into thinking that I, too, like him, had dedicated my life to Islam. Why was God making this hard on me? First that Javad kid—

A sudden wave of inspiration washed over me.

My first attempt at being an imam had taught me an important lesson. I could do what I hadn't done when Javad had asked me about his pubic hair—run, hide, and consult Google.

Hopefully, the steps involved in the ritual would be short and easy to remember, because I couldn't be in the middle of bathing the dead uncle and pull out my phone to get instructions on what to do next. I'd have to memorize the procedure and I'd have to memorize it fast.

Luckily, I was great at that. I'd been learning lines by heart most of my life. So there was hope.

"I'll be right back. I've got to go to the bathroom."

"All right, man," Jibreel said. "Meanwhile, we'll take Uncle Tariq in."

"Yeah. Sure. That's good." I didn't tell him I had no idea precisely where the unfortunate elder's remains would be transported. It sounded like there was a room designated for this kind of thing. If I didn't ask where it was located, and I needed more time to research the ghusl than a trip to the restroom would reasonably allow, I could always say I got lost looking for it.

I hurried back the way I'd come, whipping out my cell as soon as I was out of Jibreel's sight, and typed "Islam how to do a ghusl" into the world's most ubiquitous search engine. This did not work. The results that came back were instructions on how to clean oneself after having entered a state of impurity—after sex, for example—and not on the treatment of dead bodies.

I added the words "before burial," tried again, and had more success.

The first site I clicked on said the ritual had to be performed by someone who met the following criteria:

1. Was an adult—check.
2. Of the same gender as the body—check, I assumed.
3. Was Muslim—sure, kind of.
4. Was trustworthy and honest—well, shit.
5. Knew the proper way to carry out the ritual—if I knew that, I wouldn't be on this web page, would I?

I was about to browse away, when the screen was taken over by the notification of an incoming call.

I answered. "Mom?"

"Azaan. I just got your message. You're coming to stay with me?" She didn't sound entirely displeased with the idea, which was a little surprising.

"No. I said that I'll be telling people I'm staying with you. If it ever comes up, just pretend that it's true."

"It's not true?"

"No," I said. "Look, I—"

"I thought you came back to be with your father."

"I did."

"Then what is the problem, darling?" she asked. "You're welcome to come over, of course, if you must, but do know that Saqi will not be allowed to visit. I realize that may seem a bit—"

"I really have to go."

"Where are you going? To a hotel?"

"No. I'm just spending some time at a friend's."

"What friend?" she demanded.

I sighed, eager to get her off the phone so I could get back to dealing with the remains of poor Uncle Tariq. "Never mind. You don't know her."

I literally slapped a hand on my mouth as soon as the words left it.

Iqra Saifi's voice went to a higher register. A much higher register. "Her?!"

Oh, come on. That had been so careless. Panic, jet lag, and a lack of sleep were really messing with my head.

"You found a woman? How long have you been back? Two days? You work fast."

Actually, given my history with Mads, the truth was that I worked really, really slowly, but there was no reason to go into that. "Mom, please—"

"I won't tell anyone. It just doesn't seem," she noted, "very imammish."

"We aren't perfect," I said.

It took a while, but eventually she said, "Yes. Having been married to one of you, I'm well aware of that. Wait. Don't tell me that bastard, that Tiger, has gotten his claws in you. Because those pump-and-dump marriages he enjoys so much don't work in this country. You'll end up—"

"I'm not married," I assured her. "It's just . . . run-of-the-mill fornication."

"Thank God for that. Though I really think it is unfair of you to expect me to keep half a secret."

"What do you mean?"

"I believe I must know who this person is."

"Mother," I said, "don't be unreasonable."

"I am saying this for your own good. A secret is such a small thing. It can slip out so easily. A mere fraction of one is so tiny that I just would not know how to go about making sure it is safe."

"Are you seriously blackmailing me right now?"

"It's called parenting, dear."

I rolled my eyes.

"Bring her over for tea," Iqra Saifi said. "A high tea, perhaps, as this is a high occasion."

"What? No."

"Why not? You finally meet a nice Muslim girl—well, a naughty Muslim girl, at any rate—and you won't introduce—"

"She's not Muslim," I told her.

"Fine. Christian then—"

"Jewish," I said.

"There was no need to give it away. That was going to be my next guess. Now, it doesn't much matter what her religion is, does it? Everyone loves tea."

"That hasn't been my experience."

"Well, you can't go around listening to the opinions of Americans. That's how one ends up having bad taste."

"Just . . . listen, we'll talk later, all right? Right now I have to learn how to deal with a corpse."

"A what?"

I felt for Mom. Not as bad as I felt for Uncle Tariq, who was probably going to have his last rites butchered, but still this was a lot to drop on her in one conversation. "Some guy died. They want me to wash him and stuff."

"They didn't teach you how at your fancy Islamic university?"

"I . . . skipped class that day?" I ventured.

"Azaan. How typically irresponsible. And at your mosque in Dover, no one has died?"

"Well, uh . . ." I thought about saying no, but I had supposedly held the job for something like eight years. It would be highly improbable to have a congregation where no one perished over that period of time. "I . . . delegate."

"You delegate?"

"Yeah." I said. "We have a ghusl guy."

"Well, it's not a one-person job, is it? You must help him."

"Guys," I said. "I meant to say guys. They like to get the reward for it, you know?"

"Well, it isn't difficult. I have done it several times."

"Someone just told me Dad did all of them."

"Well, that person apparently forgot that women exist. You father can't very well wash them, can he?"

I nodded. I had just read about the matching gender requirement online.

"He asked me to do it often. It isn't brain surgery. I can explain it to you if you want."

"Yes, please," I said. "That would be amazing."

I was calm by the time I found the room where Uncle Tariq's body had been taken. This was, I told myself, just a performance like any other. The routine my mother had described was straightforward and made sense. It was entirely possible I would manage to do it correctly, and if I didn't, maybe my audience wouldn't know or notice.

Jibreel, thankfully, handed me a pair of latex gloves, which made the whole situation more bearable.

Uncle Tariq's clothes had already been taken off of him. A cloth covered him from his navel to his knees. They'd left his watch and a hospital tag around his wrist. I took those off and handed them to his family.

Then, with the name of Allah, I began.

I cleaned the body of impurities. Either the skin was cold under my hand or the water was, I don't know which, but the experience wasn't what I expected. I had thought I'd freak out, at least a little, but what I was doing felt like an entirely natural thing, like something people had done for centuries—because they had—and some part of me, perhaps, recognized that I was observing the traditions of my ancestors.

There was a surprising amount of peace in that.

Jibreel handed me a fresh pair of gloves when I was done.

Then I gently pressed on Uncle Tariq's stomach to get rid of anything that remained there. Nothing happened. Still, Jibreel gave me yet another fresh pair of gloves to put on.

After this, I washed the dead man's awrah—the parts of him veiled by the cloth, without removing the covering—and, again, changed gloves.

I did the ablution for him, as if I were helping him prepare for one of the five daily prayers, though I didn't put water in his nose or mouth, as my mother had instructed.

After that, with the help of the others, I washed him, starting from his head. I thought I was supposed to wash the right side first, then the left. Jibreel had to correct me. Upper right, upper left, lower right, lower left. He frowned at my mistake and maybe it was elementary, but I was beyond caring. I was glad he caught the error. I wanted to do this well for Uncle Tariq.

We did this again and again a third time.

Then it was over.

It was strange. I didn't know this person. I didn't know where in Redding he'd lived, how long he'd been here, where he was from, or whether he would have liked me. Odds were that if he knew who I really was, he wouldn't have. But there was a chance he would. Maybe there was something of what desi uncles called "a rascal" in him too. It was possible that he wouldn't have minded that this duty had fallen to me.

I hadn't thought to remember the names of his sons or even ask how he had died. Despite all these unknowns, I felt connected to him, like we were doing something solemn and immense together, like he had given me the opportunity to join him on a meaningful journey for a time and given me the ability to serve without the expectation or hope of any return.

Jibreel hadn't been wrong.

It was a gift, just a very sad and human one, that left me acutely aware of my mortality.

After all, someone would do for me one day what I was doing for Uncle Tariq then.

When I was done, Jibreel brought out the shroud, the kafan, and I tried to remember what to do with the three sheets he was carrying, but I couldn't.

"I can't do this," I said, even though it was bad for the illusion I needed to maintain. That seemed trivial and insignificant at the moment.

"What's wrong?" Jibreel asked.

"Can you all finish up?"

"Yes. You've done most of the work. You do look exhausted, Azaan. We should have just waited for Imam Saifi to return. I'm sorry, brother, if I pushed you too hard. I forgot that you have been traveling."

"It's all right," I said. "It was . . . it was my honor."

My father led the funeral prayer for Uncle Tariq that afternoon. It was being held on short notice, but everyone around was used to that. Muslims believe in burying the dead as quickly as possible after their demise. Over fifty or sixty people showed up, which was a remarkable number for a relatively small community.

I couldn't help but wonder who would be there when I died. Less than half that number, probably. Maybe less than a tenth.

Did it matter?

Afterward, I was leaning against one of the mosque's Roman pillars, waiting for the body to be brought out, when Jibreel came up to me with coffee. I took it gratefully.

"Did you get some sleep?" he asked.

"A little," I said.

He was quiet for a while. Then he said, "You haven't done that often."

"The ghusl? No. I haven't."

Jibreel smiled. "I could tell. Most people, you know, when they do it often enough, especially when they do it as part of their job . . . they're still respectful, but it becomes routine for them."

"Yeah, that makes sense."

"They don't do it with that much care. It meant something to his sons, man. They could tell you were moved. It was like you cared about him. Like you were his imam."

I took a bitter sip from the cup he'd handed me.

"I was impressed," Jibreel went on. "The Azaan Saifi I knew wasn't capable of reverence like that."

"You didn't know me very well."

"You didn't care about things like this," he insisted. "Subhanallah. The light of the Quran has opened your mind. Studying at Al-Azhar has had a profound effect on you."

"Perhaps you just had a low opinion of me."

He shrugged. "Maybe. You know, I was surprised when you got into Al-Azhar. They don't take just anyone."

This was something I'd covered with my dad years ago. He too had been unconvinced that my academic record was good enough for such a prestigious institution to accept me. I broke out the old lie I'd come up with then. "Tiger Uncle pulled a few strings."

"Ah," Jibreel said. "That makes sense. He does have his puppets, doesn't he?"

"I guess so."

"Who does he know there?"

"I don't know."

"It doesn't matter anyway. Did you know someone by the name of Abdullah Samadi when you were there?"

I shook my head, wondering why he was asking these questions. Had I made other mistakes in the ghusl, mistakes he hadn't thought significant enough to point out? Had he guessed the truth as a result?

It surprised me a little that it didn't worry me more, that my heart didn't start beating wildly at the prospect of being found out. Uncle Tariq's passing and my participation in the customs that made it bearable had numbed me, at least temporarily, to smaller consequences.

Death has a way of altering one's perspective.

"Mahmud Ghazi Suleiman? He should have been there at the same time as you."

"It's a big campus," I told him.

He nodded thoughtfully. "Well, good job today."

"Thank you."

"I should go find your father and Tiger Uncle. They're going to have to sit down with me to talk about the mosque's books eventually."

"Have fun," I said.

Jibreel grunted. "It's like taking candy from a baby."

"Doesn't that mean it's easy?"

"Spoken like someone with no children. Yes, it isn't hard to do, but you have to endure a lot of whining."

I smiled.

"I'm serious. It's been a battle with them from the start. The day after we had the board elections, your father started talking about retiring once the mosque is complete. I think maybe he has been used to doing this his way for too long. He doesn't want to have to report to people or answer to us."

"That does sound like him."

"I feel bad," Jibreel confessed. "Like I'm driving him out. That wasn't my intention when I pushed for the elections. We have a charter. We should follow its bylaws. You know?"

"I wouldn't worry about it," I advised him. "No one makes my dad do something he doesn't want to do. If he decides to walk away, it'll be because he chose to. Besides, you aren't rid of him yet. I wouldn't count your chickens."

Chapter Fourteen

THE ADDRESS KASHAF AND ILHAM HAD GIVEN ME TURNED out to be a massive, sprawling house in a posh neighborhood. A red Corvette stood proudly in the driveway, still gleaming in the fading light of the setting sun. Tiger Uncle had said these two were from a poor family. It certainly didn't look like that was true.

I made my way up to the front door and rang the bell. In mere seconds, Ilham opened it, smiling and wordlessly inviting me in. Kashaf, who had chosen not to wear her hijab tonight, stepped up behind him and greeted me by saying, "You came."

"Of course." My footsteps echoed on the marble floor and through the giant foyer when I entered. It was an enormous, empty space, with almost no decor of any kind. "I said I would."

Kashaf's smile did not reach her unnaturally dark eyes as she said, "Well, we are glad you are here, brother. Come in. As you can see, we do not have a lot of furniture yet. We only just started renting here."

I followed them to the family room where I took a seat on a

new leather couch Ilham pointed toward. "This is a nice place regardless," I told them.

"Is this like your home?" Ilham asked.

I laughed. "No. I live on . . . well, a sofa that's a little smaller than this one. I share an apartment with five people."

They looked at each other, then looked back at me, clearly expecting me to elaborate. There was serious Addams Family energy about these two. I wouldn't have been all that surprised if theme music from that show had started playing in the background.

"Uh . . . so, yeah, it's uncomfortably cozy. It is a decent location, I guess, and the rent is manageable, so—"

"Why do you live like that?" Kashaf asked. "Your mother is a doctor. She must have money."

I shrugged. "Well, my parents don't support me, so . . ."

"You got supported when you were young," Kashaf said. Or asked. I wasn't sure.

"You mean when I was a kid? Sure. Um . . . what are we talking about here?"

"Debt," Ilham said.

Kashaf spoke over him. "We are just trying to get to know you, Azaan. This is how friends are made, yes?"

"I mean—"

"You became a preacher like your father. You must love Imam Saifi very much."

"He . . . has definitely been a motivating factor in my life," I told them.

"It's amazing what he has accomplished. The new mosque is beautiful."

"It is," I agreed. "He spent his life on it. He basically raised the money to build it himself. With Tiger Uncle's help, of course. Speaking of whom—"

"How did he raise the money?" Kashaf asked. "It must have cost millions."

"It took years. He went around and did fundraisers all over California. He went to other states and even to other countries—"

"It sounds," she broke in, "like he was away a lot."

"The mosque was a priority for him," I said.

"And you weren't?"

I frowned.

"I don't mean to pry. I am just very interested in love," Kashaf told me. "I want to figure out how it works. I haven't been able to do that yet."

"A lot of ink has been spent trying to answer that question," I said.

"Wasted," Ilham muttered.

"He does not think love is real," Kashaf told me in a stage whisper. "To him, relationships are just the exchange of duties and responsibilities. What do you say to that?"

"I disagree."

"Why?" she asked.

"Because I've been in love. I mean, we all have at some point, right?"

Again, they exchanged a look. This time, they both shook their heads.

"Really? I thought it was a universal experience."

"A man who lives by a river doesn't often think of the desert, does he, Ilham?"

The thickset younger man grunted.

"Our father never had any use for us," Kashaf declared, her tone surprisingly neutral given her subject. "Our mother was his second wife, and when he had to choose between us and his first family, he chose them. I don't know why."

"Yes," Ilham broke in. "You do."

"On an individual level," she clarified, "yes, we do know. In terms of the nature of love, I've never understood. Why do some people receive it while others don't?"

"I have no idea," I admitted. "But I'm sorry that happened to you."

"Our mother loved us very much," she assured me.

"Well, good."

"That would have been enough, I think, if she had lived."

"Oh."

Kashaf got to her feet. "We are being poor hosts. Let's feed you. You should also take some food back for the imam."

"No, no. I'm not going to see him tonight. I'm spending it at a . . . uh, friend's place."

"What friend?" Ilham asked.

I scratched the back of my neck. "Just someone I knew from school."

"You must tell us what that was like, going to school here," Kashaf said.

"Why don't you guys tell me more about yourselves instead?"

She glanced at Ilham. "I heard Tiger Heart does not want you to hear what we have to say."

"Why is that, though?"

"If we tell you," Ilham said, "you will know."

"Yes, that's how it works."

"There would be no going back, is what he is saying," Kashaf explained. "Adam taught us that a man should be careful what fruit he bites into. Some of it is rotten, and some of it has worms."

"That's not an answer."

"No," she conceded. "It is not."

"You think we'll see the moon tonight?"

I looked up, startled out of my reverie by the Uber driver's question. I'd been thinking about the fact that I hadn't gotten any answers out of the twins, who seemed peculiarly interested in me and my history, but shared almost none of their own. Whenever I'd asked them any questions—even innocent ones like "what do you do for a living?"—they had given ludicrous answers.

I knew, of course, Kashaf worked as a cashier at Tiger Uncle's store, but that wouldn't allow them to afford the kind of lavish lifestyle they enjoyed. My inquiry had been directed at Ilham, who had to be making most of the money, but he'd just laughed and answered with one word: "Crime." Kashaf had chuckled, and I'd smiled politely at what was obviously a joke. I'd never actually gotten a real response, though.

It had been a strange evening.

A strange day, in fact. Part of me was still processing the morning, thinking about Uncle Tariq's ghusl and the part I had played in it. The end result of it, I was sure, was that more string would be added to the knot in my chest, making it more complex and difficult to decipher.

"Sorry," I said. "What was that?"

"The moon," the driver said. "Do you think we'll see it tonight? We haven't in days."

I peered out the car window. "I doubt it."

"It's real pretty this time of the year. Goes all red."

"Yeah?" I asked.

"It's because of all the smoke. Guess it's a little consolation, you know, for all the destruction we've suffered."

I didn't ask him where he thought this supposed recompense was coming from exactly. I had no desire to enter into a theological or spiritual debate just then. I mean, I never did, but on that night in particular, I was drained.

"I miss it," the driver said. "Wish it were there. Makes the dark brighter."

"Well, it's there, whether its visible or not, right?"

"Would be better if we could see it, though."

I nodded and this seemed to satisfy him. The rest of the ride went by in silence.

When we got to Madi's house, a sleek sports car zipped past us at high speed and parked at the end of the cul-de-sac, causing the Uber driver to grumble.

Ignoring him, I stepped out and walked up to Madison's porch. On my way, I spared a glance for the heavens and I could have sworn, for a fleeting moment, I saw a small sliver of orange in the unimaginable distance. I stopped, stood still, and searched for it again.

I couldn't find it.

One day soon, I knew the moon would reappear in the sky when I wasn't looking and I probably wouldn't even notice, at least not right away.

My phone chimed with a new message.

MADISON:

Tell me you're close.

AZAAN:

I'm here.

As I got to her door, it opened. I saw her standing there and without saying anything I reached over, tipped her chin up and leaned down to kiss her and that made everything seem better, so I kissed her again. She made a sound at the back of her throat, a growl or a whimper or something in between. It was all need and lust and my shirt was off before we thought to close the door behind us and then her back was pressed against a wall and her dress was bunched up around her waist.

After, as we lay on the cold floor, trying to catch our breath, tangled with each other, disheveled, she laughed and said, "That's some hello."

I brushed strands of her long dark hair away from her eyes. "Hey, Mads."

She turned her face in to kiss my palm. "This is the wildest thing I've done."

"Sex in the foyer?" I knew that wasn't true. I mean, our first time had been on a stage at school. Granted it had been the middle of the night and the place had been deserted, but that had still been pretty adventurous.

Madi took my hand in hers and interlaced our fingers. "I meant this. I needed . . ."

"What?"

"Someone," she said. "I'm glad it's you."

"You've said that before," I reminded her, starting to sit up. "Look, we should—"

She pushed me back down. "That's the 'let's talk' look. Can we not right now? Later."

"Sure. But do we have to stay here?"

Madi grinned. "No. We can go to bed."

"We don't have to. If you prefer, we can lay 'upon the ground and tell sad stories of the death of kings. How some have been deposed; some slain'—"

"Oh, shut up." She got to her feet, then held out a hand to me. "And come with me."

The next morning Madi was lying with her head on my shoulder. It hadn't been a long night. I'd been too beat to stay up very long. If she was disappointed, she wasn't letting on. Instead, she was running a hand over my chest lazily. She'd been doing so for a while, her blue-gray eyes fixed there intently like they were searching for something, so I asked.

"Can I help you?"

"I'm looking for that knot of yours."

I'd only ever told two other people about that, and they were both physicians whom I'd thought best to check with in case it was a symptom of some kind of awful, terminal disease. It turned out to be nothing but an indication of what my mom called a sensitive heart. I was pretty sure that could kill you too, but only slowly.

I'd had no secrets from Mads though, except—for a while—how I'd felt about her.

Well, there was also the truth of how often my father hit me, but that was the business of Saifi and Son.

"Why?" I asked. "Are you going to kiss it and make it better?"

"Do you think that would work?"

"It's impossible to know," I said.

Mads sat up, held her dark hair back with one hand, leaned down, and brushed her lips against my clavicle. "There?"

I shook my head.

She kissed me where my heart was. "Here?"

"No," I said.

Then she kissed me where my ribs met, just above where my abdomen started, where the knot lived.

"Lower. You should definitely keep going lower," I told her.

Madi grinned, rolled off me, and settled back where she'd been a moment ago. "Jerk."

"You found it on that last one."

"And?" she asked.

"I don't think you fixed it."

Madi let out a comically dramatic sigh. "Damn. I thought I was special."

"I don't think it'll ever go away. Well, dying will probably fix it, but that seems like a pretty drastic cure."

"Don't say stupid things."

"But that's my only skill."

Madi smiled, then became serious. "So, the first time we were together—"

"When I left you wanting, apparently."

"Get over it," she said. "Seriously, Azaan, the first time we were together, you told me not to ask about the scarring on your back. Can I ask about it now?"

"I don't want to talk about it. It . . . doesn't matter. I do want to talk about us. You know, you've cut me off every time I've tried to get—"

"Real. I know. And look, oops, I did it again."

"Mads."

"Fine," she grumbled. "Ask me what you want."

"Do you—"

"Am I sure what we're doing isn't a mistake?" Madi guessed. "No, but I . . . I've seen lots of therapists, you know, because of the plane crash."

I nodded.

She took my hand and started examining it, comparing her long, elegant fingers with my thick ones, not looking at me as she admitted quietly, "I've learned I'm afraid."

"Of what?"

Madi shrugged. "Abandonment, I'm told, which is stupid because my parents didn't . . . and you didn't—"

"I'm sorry."

"No, that's the thing, what are you sorry for? It isn't like you picked something or someone over me. Neither did my family. I got left behind, but that wasn't anybody's fault. It just happened."

I nodded.

"Apparently, my heart can't tell the difference. It isn't able to let people go. That's why I got married young. That's forever, right? A ring with a diamond in it. Not to mention the fact that it's supposed to be a girl's best friend, something I was in dire need of after you were gone."

"You never really explained why you didn't want me to stay in touch. I would have. I wanted to. Desperately."

She shrugged. "It was stupid, maybe. I was angry and confused and . . . just raw. It seemed best to rip the bandage off, because what? We were going to date with you in Cairo and me here? No. We'd go back to pretending we were just friends?" Madi drew in a deep breath. "I thought it'd hurt less if I was the one cutting you loose."

"Yeah."

"It didn't."

I kissed her forehead.

"Lyle was nice and already stable when I met him. His plan was to take over his father's real estate business, which meant he wasn't going anywhere. I liked that, so when he asked, I married him, and it was okay for a while."

"What happened?"

"Nothing at first. I think, slowly, he figured out I wasn't in love with him. I mean . . . it was all right, all of it, but there was no fire, at least not for me. At the beginning of our relationship, I think he didn't care or maybe he thought he could light it but when he couldn't . . ."

"He gave up?" I asked.

"He cheated. I was furious. We'd exchanged promises. His breaking them was just him leaving without leaving. The worst part of it was like . . . I understood. Not in the sense that I would have ever done that myself. It's just that I knew he wasn't satisfied, and unlike me he hadn't resigned himself to being a little unhappy all the time. I could see why he'd want someone who could give him more."

"Doesn't make it a less shitty thing to do."

"No," she agreed. "Anyway, that was it. We'd just had Julie, and she was a blessing. Here was someone who wouldn't leave me, not for a long time. I thought that meant I could be content, at least for a while."

"Why aren't you?"

Now Madi met my gaze. "I am. Sometimes. It's just . . . I feel like there's no one around who understands me, who truly gets me, you know? Maybe that's something no one gets to have, though. Maybe not being understood is what being human is."

I stroked her hair and waited to see if she would go on.

"So . . . yeah, maybe this—you and I—what we're doing, maybe it'll end up hurting us. Maybe it won't. The only certainty I have is that it'd be nice if a few more nights were like last night."

I understood more what this was now—what she and I were, what these moments together were—they were stolen pieces of a life that might have been, a life we might have had, where neither one of us was alone.

The problem, of course, was that these fragments of what had once been possible were fleeting, like the light of a falling star, and she had no idea how she would deal with the fiery crash that was coming.

I didn't know how I'd deal with it either.

I would go back home soon, which would mean a return to our regular lives with our usual pains.

Maybe because we both knew this wasn't going to last, because we had gone into this with our eyes open, being left behind wouldn't burn her this time and leaving her wouldn't incinerate me.

Or perhaps, despite all our foreknowledge, we'd end up bleeding anyway. Maybe the best we can hope for in life is to choose our wounds, and that's what we were doing.

"Does that answer your question?" Madi asked.

"I didn't ask you anything," I pointed out. "I was going to and then—"

"I interrupted."

"Yeah."

"Sorry. What were you about to ask me?"

"Do you want to get some coffee before we get started with the heavy stuff?"

She laughed. "Well, it's a little late for that."

"A little. There's still so much more to say, though. I want to hear everything. I'm excited to get to know you again, Madison Porter. Unless . . . I mean, it's still Madison Porter, right?"

"Yes," she gave me a quick peck on the cheek and got out of bed. "It is."

I spent some time arranging a surprise date for Madi, then went back to the mosque, only to find police cars and camera operators there, along with a substantial crowd. It was obvious nothing bad had happened. There was no tension in the air. Everyone was perfectly calm. I asked a bystander what was happening and learned the mayor had come to visit the masjid before its grand opening ceremony and that my father was giving her a tour.

I spotted Jibreel, waved at him, and started to head to my apartment, but he jogged over, adjusting his glasses on his face as he did so. "As-salamu alaykum."

I returned the greeting. "This must be exciting for Dad."

He frowned. "It was exciting for all of us for a moment. Someone came in last night and poured red paint all over the carpet in the prayer hall, right in front of the minbar."

The minbar was the place where an imam stood to give his sermon. I grimaced. "Dad must have loved that."

"He was freaking out, especially because the mayor was about to arrive. We covered it up with a sheet and if anyone asks, he'll say it was an accident."

I nodded as I opened the door to the studio I was staying in. My father wouldn't be thrilled at the prospect of lying while in a mosque—or lying at all—but I could understand why the board didn't want the vandalism to get more coverage.

Jibreel pushed in after me, not waiting for an invitation. "Did you see anyone suspicious here last night?"

I shook my head. "I was at my mom's place again."

"I can't blame you for wanting to stay with her." He gestured at the barren apartment. "Has to be more comfortable than this."

"Just a little bit. Hey, are you guys going to report this to the police?"

"They haven't done anything so far about everything else that has happened," he said. "So Tiger thinks that it's best to let Imam Saifi catch whoever is responsible. He's living here now, after all. He'll spot the culprit sooner or later."

Given all the shenanigans I'd gotten up to when I was a kid, relying on Dad's ability to sniff out mischief probably wasn't a good plan. I didn't say so, however, and Jibreel went on.

"Anyway, at least the mayor's visit is going well. Imam Saifi has had her trapped in there for forty minutes. He's describing everything to her in detail. What brand of toilet bowls are in the bathrooms, where we got the curtains from, everything. It's endless."

"He's very proud."

"Yes, man, and that's good. But," he joked, "I'm worried the mayor is going to die of boredom in there. That won't play well in the press." More seriously, he added, "Speaking of which, I need to talk to you."

"What's going on?"

"Has the journalist you spoke to learned anything more about the donation money that's gone missing?"

"I don't know."

"They shouldn't have. I spoke to Uncle Karar and Nadeem and told them to be careful who they speak to and what they say."

"Good," I said.

"I also finished going through all the records Tiger and Imam Saifi gave me. Neither one of them helped, by the way. They kept making excuses. I decided to just do the math as best I could and give them the benefit of the doubt at every stage."

With a preamble like that, this likely was not going to be good news.

"The best-case scenario, being as charitable to them as possible," Jibreel said, "around two hundred thousand dollars is missing."

"What?!"

My shock seemed to bring him some measure of satisfaction. "Exactly. It's a big deal, don't you think?"

"I mean, it's not a rounding error."

"Can you imagine what people would say if this gets out?" Jibreel asked. "We have to find the money. You must talk to your father. If he doesn't cooperate, I'm going to get the authorities involved."

"Hold on. That'd devastate him. There must be a good explanation. If you go to the cops, that'll kill Dad. The respect of the community means so much to him."

"I'm not doing anything yet," Jibreel assured me. "I'm not accusing anyone of anything either. I just need answers."

"That's fair."

"Soon," he added.

I rubbed my temples with my palms, trying to process the enormous number he'd thrown out and the implications of everything else he'd said.

The fact that Dad and Tiger had both been giving Jibreel the runaround didn't look good for either of them, but it was inconceivable they were thieves.

My mind flashed back to Tiger in his shop, notebooks spread out in front of him, talking about how bad business had been.

No. He wouldn't steal money from this community to which he had given so much over the decades.

Would he borrow it with the intention of paying it back, though? Tiger had made a life out of bending and not breaking the rules of the religion he followed. It could be that's all this was. He had said he wasn't liquid, after all.

"I'll talk to them both," I promised, "as soon as I can."

Chapter Fifteen

MY FATHER WAS PRACTICALLY GLOWING WHEN I FOUND him after the mayor left. Her people and the cameras that followed them around were gone. I had rarely, if ever, seen him happier. Clearly, the success of the mayor's visit had helped him get over the destruction of the carpet in the prayer hall. Bringing up Jibreel's concerns about the finances of the mosque, as I'd come to do, would poison his good mood.

"Ah, there he is, my little traitor," he said when he saw me. There was no venom in his tone despite the sting in his words. "You were at Iqra's place again last night, weren't you? It's very disappointing to see you spending so much time with that woman."

"You are the one who always says that Paradise lies at the feet of one's mother."

"It was the Prophet who said that, as you know."

"It's true then?" I asked.

"What do you mean? Of course, it is true. Astaghfirullah.

How can you ask that? If Muhammad, Peace Be Upon Him, said it—"

"It was a rhetorical question, Dad."

"I see," he muttered. "It is just that . . . well, I don't think you should be on Iqra's side."

"I'm not on anyone's side. She has a spare room. It has an actual bed. It's more comfortable than sleeping on the floor is all."

"Hardship builds character," he said, though I could tell his heart wasn't really in it. The desi in him knew that if you ever got a free upgrade of any sort, you took it.

"I'm enough of a character already, thanks. Anyway, look, there's something we need to discuss."

"Is this about the mayor?" he asked, brightening up a little. "She was very impressed with our setup here. Didn't she tell me again and again and again how very nice everything was? Didn't she say I had built a marvel? It was good of her to come, don't you think?"

"It's very exciting."

"Of course," my father muttered, "she was only doing it to curry favor. That's the only reason these politicians do anything. Not that it'll benefit her much. The congregation will vote for the liberal challenger, I think."

I shrugged. "Probably. That's what they usually do."

"I don't understand the politics of this country, Azaan."

"Well, you've only lived here for what? Thirty-plus years? Give it time."

"Very funny," he groused. "I'm serious. I am a conservative. Many Muslims are, actually, when it comes to their values."

"That's often a package deal with the whole religion thing," I agreed.

"Yet we have this uneasy alliance with liberals, who

tolerate us but don't believe the things we believe, because the conservatives, who believe a lot of the same things we do, think we are the enemy. It's not comfortable, you know, being in a marriage out of necessity and convenience."

I decided to let that remark go without comment.

"It doesn't help that there is no consistency to the views these people hold. Liberals want a powerful government but don't like the police. Conservatives love the police, but don't trust the government. It is all illogical."

"I've never really thought about it. But it doesn't matter. I need to talk to you about money."

Dad sighed. "Is this about freezing your grandfather's brain? I can't afford that, and even if I could, I wouldn't pay for it. I doubt this technique works, but if it does, Baba's brain is no good, is it? It's full of filth and disbelief and Allah knows what wickedness. Don't you think it's better for humanity if it dies with the rest of him?"

"I spoke to Jibreel."

His expression darkened. "And what did that pea counter have to say?"

"That there are a lot of funds missing from the treasury here. He can't be sure how much, though, because you and Tiger Uncle—"

"Should he be talking to you about the board's internal business? No. I don't think so. This is not your concern."

"It's just—"

"It's just nothing," my father snapped. "This is exactly why children shouldn't involve themselves in the work of grown men. He does not understand the records we kept. That is all this is. Beta, I have documentation to back up every single one of the mosque's pennies. Trust me, there is nothing to worry about."

"Then why not just show your paperwork to Jibreel? Explain your system to him and put this behind you."

Imam Saifi sighed. "Why should I have to justify myself to a child I watched grow up? Why should I get him more involved? So he can create more issues just to feel important? Doesn't he already cause enough trouble teaching our boys Sunday school? Why does he also have to be treasurer?"

"He's teaching Sunday school? So, you're making kids sit and listen to him? I would've hated that when I was young."

"They like him, actually," Dad admitted grudgingly. "He's gotten a lot of them to take the green pill—"

"The what now?"

"Some of them call it the haqq pill. It is the Muslim version of the medicine that a lot of angry men are swallowing these days. I saw something about it on the news. It comes from an old science movie or something."

I frowned, tried to figure out what the hell he was talking about, and took a shot. "The red pill?"

"Yes. That one. It's harmless, I think. They're mostly just really into working out all of a sudden and being 'alphas.' Also, they talk about Islam like they are the only ones who understand it."

"And damn it," I said, "that's your job."

A hint of a smile flitted across my father's face. "Oh, and they really seem to have harsh views about women."

"Which isn't harmful?"

He waved dismissively. "Haven't I seen young men do this all my life? They roar like lions when they are bachelors, but then they're afraid to even mewl like kittens after they are married. It isn't anything to worry about. Though I do wish he would stop making them hate-read books."

"Hate read?"

"Jibreel has his students read books by Muslim writers and then has them go online and complain about the texts, saying they aren't good representation or something like that. It's such a waste of time. If you think a book isn't good, why make your students read it? Have them read useful things instead."

"Hold on. I don't understand. Are there authors out there claiming to write on behalf of all Muslims? Because that seems like it'd be impossible to actually do."

"I don't think there are, but Jibreel says it doesn't matter what the writers are trying to do. He says that by attacking stuff we don't agree with online, we can shape the narrative about Islam and control what people get to say and publish. Apparently, liberals are very into this idea. Like I said, Azaan, I don't understand the politics of these people. This seems like the opposite of what progressives should want."

I'd come across this representation concept, which was sweeping through the film industry too, and I hadn't really had a problem with it. It seemed like it would mean more work for me and that was a net positive, as far as I was concerned.

I'd never seen it weaponized, though. Leave it to Jibreel to make a literary jihad out of it.

"Couldn't he also 'shape the narrative' by writing his own books?" I asked.

"That's too much work. At least for now. Apparently, they are working on thinking machines, and soon that is where all art will come from."

I rolled my eyes.

"I'm just telling you what Jibreel said. All poetry and paintings and literature will be made by computers. No one will talk about Tolstoy because work just like his will be produced in seconds. Ghalib will be surpassed by lines of code. That, he says, is where the next great Muslim novel will come from."

"Yeah, that's not going to happen."

My father grunted. "How can you be sure of that? I have lived long enough to see reality surpass imagination. Maybe one day our jobs will be done by machines too."

I shuddered. The rise of hard-core conservative imambots seemed like a truly horrible idea.

"Anyway," I said, "let's get back to the money issue—"

"Look, the reason I told you all this is to make you understand that Jibreel Jameel is—"

"A bag of dicks. I got it."

"Astaghfirullah, Azaan. Don't talk like that. But . . . what you said isn't untrue."

"It doesn't matter if he's likable or not. All that matters is if he's right. If you have proof that nothing is amiss, you need to offer it to him. Dad, this is serious. He is going to go public with this very soon."

Imam Saifi sighed. "How did you get old enough to give out advice without learning that you shouldn't offer it except when you're asked? For the last time, Azaan, leave this to me and Tiger. I will talk to him. He will handle it. You stay out of this. Do you understand? Don't make me tell you again."

"Yes, Azaan," Tiger Uncle said as soon as he answered his phone. "What can I do for you?"

"Uncle, I was speaking to Jibreel Jameel—"

"That is always a bad idea."

"Well, it's done now. Can you explain why you or Dad haven't been helping him decipher the mosque's accounting system?"

"He would figure it out himself," Tiger grumbled, "if he could do even fat math."

"What?"

"You haven't heard of fat math before? In Pakistan we call it 'mota hisab,'" Tiger Uncle explained. "Arithmetic, the answer to which is easy to see."

"You guys have weird sayings."

"What is this 'you guys'? You should say 'we guys.'"

"No one should say that," I told him. "Now about the money—"

"Uff, Azaan, it is not a big deal. I am sure—"

"He told me he estimates around two hundred thousand dollars are missing."

Tiger Uncle was quiet for a moment, then he cursed before he said, "What a bloody mess. I did not know it was that much. Have you spoken to Saqi about it?"

"Dad said he has receipts for everything he's spent the mosque's money on, that he'd talk to you, and that you would handle it."

Tiger scoffed. "Really? Is that what he said? What a bitch he is."

I laughed.

"I'm serious. This is not my shit. Why does he expect me to come wipe his bum for him?"

"Gross. Why would you say that?"

"Because that is what is happening. Always, whenever there is trouble, everyone looks to me to solve it. Tiger fix this. Tiger fix that. I have to admit that I like it sometimes. It is like they are coming to my court, you know, because I am the king of this jungle. Except just because I've been able to see a way out of problems before doesn't mean I can do so always. And to drop this on my doorstep without even talking to me about it first, that is not on." Tiger Heart paused, then added, "Also, I already told you to let this go. Why won't you?"

"Even if I did, what would you tell Jibreel?"

"Right. There is that stale fart. Let me think."

"What is there to think about?" I asked. "You guys can just tell the truth, especially if Dad has proof."

"Azaan, you should know by now that one should only speak the truth as a last resort."

"But there's no reason to lie here."

There was another silence. Then Tiger posed a question of his own. "Do you think I took the money?"

"What are you talking about? Dad just told me he can account for everything. That should be the end of it. I don't get why you two won't just cooperate with Jibreel and finish this."

"Everyone will for sure think I took it. It either has to be me or Saqi, right? We were the only ones with access to it. Will the community believe me, do you think, or their imam?"

I took a moment to hear what he was saying . . . or, more specifically, what he wasn't saying. Tiger was not claiming, like Dad, that were was no issue here. By moving on to wondering who would get the blame, he was essentially conceding that Jibreel had found a real, substantial problem.

As for Tiger's question about how a battle of credibility between him and Dad would go, he was exactly right. The reputations of these two men were well-established.

"I don't think you'd steal from the mosque," I told him. I wasn't just being nice. It was true. Whatever else his failings, outright crime wasn't Tiger's style. It lacked the finesse of someone who called himself a goldsmith and a technician.

Would he take the money if he needed it? Yes, but he'd fully intend to return it as soon as possible. "Borrowing" the funds was something he'd be able to convince himself was an okay thing to do.

Was Tiger Uncle's financial situation really dire enough for him to try something like this, though? I mean, sure, this was a huge amount for the average person, but this man had millions. Could things really have gotten so bad for him that he couldn't move some of his own assets around to raise cash?

I didn't think so.

Tiger, for his part, seemed touched by my statement. "Thank you," he said softly. "That is nice of you to say. It is the curse of liars, unfortunately, that their honestly is not believed. Listen, don't say anything to Jibreel. Let's stall for a while. I will figure out a way to make the mosque whole even if I have to take it up the hole. Can you do that for me, Azaan?"

"Yeah, of course."

Without saying anything else, Tiger hung up.

It looked like there was going to be a happy ending—well, an adequate ending, anyway—to the mystery of the disappearing donations. I ought to have been satisfied. Like Adam in the Garden, however, I wasn't. I wanted knowledge of who, in this situation, was good and who was evil.

Tiger Uncle was admitting that funds were missing from the mosque's treasury, which was something Dad adamantly refused to do. Was that because Tiger knew what he had done while my father didn't? Or was Dad just feigning ignorance?

It helped Tiger's case that he had spoken not like a guilty man, but like an innocent one resigned to his fate.

The fact that he was willing to move his assets so he could raise money now begged the question of why he wouldn't have done that in the first place instead of reaching into the mosque's pockets.

It could have been simple greed. I was pretty sure that the Prophet had once said that if the children of Adam had a valley full of gold, they'd desire a second, and if they had a second, they'd want a third. It is human nature to constantly lust for more even when one possesses more than enough.

Still, my instinct was to believe Tiger. He had sounded genuinely surprised by the amount in question.

Except, in order to believe him, I had to also believe Dad was lying. For all his many and deep faults, he was Imam Saqlain Saifi, and it was inconceivable that he would do something like this. Even at that very moment, I was standing in a building that was a monument to his faith. How was it possible that he could be faithless?

Yet it was undeniable that a lot about my father's circumstances didn't make sense. His being behind on his bills, for example, while announcing his intention to retire.

According to Jibreel, Dad had started talking about retirement as soon as Jibreel had been elected treasurer. Jibreel had chalked it up to my father not wanting to give up control over the mosque's operations, which made sense.

But it was also possible that Dad just wanted to make an exit before what had happened to the stolen funds was discovered. Selling the house in those circumstances would also make sense, either because he planned to run—which sounded ridiculous—or because he hoped to repay what he had taken with the proceeds of the sale.

For him to do something like this, however, his need would have to be beyond desperate, and he'd have to be motivated by something he loved more than the mosque, more than Islam, and more than God.

There was nothing like that in the universe.

Was there?

A voice called out, "Imam Saifi?"

I looked around, searching for my father, before I realized that I was the one being addressed. Pasting on a smile, I turned to see who had spoken. One of the board members, the one who had opposed the teaching of yoga to women at the masjid, was hurrying to catch up with me.

"Call me Azaan," I said as he shook my hand.

"You can call me Uncle Nadeem. We met before."

"You're in charge of interfaith outreach."

"Yes, exactly," he beamed happily at being remembered. "In addition to that, I am also responsible for giving the Friday sermon here. That is what I wanted to talk to you about."

"Isn't that something Dad does?"

"Imam Saifi—the original one, that is—he's still doing the service at the old mosque. This one, as you know, won't technically be open until the ribbon cutting happens. That's when he will speak here on the pulpit for the first time."

"Okay," I said.

"The problem is that some people keep showing up here anyway because it is closer to where they live or work. Instead of turning them away, I've been leading the service. I am like your father's . . . what do they say at concerts? Opening act? I am like Beyoncé opening for Atif Aslam."

"Uh-huh."

"What I'm forced to admit is . . . well, you see, I am not really qualified to do this. I talk about basic things that everyone knows. For example, I've told the congregation that men should not be wearing silk ties because that is a sin, and how music is a tool of the devil, and how birthdays are forbidden—"

"Wait. What are you talking about?"

Uncle Nadeem blinked, surprised by my surprise. "Birthdays. They are not of Islam, yes?"

"I mean—"

"They are an innovation from the West. It's like that whole yoga nonsense, except that came from the East. Let me ask you. Did the Prophet ever celebrate a birthday? Not that I know of. In fact, he said that for Muslims there are only two Eids. And what is an Eid? It is a celebration that comes every year. Are we not going against this when have parties and make special the day of our birth? This practice is just an imitation of the nonbelievers and, as you know, that is haram."

I pinched the bridge of my nose.

"Have you not told the brothers and sisters at your British mosque about this? You should warn them about these dangers, shouldn't you?"

"I figured it was harmless to let people be happy every once in a while."

"Ah," Uncle Nadeem said knowingly, "I see what happened. You fell into the trap of thinking for yourself."

"Yeah. That was careless of me."

"Maybe this would be a good topic for your sermon?"

"What sermon?" I asked.

He was already on a roll, though, and going downhill fast. "You could talk about how we should not be following our own thoughts and desires. We must instead look at what the Quran and the Prophet say about things. We must all dissolve in the Sharia."

"'You will be assimilated. Resistance is futile.'"

Uncle Nadeem clapped me on the shoulder. "Exactly right. What a brilliant line. You should use that."

"I'm pretty sure it's copyrighted. Anyway, I don't think I should give a sermon," I told him. I was still resolved not to give out any more spiritual advice than I absolutely had to in order to remain in character. Also, to be honest, I didn't want the homework.

"Why not?"

"Well . . . uh, there shouldn't be a service here at all. With the prayer hall carpet being destroyed and all."

"Don't worry about that," Uncle Nadeem said. "We'll fix that long before you speak."

"If I speak, though, then you won't be speaking and . . . well, honestly, listening to you now, I'm . . . I'm in awe of your profound wisdom."

He grinned. "You are too kind, really, but like I said, I'm not trained for this work. You went to university for it."

"Sure. But what university did the Prophet go to? What about his Companions? Isn't this whole business of getting degrees just another Western innovation like—"

"Birthdays," he exclaimed.

This wasn't strictly true. Al-Azhar was ancient, as was the concept of giving out what in Islam was called ijazah, which was a license allowing someone to teach or transmit their knowledge onward to future generations. It essentially served the same purpose as the pieces of parchment paper modern institutions handed out to their graduates. Formal education had deep roots in the Muslim tradition.

In fact, my father had given a whole speech once about how the University of al-Qarawiyyin in Fez, Morocco, founded by a woman called Fatima al-Fihriya, was the oldest center of higher learning in the world, and how we should all be proud of that fact.

It was the kind of historical nugget Dad dropped often. Modern Muslims spend a lot of time talking about the accomplishments of the people who came before them while having few of their own, like an adult kid who gets by on a prestigious family name, always willing, eager, and desperate to remind people how awesome their grandparents and great-grandparents were. We slumber on the shoulders of giants.

Anyway, Uncle Nadeem's enthusiasm about condemning innovations in religion outpaced his logic, and he said, "You make perfect sense, Imam. Maybe there is no harm in my continuing to give the khutbah on Friday, just to remind everyone that there is nothing wrong with a layperson taking on a leadership role."

"Whatever you think is best."

He shook my hand and was about to leave when a thought occurred to me.

"Uncle Nadeem?"

"Yes?" he asked.

"Did you talk to a reporter about a possible issue with the mosque's finances?"

"No, no, no. That would be very wrong. Jibreel told us not to mention that to anyone, and I did what I was told."

"You do seem to be very good at that," I conceded.

"Thank you. Imam Saifi, if you don't mind my asking, why do you want to know?"

"Oh, it's nothing. Dad told me it was no big deal and that he had paperwork to account for everything. I just thought you should know that in case you give any more interviews."

He nodded. "Your father is a careful man. I'm sure he has proof of everything he spent money on either in his office or at home. We all know Jibreel is probably overenthusiastic about his new role, like Tiger says."

Uncle Nadeem was right. The documentation that Dad was refusing to produce ought to be easy to find. There were really only two places it could be. I could just look for it myself and share it with Jibreel if Dad wouldn't. It was a simple, easy solution.

"So, Uncle, you know that I am staying in one of the mosque's apartments, right?"

"It's our pleasure to host you."

"Thanks. Are there spare keys for the units? I locked myself out."

He smiled. "It's no problem at all. You know the conference room where we first met?"

"Yeah?"

"In the top right-most cabinet, behind some books, there is a shoebox in which you will find extras. You let yourself back in anytime. Just make sure you put everything back like you found it."

"I will."

"I suppose," Uncle Nadeem added, speaking more to himself than to me, "we should lock those away soon. It's just that we haven't really started renting those places out, so—"

"Don't worry about it. It's not a priority. I mean, everyone who knows where to find them is trustworthy, right?"

Just as I retrieved the spare key to my father's apartment from the hiding spot Nadeem had told me about, the door behind me opened and someone walked into the conference room, making me jump out of my skin.

I recognized Uncle Karar, the other board member I'd met, the one arguing for yoga classes to be allowed on mosque property.

"So sorry, so sorry. I didn't mean to startle you. Didn't mean that at all. But I was looking for you. Do you have a second, Sheikh?"

"Sure," I said, slipping the key into my pocket. "What do you need?"

"I just saw Nadeem, and he says that you're going to let him continue doing the Friday sermons. I must protest."

I smiled. "I take it you're not a fan?"

"Well, between him and your father, I haven't been preached to in a manner I've liked in some time. No offense. It's just that I find the brand of Islam practiced here rather . . . well, it's a bit extreme. It wouldn't hurt to ratchet down the intensity just a smidge and be flexible. Like they weren't with the yoga. You remember that business?"

"It'd be difficult to forget."

"My daughter is still upset about it. She won't come to the mosque now. Feels like she's being judged for her hobby, which is perfectly innocent. All over the world, people exercise in this fashion. In Saudi Arabia and in Pakistan they have classes to teach it. They do. But here, suddenly, it is forbidden. Haram. It doesn't make sense."

"I don't disagree, Uncle."

"I remember you said so. Thank you."

"I tried."

"Maybe you could have tried harder."

"My father doesn't listen to me."

Uncle Karar pulled out a chair for himself and sat down. "I don't understand what happens to some Muslims when they leave their lands. Many become super conservative, thinking God has them under a microscope all the time, or they become . . . well, crazy liberals like you. Before you were reformed, I mean. You used to do whatever you liked. The middle road is what Islam is really about. Life has to be lived in balance. We are lucky the majority of our people everywhere understand that."

"What do you want me to do about it?"

"Get Nadeem off the minbar. I can't take another lecture about how parts of my feet will burn in hell because the hem of my pants extends below my ankles. It is too much. Much too much. Please help."

"Look, I'll be gone soon, so I don't want to mess with the status quo. I hear your concerns, I really do, but all you have to do is hang in there for a few weeks. Then Dad will be the one addressing the congregation again."

He pulled at his beard. "That is not much better. Did you know your father yelled at a young man the other day because he had a mohawk? Haram, he said. Forbidden. Have you heard of this?"

"Oh. Um . . ." I pulled out my phone. "Excuse me. I just got an important text. My grandfather is in the hospital, as you know. Do you mind if I respond?"

"No, no. Go ahead."

I went to the internet looking for religion again.

When I was done, I set my cell aside and, trying to sound like an authority on the subject, declared, "Sorry about that. Now where were we? Right. Mohawks. My father isn't wrong. They are actually not allowed. You can't shave part of your hair and keep the rest. Fauxhawks apparently are okay, though." There was, in fact, a lot of material on this issue. Whatever else you could say about Muslims, you couldn't accuse us of not taking our religion seriously, that's for sure.

Uncle Karar deflated a little upon hearing this. "Well, there was no reason to scream at the boy, was there? He could have spoken to him gently."

"Dad doesn't really do gentle," I said. "Uncle, I sympathize, but I don't think it's appropriate for me to fly in and take over here, even temporarily. It's not right."

"So we're doomed then, doomed forever, to have hardliners speak for Islam."

"Well," I said, "perhaps it's their province."

Uncle Karar blinked. "What do you mean?"

"Generally speaking, conservatives make good religion and liberals make good art."

"And what about the rest of us? What do we make?"

I grinned. "Audiences."

He was clearly not amused.

"I'm kidding. If it's any consolation, you've done your part. You got on the board. You got involved. Maybe you'll inspire other moderates and they'll run for election too." I paused, realizing that perhaps he had done more than that. If neither my father nor Tiger nor Jibreel nor Uncle Nadeem were Madi's source on the story, that meant Uncle Karar was. Had he gotten so fed up with how this place was run, that he'd resorted to gossiping with the media in the hopes of forcing a change? I figured it didn't matter now. I had access to Dad's apartment and soon I'd have the evidence necessary to help close Jibreel's investigation. So instead of bringing up Mads, I just said, "Things will get better eventually."

"Until then we're supposed to just keep suffering?"

"If it makes you feel better, Catholics say that's good for the soul."

"We," he huffed, "are not Catholics."

"True. But that's not a problem I can help you with."

I broke into my father's office. Well, that's not exactly true. It overstates things quite a bit since none of the doors in the mosque had any hardware on them yet and were, therefore, incapable of being locked. However, it sounds badass and I do like sounding that way, so I'll go with it.

Anyway, there was nothing there except for a ton of boring-looking, neatly arranged documents with a combination of Arabic and English on them. All of them had something to do with faith and nothing to do with banking.

I had to wait around a bit for a chance to go through his apartment. I did that when he went to visit Baba. There wasn't much that was useful there either, though I did rediscover my father's old office safe, which he'd had for years. I remembered him moving it from our old house to our new one when I was eleven. Apparently, he'd dragged it here too.

Unfortunately, I didn't know the code.

There was someone who probably did, though. All I had to do was convince her to give it to me.

I'd have to reach out to Iqra Saifi.

I called Madi on my way to my mother's place. She sounded far away when she answered, like people sound when they've got you on speaker.

"What's going on?" she asked.

"I'm in an Uber and going to see Mom."

"How's your grandfather?"

"Ask for him tomorrow and you shall find him a grave man."

"Come on. Really?"

"It had to be done," I told her. "Anyway, listen, I'm calling to ask you out. Tonight."

"Where are we going?"

That was an excellent question. When I'd googled "the most romantic places in Redding, CA," all the results I'd gotten were outdoors. This would have been irritating at the best of times, given my passionate and enduring aversion to nature, but it was ludicrous now, as the atmosphere around us was still unpleasant to breathe in.

According to the news, the wildfire in the area was almost fully contained. Its effects, however, would linger for a while after it was put out.

Faced with a lack of options, I'd taken the time to arrange a romantic setting myself.

"It's a surprise," I said.

"What should I wear?"

"The answer to that question will always be 'very little.'"

"Don't be an idiot. Tell me. Is it a fancy place?"

"It's most definitely not. Just wear whatever. It'll be fine."

"What time?" she asked.

"Nine."

"That late?"

I shrugged. "We have to make sure no one is around."

"Why?"

"Don't worry. You'll love it," I promised her. "I have to go. I'm almost here. See you tonight, babe."

"Wait, wait, wait. Did you just call me 'babe'?"

I thought about it. "It may have slipped out."

"Slip it back in, please."

"That's what she—"

"Don't," Madi warned.

"Okay. I'm sorry. I—"

"It's not that I mind," she explained. "It just sounds . . . it sounds like something someone in a relationship says. No strings, right?"

"It wasn't a 'I think of you with affection' babe," I hurried to explain. "It was a 'I truly love fucking you into utter incoherence' babe."

There was a pause. Then Mads asked, "You forgot you were in an Uber there for a second, didn't you?"

"Yeah."

"The driver is looking at you, isn't he?"

He had, in fact, turned his head completely around to stare at me. I met his eyes for a long, uncomfortable moment before he turned back to face the road. "Uh-huh."

"Be less embarrassing," she suggested.

"I'll try."

"And Azaan?"

"Yeah?"

"Sex sounds a lot hotter if you can describe it using three syllables or less."

I smiled. "Thanks for the note, Mads. I'll see you tonight."

As I hung up, I saw that the driver was still staring at me, now through the rearview mirror, and grinning. I slunk back into my seat and read the brass numbers on the homes we were passing by.

Forty-three excruciating Mississippis later, we pulled up in front of my mother's new home. Mercifully, no words were exchanged as I got out except for a quick "thank you" from me.

Mom's new neighborhood was in a swanky gated community, with perfectly manicured green lawns and signs forbidding street parking. It was a slightly upgraded version of where Kashaf and Ilham lived, which was just a bit better than where Madison's home was, and that was slightly nicer than where I had grown up. These small improvements and modest gains, this climb up a ladder that never ended, were the dreams and aspirations of many and the life's work of a few successful Americans.

I made my way past a gardener who, despite the awful air quality, was being made to paint a neighbor's grass so that it would look as pristine as everyone else's. I nodded at him and made my way to the door.

Iqra Saifi greeted me, a spicy romance novel—judging from its provocative cover—in her hands. Her hobbies apparently hadn't changed. This particular one used to make her pious imam husband furious.

"Your timing is terrible, dear. I was just about to get to the good part. Anyway, you've already interrupted, so you might as well come in. What was so important that you had to see me right away?"

I followed her through a pristine, professionally decorated house that looked like it had sprung out of a magazine with a maximalist aesthetic, with paintings in gilded frames everywhere, along with elaborately carved furniture and expensive-looking, busy rugs. It was the exact opposite of the kind of home she'd had with my father, which was likely the point.

"I need a favor," I told her. "And I thought I'd have a better shot at convincing you to help me if I spoke to you in person."

"Direct. That's the one thing I like about you, Azaan. You're always honest."

"Well . . ."

"Tea?"

"No, thank you."

She nodded and gestured for me to sit. I sank into a green velvet sofa.

"What do you need?"

"Information," I said. "It's important. Only I can't tell you why I need it, and I can't have you telling anyone I asked for it."

My mother crossed her legs and leaned forward. "Pray tell, darling, what do I get out of this, aside from the novelty of finding you, for a moment, interesting."

"What do you want?"

"I'd like for us to talk."

"We are talking."

"I am saying I would like us to sit down together and have a proper conversation."

I blinked. "Really?"

"Don't act like it's unusual. It's something other families do all the time."

"Yeah. But we don't."

"I would like it," Mom insisted. "Come on, it'll be fun. When was the last time we had fun together, do you think?"

"Um . . ."

"Never," she told me. "Because children are tedious and boring and you chose to move away before you grew up."

"Yes. I 'chose' to move away. Anyway, listen, do you remember that combination safe Dad had?"

"I do. Talking about your father, however, is not what I had in mind. Let's discuss something we are both interested in. Why don't you tell me who the young lady you are currently railing is?"

"Can we not say it like that?"

"Is that not how young people talk these days?"

"Maybe," I conceded. "You aren't one of them, though."

"Well, there's no reason to be rude. Now tell me—"

"It's Madison Porter, okay? How does that help you?"

"The girl the Altmans took in after her family passed in that plane crash? The one from across the street?"

I nodded.

"I'm impressed. That young lady is . . . what's the word?"

"Nice?"

"A smokeshow."

"I don't want to talk about Madi."

"Why not?"

"I came here because I need the combination to Dad's safe. Do you know it?"

"I used to," she said. "We kept our passports and official documents in there, along with all of his papers from his precious mosque. I had to have access to it. The code is probably still good. Saqi always was a creature of habit."

"True."

She leaned forward, as if to hear better. "So how is it that you are schlepping Ms. Porter?"

"First of all, I don't know what that question means. Second, I'm pretty sure the word you're looking for is 'schtupping.'"

"No, dear, it's schlepping."

"Whatever. Mom, I feel like we're talking past each other. Could you just please—"

"I'm asking how you and Madison met?" Mom interrupted.

"In high school."

"I meant when did this whole thing start?"

"In high school."

"Wait. That's right. She was the girl you had topless in that old mosque's parking lot, isn't she?"

"No! That's not what happened."

Just how many versions of that story were in circulation?

"Calm down, dear. There's no reason to get excited. I am simply going off what I've heard." She studied me appraisingly, then asked, "Have you really been carrying a torch for her all this time?"

"A candle maybe."

"That's very sweet."

"Anyway," I tried forcing us back to the business at hand, "I need the combination to Dad's safe."

"Why?"

"Like I said, I can't tell you that. I'm looking for something. I searched Dad's office at the new mosque and I searched his apartment—"

"You did what?"

"I found a spare key," I explained. "It wasn't difficult."

"That was not the part that concerned me."

"Look, Mom, that safe is still there. It's really the only place I haven't looked. I'm not going to take anything. I just need to see if he has . . ."

"What?" she demanded.

Some record of where two hundred thousand dollars of the mosque's money went, I thought but didn't say.

"It's nothing," I said.

"You are certainly going through a lot of trouble for nothing."

"Mom—"

"I want to meet Madison. Bring her over for tea."

"I can't, Mom. It isn't that kind of . . ." I would have used the word "relationship" if Madi hadn't objected to it a little while ago. "Arrangement. It's very casual."

"Your decade-long crush on this woman is 'very casual'?"

I nodded. "No games. No strings. No promises."

Mom snorted. "I see. Well, good luck with that, dear. I am sure it will go smoothly for you."

"Will you help me?"

"I want you to at least extend the invitation, Azaan. If she doesn't want to meet me, that's her prerogative, I suppose. Do tell her it would be nice for me to speak to the woman my son is in love with."

"Was in love with," I corrected. "A lifetime ago. I'm not now and I don't intend to be. It's impossible. It's like they say, lightning never strikes the same place twice."

"What are you talking about? It does that all the time."

"But I heard—"

"You can't listen to people, darling," Mom drawled. "That's how one ends up being ignorant. I am aware of the popular misconception. I am telling you that it is very wrong."

"Oh," I said.

"Anyway, methinks the larka does protest too much."

"Please don't do that to Shakespeare," I begged.

"Fine. Back to my invitation—"

"Okay. I'll tell Madi. But she will say no."

"That remains to be seen," my mother said. "Now, here is Saqi's code . . ."

Chapter Sixteen

THE ALBION WAS A SMALL THEATER THAT COULD ONLY seat around a hundred and fifty people at a time. It was venerable, though, in that it had been around for sixty-one years and was housed in a brownstone—or at least a building with a brownstone facade—downtown. Standing in front of it, I waited for Madi to arrive and took a moment to feel sorry for myself.

I had never gone through this much trouble to plan a date. My default was the classic dinner and show routine, which worked just fine. It was a low-effort, high-reward move. Even if there ended up being no spark, at least you got a good meal and some entertainment out of the experience.

That isn't to say all the dates I went on were tame. A woman who was pretty enough to tempt even me into outdoor activities had convinced me to go rock climbing and bungee jumping once. Of course, she'd had to arrange all that. I would have had no idea where to start. I shouldn't have gone. We were too different. I'd realized that when she'd said her dream was to have adventures in the wilderness and one day maybe even go to the South Pole. Thousands upon thousands of years of human effort to build up a civilization and she wanted nothing more than to escape it. Some people, honestly.

At any rate, tonight was different. I had come up with an idea I thought Madi would adore and, if it had gone off like I'd imagined, I know it would have been perfect.

It hadn't, though.

Madi's car pulled up and she stepped out. I noticed that she had done her hair differently. It was up in some sort of loose, messy side braid that somehow still made her look put together. She'd chosen a high-neck skater dress with cutout sleeves. It was red, and it lit the blue in her eyes on fire.

She smiled when she saw me. I'm not sure what my expression was just then, but it made her shake her head, glance away, and bite her lower lip.

Okay. I've talked quite a bit about how I prefer art to nature.

I take it all back.

Nature kicks art's ass because nature has Mads.

That means nature wins.

It's not even a contest.

"You've got to stop looking at me like that," Madi said when she was close enough to touch. "You're killing me."

"It's just . . . you look like He spent a full seven days on you."

"What are you talking about?" she asked.

"God. Genesis."

I didn't have to explain further. She got it. In the Torah, just like in the Quran, it had taken six days to create the heavens and the earth.

"That's so cheesy. I mean, it's aged, sharp cheese, but it's still cheese."

"Only the best for you, Mads."

"Speaking of which," she nodded her head at the barely lit theater behind me, which looked dead, "what are we doing here? It's shut down because—"

"Of California's latest natural disaster, yes. Look, you know how they say that when you're giving someone a present, it's the thought that counts, right?"

She nodded.

"That goes for tonight as well. My concept was amazing. The execution . . . well, that's the problem—"

"What was your plan?"

"I wanted to take you someplace that . . . well, someplace that meant something to us, and I figured a picnic on our high school stage would be a good idea. But—"

"They cut the after-school drama club and turned that space into a basketball court," she finished.

"So," I waved at the Albion behind me, "I thought this would do."

"But it's closed."

"For other people. I have connections."

Madi smirked. "Do you really?"

"I've known Ben—the facilities manager here—since I was, like, ten or something. He was in the same troupe my babysitter was in. I hung around with them a lot. Anyway, I reached out to him and he remembered me. Turns out he was willing to do me a favor for old time's sake, and he let me in."

"Then what's the problem?"

"Well, for one," I said, "it never occurred to me that a deserted playhouse is more eerie than romantic."

"I don't mind," Madi said.

"Okay, but . . . well, it's not what I had imagined. Come and see."

She took my arm and let me lead her inside. Her voice echoed in the empty lobby as we walked through it. "Have you ever even been on a picnic before?"

"I've eaten in a car," I said.

"Okay."

"How was work?"

"Fine." She sighed. "I had to do film reviews. Another day, another remake. That's the life of a media critic these days."

"I can see how that'd get old."

"It's just . . . modern writers, you know, they—"

"Suck?" I suggested.

"That's a little harsh. I mean, studios and execs are the ones running a train on old franchises because they think it guarantees them an audience. It's just that when it comes to scripts nowadays . . . it's like everything is about teaching people a lesson. We left morality plays in the Middle Ages for a reason. They're preachy, and preachers are boring."

"Amen."

"It's an affliction all art is suffering from. I was talking to this novelist a while back . . . what was his name? The guy who wrote *The Bad Muslim Discount*."

"I don't know. I've been wanting to read that, though. Sounds like something I'd like."

"Maybe you would."

"A ringing endorsement."

She made a despairing gesture with her hand. "No, it's actually all right. Most of it. I didn't like the ending. You could tell the author was trying to send his readers a message. It's like

. . . obviously, every story has a theme, a moral, a point. But just tell us what happened and shut up and let us figure out what we want to take from it, you know?"

I nodded.

"I do love the characters he comes up with, though. They're great."

By this time, we'd reached the doors leading into the auditorium. I gently extricated myself from Madi and went up to pull them open for her. "Here we go. Brace yourself."

She laughed. "For what? I have no idea what's happening."

"I'm taking you to Paris."

"That doesn't sound bad at all."

"Yeah. Except it's 1792."

With that, I let her in so she could gape at my failure.

The Albion had closed unexpectedly because of the wildfire, in the middle of a workday, while the cast and crew were preparing to put on an adaptation of *The Scarlet Pimpernel*, which was set during the Reign of Terror in the French Revolution. As a result, on stage, behind where I'd set up a small table covered in white cloth with a candle, take-out containers, and a bottle of wine, sat an enormous guillotine.

It came complete with a wicker basket in front of it to catch any heads that might roll. Its blade was coated in "blood," a mixture of corn syrup—which is in everything these days—titanium dioxide, red coloring, and gore. Some of this was also splattered on the base of the cruel machine and was clearly meant to be evidence of grim punishments recently doled out. The backdrop was a rabid crowd gathered to witness the dispensation of death in a squalid, miserable, grim city.

Like I said, my idea had been sound. The execution—and, more specifically, the presence of a contraption designed for executions—was the issue. Plus, the lighting was deliberately unnerving and dim. It didn't exactly provide a romantic ambiance for what was, in a way, our first actual date.

I waited for Madi to say something.

When she was done surveying what I'd managed to pull together for her, she looked up at me and with an entirely straight face said, "Please tell me we're having cake."

One of the joys of living in London was the food. From Poppie's Fish & Chips to some of the best Indian food anywhere at Dishoom, excellent cuisine from all over the world was on offer. Redding wasn't like that. There were a few good eateries, of course, but on the whole . . . let's just say it wasn't exactly the gastronomical capital of the world.

It did, however, have some solid Thai restaurants, and so that's the direction I'd gone in. It had turned out to be a good choice.

I'd paired the meal with the best Riesling the local Liquor Barn had, which was from Canada for some reason. According to the internet, the white was the best pairing with Thai food, and I didn't know enough about the subject to have an opinion of my own.

I'm not a wine guy. I don't drink for pleasure. I drink to forget myself, and there are more efficient and cheaper ways to achieve that goal.

It was, all in all, a very nice experience, even given the incongruous backdrop.

Madi was full of questions that night, and I answered them for her. After all, I had wanted to hear her story. It was only fair that she got to hear mine.

"What are you going to do if you get the part in this movie you're trying out for?"

"I don't understand what you mean."

"What are you going to do about your family and the people at your mosque? Everyone is going to realize that you aren't what you are pretending to be once it gets released."

"I've always known that might be a problem I'd have to deal with."

"And?" she pressed.

"I figured I'd burn that bridge when I got to it."

"It's good that you've thought this through."

I shrugged. "I made this bed when I was seventeen. It sucks that I have to sleep in it, but there's no other choice."

Madi skewered a shrimp on her plate with a fork. "Not one you're willing to make anyway."

"Please don't tell me to just be honest. I don't like doing that."

"Funny. I could have sworn I read something by an author you admire a little that's relevant. How'd it go? 'This above all: to thine own self . . .'"

"Oh, shut up."

She chuckled, picked up her glass, studied it for a moment, then took a sip. "But seriously, why haven't you come clean? It has to be exhausting, this pretending to be Muslim."

"I'm not pretending. I am Muslim," I said. "I just don't practice."

"Isn't that like saying you're a vegetarian who eats meat all the time?"

I sat back and thought about that for a second. Finally, I countered, "Aren't you Jewish?"

"You know I am."

"But you don't practice either."

"Judaism is my clan or family or something. It's not just my faith. I don't have to practice to say it's part of my identity."

"I feel the same way about Islam. Not that it's my family. I wouldn't claim my family if I had a choice."

Madi gave that a small smile, which was probably more than the joke deserved.

"It is in my bones, though. It's my marrow. It makes up a lot of who I am and how I see the world. It's like . . . if I'm Wolverine, then Islam is like that metal they fused to his skeleton or whatever."

She raised her eyebrows. "That's an unusual reference for you."

"Oh, I watched all those mutant people movies. I'll go see anything with Patrick Stewart in it. My point is—"

"I get it."

I could see that she did. "Anyway, people like my father have a lot of contempt for people like me, those who don't or can't walk the true path."

"That's why you pretend."

"I didn't used to. I used to just do whatever I wanted."

"I remember," she said. "I thought you were so brave to just be yourself all the time. It seemed really cool."

"I mean, I was cool, but that was because of the leather jacket I wore all the time."

"No, it wasn't."

I laughed. "Anyway, I guess I just got tired of him beating the shit out of me, you know? We adapt to survive."

Madi frowned. "I thought that night we kissed was the first time he hit you."

I shook my head.

She held out her hand, and I reached across the table to

take it. There was sudden, genuine pain her voice. "I'm so sorry. I didn't realize—"

"It's not your fault."

"Why didn't you tell me?"

I shrugged. "I don't know. I've never told anyone."

"After the plane crash," she said softly, "you were my rock. You were the only thing in the world I trusted. You were there for me. I could have been there for you."

I squeezed her hand. The knot was flaring up again, but it didn't feel as thorny as usual. "You were, Mads. You absolutely were."

"I hope," Madi said as we started to clear the table, "that you weren't planning on recreating what happened the last time we were on stage together."

"Well, no, we can't," I told her. "Ben's in the building somewhere, waiting for us to be done so he can lock up."

"And there is a death machine looming over us," she reminded me.

"That too."

"Besides, it'd be very uncomfortable. We're perfectly capable of keeping our hands off each other until we're in bed."

"Foyer," I reminded her.

"Oh. Right."

"Anyway, to answer your question, no, that wasn't the plan. I just wanted to do something nice for you."

Madi leaned over and gave me a quick peck on the cheek. "What do you say we get out of here?"

Later that night, in my arms, when I was close to sleep,

absently tracing shapes with her long fingers where my heart was, she said, "I can't get over it."

"Right?" I mumbled, turning to kiss the top of her forehead. "I'm very good."

She shook her head. "I was talking about what your dad did."

"I know."

"The scars on your back? That's how you got them?"

"Yeah."

"Shit. Why didn't your Mom ever stop him?"

I yawned. "I don't know. You can ask her yourself if you want."

"What?"

"She told me to invite you over to her place for tea."

"Wait." Madi propped herself up on an elbow and looked down at me. Her dark hair tumbled like a curtain down on my face until she pulled it away. "You told her about me?"

"I needed the code."

"What code?"

"It's a long story, Mads."

"I'm tired of hearing that. No. You've used that line way too many times. Come on. Spill."

"Okay," I said. "But you have to promise me we're off the record."

Her eyes narrowed and turned scorching, but not in a good way. "Seriously?"

"What?"

"We're naked. In bed. Off the record? Do you really think I'm being a reporter right now? Are you fucking with me?"

"No, I did that earlier."

Madi sighed. "Azaan."

"It's just that you wanted to do another story about the

mosque. I don't want you to have to choose between listening to me and your work. That's not—"

"I choose you," Madison said.

"Just like that?"

"Just like that," she confirmed.

I raised my eyebrows.

"My editor wants me to drop it anyway. He thinks I've done too many follow-ups on the vandalism stuff. It's niche, we don't have any real evidence about any financial issues, and even if we did, it's not as sexy as a hate crime anyway."

"Okay. Well, in that case, here's what's going on . . ."

I explained the issue of the missing money to Madison, walking her through everything I knew, from Tiger Uncle's first call to Baba's concerns to the sale of the house and to Dad's inexplicable financial woes.

After she'd heard it all, she was quiet for a while.

"You're regretting going off the record, aren't you?" I teased.

"A little bit. But seriously, can I ask you something?"

"Sure."

"Are you hoping Mr. Saifi did it?" Madi asked.

"Of course not. Why would I?"

"It would give you a reason to hate him if he did."

"I already have reasons for that," I reminded her. "No, I'm actually hoping it wasn't him. I mean, he's still my dad, after all. And . . ." I paused to take a deep breath as the knot started to act up again. Madi placed a light hand where she now knew it was. "And because if he did take the money, then he wouldn't be what I spent my whole life thinking he was. He'd be a hypocrite instead of a holy man. If that were true, then . . . then it'd mean I didn't know him at all. It'd mean that all that discipline he inflicted, all that hurt, it was all just meaningless."

Mads kissed my shoulder.

"Worse, it'd mean that Dad is the better actor in the family, because I've only ever fooled other people. But if he's capable of stealing from God, if he's found some justification for it in his mind, then I think maybe he's even fooled himself."

She didn't say anything, and I wasn't sure there was anything to say. Besides, we were deep into the night and dreams were calling.

"Hey," Madi whispered a while later.

"Hmm?"

"About your mom . . ."

"It's nothing. I'll tell her you said no."

"Don't do that," she told me. "I want to meet her."

I literally couldn't take that lying down, so I rubbed a hand over my face and sat up. "I'm sorry. What?"

"I'd like to—"

"I heard you. I just don't understand. You were upset earlier today that I accidentally called you babe—"

"I wasn't upset," Madi protested. "I just—"

I held my palms out like someone looking for alms. "No, I'd like you to help me out. Using a harmless endearment is too much like a relationship but meeting one of my parents isn't?"

"I wouldn't be going as your . . . your . . ."

"Bone Ami?" I suggested.

"'Stay classy, San Diego.'"

"Sorry."

"Look, we aren't just . . . this, right?" She gestured to the bed and then to us. "We're friends. You met my parents. You got to see that part of me. I, on the other hand, had to be hidden away from yours. I'm not saying I didn't understand that, but if that isn't the case now . . ."

"Madi, it's not a very pretty part of my life."

"Is there a pretty part of your life?" she teased.

"There is when you're in it."

Mads groaned dramatically and buried her face in the crook of my shoulder. "So. Much. Dairy."

I laughed. "If you want to meet my mom, it's fine with me. Just . . ."

"What?"

"It's going to be weird. Don't say I didn't warn you."

Chapter Seventeen

"IMAM SAIFI?"

I resisted the urge to bolt as soon as I heard those words. Long experience had taught me that nothing good ever happened after they were spoken. It didn't even matter who said them. They were always portents that I was going to have a bad time.

Following a morning workout with Madi—that's not a euphemism, by the way, we went to her gym—I'd spent the rest of the morning listening to and then mimicking lines of the Quran read out by famous reciters on the internet. I needed to knock some of the rust off my Arabic pronunciation.

I would have liked to learn the language, I think, instead of just memorizing its phonics. That might have kept my interest as I would've had the lure of getting access to a whole corpus of literature and poetry I wouldn't otherwise understand. Instead, Dad had made me learn how to properly voice the words the Quran was made up of without teaching me any grammar or vocabulary or idioms, which was the practice in Pakistan and, I suspected, other parts of the Muslim world as well.

They called it reading, but in the absence of comprehension, it was just a ritual, and to me those are just sanctified chores that have no meaning. So I wasn't exactly in a great mood.

It didn't help that my dad had been hanging around his apartment all day, not giving me a window during which I could sneak in to get to his safe and use the combination I'd gotten from Mom.

Now, when he was finally leaving after Asr prayers, someone was calling out to me.

It turned out to be a group of three girls. Only one of them had spoken, however. She was maybe fifteen and with restless, anxious hands that zipped around without meaning or purpose as she spoke.

"Um . . . I'm sorry to bother you. I'm Badr and that's Rumaisa and that's Aliza."

There was no way I was going to remember their names, so I didn't even bother trying. I simply nodded for her to go on.

"I have a question."

Of course she did. "You really should talk to my dad."

"But you're right here."

I resisted the urge to make a face. "This is true."

"I need a ruling on board games."

I blinked. "Board games?"

"Right. My mother won't let us play most of them."

"Why?" I asked.

Her fingers went to her hijab to straighten it unnecessarily, then she dropped her arms down to her sides before folding them behind her back. Finally, she released them and they started speeding through the air again. "She says they're a sin."

I had to be missing something. Just to make sure, I repeated, "Board games?"

"My cousins and I were playing Monopoly and my mom made us stop. She told us we couldn't because playing Monopoly is the same as dipping your hand in the blood of a pig."

"What now?"

"She says we're not allowed to play it because the Prophet, Peace Be Upon Him, said not to, so . . . I want to get your opinion."

"Well, I agree that you shouldn't play Monopoly."

Her face dropped.

"It's terrible. First of all, it takes forever for anyone to win. Also, it's basic. There is much better stuff out there. My roommate back in London has this one game called Scythe. You should check that out."

The girl looked confused. "Um . . . I meant your opinion about what the Prophet said."

"Monopoly wasn't around back in his time . . . Uhud, was it?"

"Badr," she corrected, sounding properly exasperated now. "You're totally not getting what I'm saying. My mom says I can't play any games that involve dice because the Prophet said not to play with them."

"Oh."

"I mean, can we have any fun? I already have to play video games with the sound off and my—"

I frowned. "Why do you have to have the sound off?"

"Because of the music, obviously."

"Sure," I said. "Of course."

"At least I get to play them. My brother isn't even allowed to." Anticipating my question, with her arms flailing around, she said, "Because a lot of the female characters aren't covered properly. Like I was playing Tomb Raider, and I searched for mods that would put Lara Croft in an abaya so he could play it, but they don't make those. I mean, there are mods that make it so she's naked all the time, but none that cover her up. Why do you think that is?"

I scratched the back of my head. "Basic economics?"

"What?"

"Supply and demand, I mean."

Badr didn't seem to think my analysis was worth pausing over. "Also, she doesn't like that in some games you play as American soldiers killing Muslims. Everyone else gets to have them, but in our house—"

You get the hand you're dealt, kid, is what I wanted to say, but I didn't. Instead, I asked, "What is it that you want from me?"

"I just want to know if my mom is right about the dice thing."

"I'm pretty sure that back in the Prophet's time playing dice meant gambling. Just don't play Monopoly with real money and you'll be fine."

She broke into a smile and turned back to look at her friends in triumph.

"Of course, you're also supposed to obey your mother, so if you can't convince her," I said, "maybe play a game where dice isn't required. Like . . . I don't know. Chess?"

"She says chess is also forbidden."

"Seriously?"

Badr nodded. "And she ruined our set anyway. She threw out the knights because she thinks they're tiny horse statues and statues are—"

"Forbidden. Yeah, I get it."

"What do you think I should do, Sheikh?"

I thought about telling her that the Mughals of India, rulers of a Muslim empire, had loved chess so much that a king was reported to have played using human pieces. The culture of those past Muslims, however, was very different than the . . . well, I suppose you'd have to call it a more puritan brand of Islam, which had gained a following in our time. That knowledge would do nothing to solve her problem.

I knew that because the issue Badr was facing was, in some way, the same one I'd faced growing up. Her problem wasn't Islam. It was the home she'd been born into and how the religion was practiced there.

As we were speaking, there were hundreds of thousands of young Muslims merrily basking in the radiation of their gaming consoles or enjoying games of chance. The fact that Badr and her brother couldn't was more about the interpretation of Islam that her mother chose to follow and impose rather than the doctrine itself.

Even though people everywhere on the political and devotional spectrum like to pretend otherwise, Islam isn't a monolith. Or, more accurately, Muslims aren't one.

Yes, the Quran and the sayings of the Prophet were recorded and fixed, but their interpretations are legion, and misunderstandings of them are greater legion still. There are people who choose to follow every word as they hear it and people who stray entirely and also those who do not take a literal approach to the faith.

The problem is that all of them are convinced that they hold the high ground, if not necessarily spiritually then intellectually or morally, and they are all willing to lecture each other and very few are willing to listen.

I'd told Madi that Islam was part of me. It had made my

moral compass and shaped the lens through which I saw the world. If I asked Badr if she felt the same way, she would likely agree with me.

Yet for all the similarities in our circumstances, I hadn't faced the same problem she was facing. My father, despite his religiosity, had never had a problem with board games.

Our religion was the same.

Our experience of it was different.

Since Muslims believe in predetermination, it must be our view that these differences are given to us by God. That is to say, I was born to my parents in the age of dial-up, when machines had screeched angrily at each other when they were forced to socialize, and Badr had been born to hers in the age of social media, when the machines had gone silent and the humans were the ones who were angry.

God had given me the Islam I had lived through, and He had given her the Islam she was being raised with. In other words, it was fate, and she couldn't change hers any more than I had been able to change mine when I'd been her age.

"Sheikh?" Badr asked again.

"Yeah?"

"What should I do?"

"Turn eighteen," I told her, "and move far, far away."

As I let myself into Dad's apartment, I couldn't help but grin at how Badr's jaw had dropped open at the advice I'd given her. It was probably not the kind of thing imams were supposed to say. Still, I felt good about it, even if it meant that I had broken character. It was, after all, the course of action that had worked for me.

It was possible that there'd be fallout. If Badr or her friends told anyone what I'd said, her parents—at least one of whom sounded like a formidable amount of work—might come looking for me. That was fine. I'd deal with it.

One of the few lessons I'd learned from the many punishments my father had inflicted upon me was this one truth about the world: there is very little you can't do if you are willing to accept the consequences.

Speaking of which, it would probably be smart to move quickly and get out of Imam Saifi's unit as soon as I could. I didn't want to have to explain my presence here.

I made my way over to Dad's closet. The scent of a woody attar, a type of non-alcoholic perfume, which was the only scent Dad had ever used, washed over me as I entered his combination.

My heart was beating a little faster than usual, but not by much. Even though I'd been delayed by Badr's questions, our conversation hadn't taken long. Whatever my father was off doing, I figured it was unlikely he'd be back soon enough to barge in on my little investigation. This would only take a second.

Was I feeling guilty about snooping around? Was my mind "full of scorpions," as an Englishman of some renown once wrote?

No.

I suppose it should have been. I believed in the sanctity of private spaces and hadn't ever even considered doing something like this to anyone before. The fact that I was wronging my father, and doing so for his benefit, made it feel . . . not okay, exactly, but at least justified. That was what our relationship was, after all, an exchange of hurts dealt out in different currencies.

There was a soft beep and the safe popped open.

The damn thing was nearly overflowing with documents. It would take more time than I had to read them all.

I found passports, birth certificates, social security cards, tax returns, title deeds for the house and for the land the mosque was built on, a rental contract for the business park in which the community had been making do for ages, the lease for his current car and the car before and the car before that, a copy of every traffic ticket he had ever gotten, an invitation for his wedding to Mom, the marriage certificate that had resulted and the divorce judgment that had followed, a stack of expired driver's licenses and credit cards for reasons passing understanding, and a ton of correspondence going back decades.

I flipped through it carefully. It was clear that things were organized in a certain way. My father was a painfully neat person. He might notice if things were out of order.

I found the fake acceptance letter from Al-Azhar University that I showed him. I'd had to pay some guy online to write it in Arabic. It was kind of sweet that he'd kept it.

Most of the mail appeared to be legal in nature, dealing with either issues that had arisen during the construction of the mosque or the deconstruction of his marriage.

I pulled out my phone, checked the time, and glanced at the door.

This was taking too long. Maybe it'd be a good idea to stop now and come back later. Only I had gotten used to a world where you never had to wait for answers to your questions, so I wanted to know now. I kept going.

I was able to get to the end of the stack.

There was absolutely no accounting here of every penny Imam Saifi had ever used of the mosque's money, like he had claimed.

However, I did find a few letters written to my father from an address in Pakistan, by a woman I didn't know, claiming that she was his wife and the mother of his twin children.

Chapter Eighteen

I PUT EVERYTHING BACK THE WAY I'D FOUND IT. I THINK. I can't be sure. My mind would not focus on what I was doing. All I could think about was getting out of my father's apartment, away from the familiar smell of his attar and his box of memories and hopes and victories and heartbreaks and follies and sins.

It was only when I was back in my own studio that I realized maybe I should have held on to that woman's note, whoever she was. I hadn't even thought to check for a name. I should have looked at the date too. When had this happened?

I considered going back to fetch them, but I heard a car pull up. I heard its door open and close. I went over to the nearest window to see if it was Dad.

It was.

He looked the same as he had before I'd read those letters, with his unruly, large, mustacheless beard and his ever-unhappy face. Of course he did. I hadn't expected anything different. Yet part of me felt that this was a stranger, this familiar man, this man who had known of me before I had known of him.

Who was Saqlain Saifi?

Was Mom aware?

I called her without knowing exactly what I was going to say, but as was typical, she didn't answer. I couldn't bring myself to leave a message.

I paced around the empty apartment, wondering what to do next. I thought about reaching out to Tiger to ask him if he had any idea this had happened, and that was when it hit me.

Kashaf and Ilham.

They were twins. Were they the same twins mentioned in the letter my father had saved? And did Tiger Uncle know? It seemed like he did. That would explain why he'd lied at first and claimed Kashaf was his daughter. It would make his bizarre insistence that I stay away from her and Ilham logical.

He had been covering for his friend.

I had siblings. I had gone to their home and eaten with them, and when I'd asked them why they wanted to get to know me better, they'd told me it was because I was Azaan Saifi. That had seemed weird then. It didn't anymore.

Their persistent questions about how I'd been raised made sense too. They had been trying to imagine what their lives would have been like if they had grown up in their father's presence like I had.

Were they jealous of my childhood?

A wild, hysterical little laugh bubbled in my chest at the thought.

It also explained why Kashaf hadn't worn her hijab the day they'd hosted me for dinner.

She didn't have to wear it in front of me. She was my sister.

I had a sister and a brother.

They were so different than I was.

"You don't look like him," Kashaf had said to me once.

"My dad?" I'd asked.

"He has weak genes."

I'd made a joke. *"Well, thank God for that."*

I ran a hand through my hair.

Unbelievable.

When could it have even happened?

Those long trips with Tiger to raise money for the mosque?

What was it Mom had said when she'd found out about Madi, before she'd known who I was with?

"Don't tell me that bastard, that Tiger, has gotten his claws in you. Because those pump-and-dump marriages he enjoys so much don't work in this country."

Is that what Dad had done? Taken up his old friend's lifestyle?

How many more women had there been?

What was I supposed to do with this information now that I had it?

I decided to call Tiger after all. It was almost instinct. He was the one who told me what to do, after all, when I couldn't figure it out for myself.

He answered on the third ring.

"Azaan," he greeted when he picked up. "How are—"

"You lied to me."

"What are you talking about?"

"Kashaf. Ilham. Dad."

Tiger sighed. "So those bastards told you, did they? I warned you to stay away from them. I said no good would come of it. So now, after playing with fire, if you are feeling burned, whose fault is that, beta?"

I shook my head.

In a much more conciliatory tone, Tiger asked, "Where are you?"

"The mosque's apartments."

"Have you spoken to Saqi?"

"No," I said.

"Good. That's good. Don't do it. Not just yet. Come see me at the store."

"Why?"

"You know less than you think. I suspect that what you have heard is less than the tip of the dick. Let's meet and I will tell you everything."

When I got to Tiger's store, I found it closed even though the lights were on. I knocked on the glass door, and Kashaf came to open it. She had a strange smile on her face. I struggled to read the emotion behind it. It wasn't friendly or warm. I could tell that much. It was . . . satisfied, which made it seem malicious given the circumstances.

"We are glad you are here, brother." That was exactly what she'd said to me when I'd visited her and Ilham in their home. This time, however, there was mockery in her tone that hadn't been there before. It wasn't clear what I'd done to deserve it. Maybe it was just that I had taken too long, in her eyes, to see the truth or maybe she was just enjoying the fact that I was suffering a fraction of the emotional turmoil she and Ilham must have lived through. "Follow me."

She took me to Tiger's office, which looked like the lair of a nineties Bollywood villain, with a leopard skin rug on the floor, the mounted head of a lion—fake, I hoped and assumed—on the wall behind his desk, and a large wooden sculpture of what looked like a jaguar on his desk.

A painting of the large cat after which he'd been named, pouncing on a grazing gazelle, was the most dominant feature of the space. He was certainly very committed to the motif he'd selected.

"Kashaf swears that she didn't tell you who she was and that her brother didn't either," he said as we entered. "Is that true?"

I nodded.

"How did you find out?"

"I found letters that Dad had from their mother."

Tiger grunted his annoyance and waved his hand dismissively in Kashaf's direction, clearly bidding her to go. I thought she'd argue, but she didn't. She just turned and left me alone with the most unique man I knew, to whom I owed so much of my life.

"Sit. Tell me, were you not happier when you didn't know all this? You just had to go take the apple from the tree and bite into it. Now you have information but you also have misery, no?"

Not sure what to say to that, I pulled up a chair and did what I was told.

"Have you ever met a lust bomb?" Tiger asked.

"Uh . . . no?"

"Too bad. That would have made this easier to explain. It would have also made your life more exciting, beta."

"I'm all right."

"If you say so." Tiger leaned back in his chair and waved his arms around in front of him, like Prospero trying to explain some kind of arcane spell his words alone couldn't describe. "I don't think without that experience you'll get what effect Reysham had on your father. As the rules of love say, where there is no understanding, there can be no peace."

"If you have an explanation, could you get on with it, please?"

"Okay, okay. It is no surprise to you, of course, that your parents have had a challenging marriage."

"I picked up on that, yeah."

"Saqi was miserable. He didn't want to leave Iqra. She supported him to a large degree financially, you know, and besides we desis have an aversion to divorce that people like you will never grasp."

"People like me?"

Tiger shrugged. "Children of immigrants, you diluted, skim, half-and-half people, who are never fully of the West or of the East."

"I know divorce is discouraged in Islam."

"Well, yes, but we have a compounded problem, because our culture agrees with our religion here. The divorce rate in India is around one percent. I think in Bangladesh, it is less than that. In some states in America, it is over ten. Our people stand by our mistakes."

"And that's not a bad thing?" I asked.

"I'm just telling you how it is. I don't concern myself with what is good and what is evil. Who said judge not unless you want to get judged?"

"That's in the Bible, right?"

"Haan, maybe. My point is that Saqi didn't want to be with Iqra and he didn't want to leave her either. She was probably more inclined to end their relationship, but maybe she was afraid of the custody battle."

I frowned. "She was worried she'd lose?"

"She was worried she'd win, I think. Also, she knew her parents would not react well. From what I've heard, her father was as frightful as yours. She didn't want to have to deal with his disappointment."

"Mom was independent. Why did she care what anyone else thought?"

Tiger gave me a small smile. "Why do you care what Saqi thinks? Why does anyone care what anyone thinks? It is a terrible and human thing to value the opinion of others. Anyway, Saqi and I started taking longer and longer trips abroad. It gave him a respite from being at home. He also got to attend a few of my weddings. He got to see how my system worked. He got to see me being happy when he was not."

"That's when he met this Reysham person?"

"Right you are. He wanted her from the very first time he saw her. She was the kind of woman who had that effect on people. I told him not to marry her, but—"

I couldn't keep the skepticism out of my voice when I asked, "Did you really?"

"She had a reputation. Frankly speaking, she was little better than a call girl. Why go through the song and dance of marrying someone who will give you what you want without the trouble? It is not good business. But Saqi was charmed by her sex magic and there is nothing you can say to a man who is under that spell that'll make him listen."

"When was this?" I asked.

"Twenty years ago. You were . . . what? Nine?"

"Yeah."

"It was in Pakistan, on an international fundraising trip that ended up being a lun-raising trip."

"A what?"

"How are you so uncultured? Lun is what they call a penis in Urdu. It was a joke."

"Good one."

Tiger didn't seem bothered by my caustic sarcasm. "Look, I know you are upset with Saqi. Lekin, a man has needs, bhai, emotional and physical. He needed to pound something other than the ice cooler he had at home. I don't know how he even did it with your mother. I don't think they make thermal condoms."

"Don't talk about my mom that way."

Tiger Uncle held his hands up in a gesture of innocence. "You asked for the truth. Can you bear it or should I stop?"

"Go on."

"There is not much else to tell. Saqi wanted Reysham, and there was no way he could have what he wanted, Islamically, without tying the knot, so that's what he did."

"I still can't believe it."

"Why not, Azaan? He is allowed four wives. This was only his second."

"He cheated on Mom."

"No, he didn't. He didn't make his second marriage a secret. It just happened in a different country, and he didn't tell her about it. That is not the same thing."

I buried my face in my hands.

"There is no religious requirement that either I or your father know of that compels a man to inform his first wife that he's taken a second. I told you once, didn't I, that technicalities can be your friend? As they say, the fun is in the details."

"The devil is in the details," I corrected.

"That's what I said. Anyway, what happened next was predictable—trouble in Paradise. The time came for us to leave. Reysham wanted Saqi to stay with her or bring her back to the States. He refused. She got upset, went to one of her friends—who used to be a lover—for advice and comfort, and he comforted her hard, if you get my meaning."

"You're very subtle."

"Saqi found out, divorced her on the spot, and back home we came. It was only later I learned that he had committed a grave error. He hadn't used birth control, even though I had told him to. The cornerstone of my philosophy is that we plow but we do not plant. He left Reysham with two little poison berries growing inside her."

"And he never told Mom?" I asked.

"Iqra did find out eventually, five or six years later, when Saqi and I were on another trip. Reysham was writing Saqi many letters at that time, and your mother got curious and opened one of them. They had a huge fight right after he came back. You would have been around sixteen then."

"How many women have there been?"

"For Saqi? Only Reysham. I never could convince him to try again, even though he saw me get married two or three more times."

"Honestly, Uncle, how do you even convince these women to marry you?"

Tiger shrugged. "I go through people who arrange marriages, and they talk to the families of these women. I flash cash. It is easier when you go to a poor village or if you know the family needs money because someone is in the hospital or needs treatment. They think they are setting their daughter up with a good, if slightly older, match and they know once she gets paid her mehr, that is—"

"The money the groom agrees to gift the bride at the beginning of their relationship. I know."

"Exactly right, beta. They know that when she gets the mehr, the girl will be able to help them financially. Some think you will, too, as an in-law. They jump at it. You seal the deal, have your fun, and when you're done, you say 'I divorce you' three times and ride off into the West."

"That's . . . terrible. I always thought you told the women you married that you were going to leave them soon."

"That would make things a lot more difficult for me. No, that wouldn't work at all. What is that look?" Tiger Uncle tsked. "Are you judging me, Mr. Fake Imam? I expected better from you."

"I didn't set out to hurt people. I just wanted a little freedom."

"I never wanted to hurt people either, meri jaan. I just wanted to fuck them. Look, you can think of me as a bad guy, but all I have ever done is pursue happiness and fulfill my contractual obligations. For some, I imagine, I have even been a way out of poverty. It is all a matter of how you look at things."

"Whatever. This isn't about you anyway. Tell me about Ilham and Kashaf."

Tiger sighed. "Right. Those fools. Reysham told your father about them, but since she had cheated on him—and also given her reputation—he didn't believe they were his kids."

"A DNA test—"

"He absolutely refused. You have to consider his position. Even though he had not done anything wrong, your own reaction should tell you that his conduct would not be well received here. He would have lost the moral high ground he needed to continue being the imam. It would have jeopardized his mosque project. He had too much to lose. So, he bought her off.

He borrowed thirty thousand dollars from me—which he very slowly paid off—and gave it to her. In exchange, Reysham agreed that neither she nor her children would ever contact him again."

"How come they're here then?"

Tiger stared at the many rings on his fingers, then rotated one that was slightly askew to put it back into place. "Things took a bad turn for Reysham. She got sick, had a bunch of strokes, and died. We had no contact with her at the time, so where the twins went, what happened to them, I don't know. They won't tell me. What they have said is that they knew who their father was and they knew he had paid once to keep their existence a secret. They figured he would pay again. They showed up a few months ago, threatening to expose him."

"Dad's being blackmailed?"

Tiger nodded. "The problem is that he doesn't really have any money, that's why—"

"That's why he's selling the house," I guessed. Then, taking a deep breath, I added, "And that's why Dad took money from the mosque."

"I feel bad about that," Tiger admitted. "When he came to me for help, I told him I was having cash flow issues and couldn't manage it. So Saqi borrowed some of the mosque's funds. He was going to return what he took once his home sold. The rest he'd give to the twins, keeping only what he needed to survive."

I shook my head. "What he didn't count on was Jibreel becoming the treasurer of the mosque before he could do that."

"Congratulations, Sherlock. You have figured out where the missing money went. Now what are you going to do about it?"

A scraping sound from my teeth made me realize I had

started grinding them together at some point during Tiger's explanation. I exhaled forcefully and sat back, trying to calm down. It was rare for me to get worked up about . . . well, anything, really.

Fury and indignation, even if they were becoming the most common emotions of humankind because they were sponsored by Big Tech, were a rare experience for me. I didn't quite know what to do with them. My father had taught me that acting out of anger was never good, not just by quoting the Prophet but also by practically demonstrating how much pain doing so could cause the people around you.

I took a moment, therefore, to compose myself.

Then I asked Tiger Uncle, "In one of our calls, you told me you would replace the money Dad took. Are you still going to do that?"

He nodded. "I will have to sacrifice some assets I would rather keep, but I have discussed this with Saqi. Instead of going with his original plan, he will pay me back once his house sells. It will work out for everyone, more or less. No serious harm has been done—"

I snorted.

"Not to the mosque. Can we agree on that? I will think of something to tell Jibreel. His investigation will end."

"And Ilham and Kashaf are happy with this?"

"They should be. They're still getting what they want. But it is difficult to tell with those two," Tiger explained. "They are disturbed children. I'm not sure if you have figured it out, but they are the ones who have been vandalizing the mosque."

I stared at him. "Are you serious? Why?"

"What better way to hurt Saqi than to wreck the thing he loves most in the world?"

I was about to say that was ridiculous but stopped myself.

Tiger was right. Attacking Dad's mosque was the best way to get to him. He'd poured more of his heart into it than anything else. My siblings had found what was basically his horcrux.

"Now you understand why Saqi hasn't caught the perpetrators," Tiger continued, "despite being on the premises all the time. If he reports them, the twins might give away his secret. He's powerless to stop them from doing anything. They enjoy that."

I couldn't help but let out a bitter chuckle. After a lifetime of handing out severe punishments to me, my father found himself unable to discipline children of his who were doing much worse than anything I'd ever done. The world was hilarious, it just wasn't always funny. "You guys are unbelievable."

"I understand why you are angry with your father. But, Azaan, why are you upset with me? What fresh sin have I committed? You have always known that I have married many women."

"I didn't realize you deceived them. I thought you told them beforehand that you intended to leave them in a few months."

"Don't be silly. Most Sunni scholars agree that temporary marriages are not allowed. That would not be Islamic," Tiger Uncle protested. "Besides, I already told you, it would make it harder for me to achieve my goals. Why would I want that? Look, beta, in the end you and I are the same. We both use lies to make our lives easier."

"I haven't broken anyone's heart."

"Only," Tiger said, "because you haven't gotten caught."

[#]

Kashaf was waiting for me outside Tiger's office. She fell in step next to me as I walked back out to the store proper. With her unnerving dark eyes fixed on the ground before us, watching the rise and fall of our feet, she said, "I would have stayed but I don't think it's pleasant to hear someone else tell your story. They leave out so much either because they do not really know what happened or because they don't understand what was important and what wasn't."

"You and Ilham could have told me the truth from the beginning," I pointed out. "You chose not to."

Kashaf's lips twisted into a smile as we got to the cashier's counter where she stopped. "If your father's . . . our father's secret got out, he would have no reason to give Ilham any more money. Ilham didn't want that."

"What about you? What do you want?"

"I want something purer than money."

"Love?" I asked.

Kashaf laughed. It was a short, chilling bark, like that of a ruthless scavenger in the wild. Then she answered by spitting out one word, acidic and virulent. "Revenge."

"I . . . I don't know what to say to that. Look, I'm still trying to process all this. It's a lot, you know? Dad is . . . I have no idea how he could do what he did. I thought he was someone else, someone better."

"Why do you speak like a man who has hidden no bodies?"

"I don't know what you are talking about."

"You are just like Imam Saifi, another unholy man pretending to be a holy one. We followed you that night when you left our house."

"Why?" I demanded.

"You wouldn't tell us who you were visiting. You wanted to keep it a secret, and we have learned that secrets are profitable. We saw where you went. We saw you start to sin even before the door closed behind you. We know about the woman you are involved with."

I scowled. "So?"

"Keep what you have learned about our father to yourself. One day, when he has nothing left to give us, people will learn the truth about him. I want to be the one to speak it. You will not deny me this."

I could have told her that I wasn't planning on exposing what Dad had done, but I didn't. The way she was speaking grated at me. She was commanding me, gloating and reveling in being able to control me. I'd never responded well to someone trying to do that.

"If you take this from me," Kashaf warned, "if you tell anyone what our father has done before I do, we will destroy you. Think about how the community will react if they find out how you spend your nights."

"I don't live here," I told her. "I don't care about that."

"But our father—"

"Is in no position to judge me."

Kashaf frowned. "Your mother—"

"Already knows."

That gave her pause. "Fine. Then we will find your mosque in England and get you fired."

"Go ahead. Do it. You won't be successful. Here is the thing you don't understand. I'm not Saqlain Saifi. I don't care what people I don't know or respect think. I'm unafraid, so I'm free."

I waited to see how she would respond.

When she didn't say anything, I turned to leave.

"Madison Porter," she called out.

I spun around to face her. "What about her?"

"We know where your 'friend' lives. We know she has a

daughter. While we do not like hurting people or scaring them or breaking their things, we will do it if there is no other choice. We already had to warn Porter not to write about the property damage happening at the mosque. Don't make us go after her again." She gave a broken little smile at what must have been a stricken look on my face. "What was it you said? That love is a universal experience? It is a universal weakness. Through it anyone can be wounded. You are no exception."

Chapter Nineteen

It took me a while to figure out what to do about the threat Kashaf had made against Madi and her daughter. On one hand, awful as it was, it wasn't ever going to be carried out. I already intended to hold my tongue like the twins wanted. They would never have cause to harm the Porters . . . or whatever Julie's last name was. There was no reason to worry Madi about what was, essentially, a moot point.

Still, not telling her about it felt wrong. She had a right to know that my presence in her life was causing these people to use her as leverage. While I didn't expect the danger posed to come to pass right now, it was possible that what they wanted from me would change in the future. Would they try to go after her then?

I decided to make my way over to her place. This had the virtue of delaying, at least for a while, the inevitable confrontation my father and I would have to have. At least this time I would have the novel experience of being the one getting the explanation and excuses instead of giving them.

It was only after ringing Madi's doorbell that I realized I hadn't called her to let her know I was coming over. It was entirely possible she wasn't home or—

A man answered the door.

He was a little shorter than me, with a pleasant, round face and distressingly thin eyebrows. He had a broad, quick, practiced smile, which showed all his teeth. They were unnaturally white and contrasted sharply with his black polo shirt. The guy was in desperate need of more subtlety from his dentist and more restraint from whoever was doing his threading.

"Yes?"

"I'm looking for Madison," I said.

"And you are?"

"Azaan Saifi. I'm an old friend of hers."

"Lyle Preston," he said, extending his hand. "But you probably already knew that. My billboards are all around town. Preston Real Estate."

"Sure," I lied.

"She hasn't ever mentioned—"

"Who is it?" I heard Madi call from behind him before she rounded the corner and came into view. "Azaan. Hi. Did we have plans?"

I shook my head. "I just—"

She stepped forward and studied me more carefully. "What's wrong?"

"Nothing," I told her.

Mads frowned, glanced at Lyle, then said, "Well, don't just stand there. Come in."

"I should go."

"Why?" Lyle broke in with magnanimity that sounded just a little fake. "We were just sitting down to a family dinner. You should join us."

"Mads—"

Her ex-husband's eyebrows rose a fraction at my use of her nickname.

"I don't want to get in the middle of—"

"Lyle," she said without looking away from me, "can you please go see what Julie is up to?"

He blinked. "Wasn't she just here?"

"Lyle."

"Right." He cleared his throat, reached into his shirt pocket, took out a business card, and handed it to me. "In case you decide not to stay. Call me if you're ever in the market for a house. Are you a homeowner?"

Madi rolled her eyes.

"It's a great time to buy, you know, but it's always a great time to buy in California."

"Lyle," she said again.

"Fine. I'll go check on Julie." Before departing, he added, "That's our daughter."

"He knows. Can you please . . ."

With a nod of his head and a flashy smile, he disappeared back into the house.

"Sorry about him," Madi said. "He takes ABS very seriously."

I scoffed. "He doesn't look like he takes abs seriously. I take abs seriously."

"It's an acronym, you idiot. A. B. S. Always be selling."

"Oh."

She chuckled. "So, are you going to tell me what's wrong? Don't say it's nothing. It's written all over your face."

"It's a long—"

"I swear, Azaan, if you say it's a long story again, I'll fuck you up."

"Drop that last preposition and we have a deal."

Madi sighed. "Stay for dinner, will you? Guppy brought her lasagna over. It's always good."

"Guppy?"

"Lyle remarried," Madi explained.

"Okay. But—"

"Her father is really into fish. Just let it go, all right? But come in. You can meet Julie."

"I didn't think you'd want me to."

"Why? You're a friend of mine. It'll be fine. The fact that we're . . . having fun doesn't have to come up in conversation."

"You're sure?" I asked.

"Absolutely. And when they're gone, you can tell me why you look like someone walked over your grave."

Julie turned out to be a nerd-in-waiting with a very serious Pokémon obsession. She was shy and reserved around me until Madi mentioned her hobby and I told her I used to collect cards, just like her, when I was a kid.

The rest of the dinner conversation—aside from praise for Guppy's lasagna—was almost entirely devoted to that franchise's lore and how Julie had recently pulled an Arceus card, who as everyone at the table knew, was the creator of that universe and, by extension, was known as "The Original One."

I couldn't help but think of Badr, the girl at the mosque who wasn't allowed to play board games, and how completely haram her mom would think all this was.

Conversation then turned to the latest Pokémon movie, which I didn't know anything about, but which was Julie's absolute favorite thing ever, with the exception of her family, of course, and the aforementioned Arceus card. When I said I hadn't seen it, she described quite a bit of it shot by shot before Madi suggested she eat something instead of talking through the entire meal.

All of them ate together, I learned, once a month. Sometimes the Altmans, Madi's foster family, joined them too. It was the birthday present Julie had asked for a few years ago, and when her parents had balked, she had managed to weep and beg and guilt them into it. Now it was something of a tradition.

Imagine actually wanting to be around your family.

During dessert, Julie grilled me about what Madi had been like as a teenager and why Julie hadn't met me before, and when she found out that I'd moved away, nodded sagely and said, "Sometimes friends have to go away, but a part of them stays behind with you."

I thought this was very profound for an eight-year old. I told her so and was informed that this was, in fact, something Ash Ketchum, the protagonist of the Pokémon anime, had once said.

Lyle and Guppy exchanged significant glances when they realized they were leaving and I wasn't. Julie, for her part, shook my hand solemnly and told me it had been a pleasure to meet me.

"Cute kid," I said when Madi and I were alone together again.

She stood on her tiptoes and kissed me lightly on the lips. "You were fantastic."

"Wrong tense, Mads."

"You're impossible. Anyway, you didn't come here to learn about the prehistory of a cartoon world. Tell me what's going on?"

Madi listened in silence as I relayed the story I'd heard

from Tiger to her. When she heard Kashaf's warning, she frowned. "So these two people, they're the ones who vandalized the mosque and threatened me before? Are they really dangerous?"

"I don't know them. They could be. There is something off about them, that's for sure."

"Well, it sounds like they had a rough time of it."

I nodded.

"Honestly," she said, "I'm not too worried. It isn't like you're doing something they don't want you to do."

"Right now," I said. "In the future—"

"What future? You're only here for a little while. Most likely, you'll be gone long before they want something from you. And, from what you've told me about your life, there really isn't that much they'd be able to get from you even if they tried."

"Hey."

Madi grinned. "Am I wrong?"

"No, but there had to be a nicer way to say that."

"Julie and I will be fine. Once you leave, they'll rightly assume there isn't anything between us anymore. Even if, for some reason, you end up upsetting them later, I don't think they'll come after me at that point. It wouldn't make any sense."

"That's a comforting thought," I agreed.

"It's much more likely they'd go after your mom."

"That's not so comforting."

Madi reached over and gave my hand a squeeze. "It was a joke. Look, everything will be fine. I told you before, I deal with threats all the time. Much worse ones, in fact. Julie and I have protection in case something goes wrong. I can take care of us."

"What 'protection'?"

"A gun, Azaan."

"Really? You have a gun?"

She laughed at my surprise. "Welcome back to Shasta County, where we have a hundred and eighty thousand people, and we sell twelve thousand guns a year to them. We like pickup trucks too, in case you've forgotten."

"But you—"

"I've taken classes and know what I'm doing. But I hope to never have to use a weapon outside of a range. So please try not to cross them while you're here."

"I won't," I promised.

"Tell me how you are. How are you dealing with the news about your father?"

I shrugged. "It is what it is."

"Talk to me, babe. I know it's bothering you."

"Did you just call me—"

"Don't try to change the subject," she warned.

"I'm telling you, Mads, it doesn't matter. I don't care about him. He can do whatever he wants. It makes no difference to me."

She didn't say anything, but her blue-gray eyes never left my face.

"I mean it."

"No, you don't. You walked into town with someone else's hair pasted onto your face, pretending to have lived in Egypt, looking like your eyesight had gone bad, and claiming you'd become an Islamic scholar all because you don't care about your dad? No. You care a great deal. After what you've told me, after what I've seen, I don't know why you would, but . . . you do."

"I can't explain it," I told her.

"You don't have to. I know about being messed up better than most people."

I felt it again, that tightening in my chest, which made it so difficult for me to talk about things like this, and I looked away from her. I touched the knot gingerly and took a long moment to mentally soothe it, to make sure my voice would be steady when I spoke, then asked, "What do I do, Mads?"

"I got therapy," she said.

"There's no time for that."

Madi put her hand on mine. "Then let me kiss it and make it better."

"You did that already. It didn't work."

"I think you should let me keep trying."

I was feeling better the next morning, not because my issues had resolved at all, but because Madi's gym had a couple of punching bags and I'd been able to vent some of my frustration on them. Then I pushed myself to the limits of my endurance on the treadmill and with weights. My theory was that if I was exhausted, I'd feel less. Mads seemed skeptical, but she didn't try to stop me.

My chest still felt constricted when I went back to the mosque's apartments where I would have to face Dad. However, it wasn't as bad as it would've been if I hadn't hit the gym with everything I had.

When I got there, I realized something was up. A group of people, including Jibreel and my father, were gathered around Dad's van. It looked like someone in the passenger seat was struggling to get out and they were trying to help him.

Behind them, the door to my studio was open and a couple of young men were carrying a queen-sized mattress in.

My father was the first one to notice me. His expression

didn't change much. He continued to look like he was locked in combat with some pretty serious constipation, except maybe now his condition was a few degrees worse. He nodded to acknowledge my presence and said, "Azaan."

"Dad."

Jibreel, not picking up on any tension, said, "It's good you are here, brother. We need help with your grandfather."

"They let him out of the hospital?"

In response, Baba's raspy voice answered from within the van. "I have ruined their plans, hmm? I have lived past my expiration date. They've thrown me out. It is not necessary for me to take up a bed, they say. I am a waste of space. Discarded. Unwanted. I saw it on your face, Saqi. You were hoping I would die in that place. Don't deny it."

"Was I hoping for that?" Dad asked. "No. Did I assume it would happen? Yes."

"So sorry to inconvenience you, Imam Sahib, by continuing to exist. Why won't you leave me here then, hmm? Roll up the windows so I'll die like a dog. You will be relieved of a burden."

"He refuses to come out," Jibreel explained softly. "We don't want to force him. We might hurt him."

"I hear you conspiring out there," Baba called out. "Do you think you can force me to die in a mosque? No. It won't happen. I did not go into one when I planned to live. I won't go in one now when I plan to die."

"Baba," I said, "no one is taking you inside the mosque. These are apartments the mosque owns."

"That is close to being the same thing. Saqi will use me in his sermons one day. This man who never came to the mosque but was forced by God to come there at the end of his days. No. No. I will not be a . . . a . . ."

"Parable?" I suggested.

"Yes. I will not be a parable for his sheep. I was never an example, and I never want to be an example."

"Maybe," Dad suggested, "we should leave him."

Everyone turned to look at their imam.

"He is being a child—"

"And it is your habit to leave children behind," I said before I could stop myself.

The gathered crowd seemed confused. My father stared daggers at me.

Ignoring them all, I went up to see Baba. "Let's get you inside."

"But—"

I leaned forward and whispered in his ear. "If you cooperate, I'll ask Madi to visit you."

"Your friend in the yellow dress?"

I nodded.

"What will she be wearing?"

"I don't know."

"Hmm." Baba thought for a moment. "Can I pick what she wears?"

"No," I told him.

"Maybe you can ask her to wear a skirt. A short one."

"I'm not going to do that, but I'm sure she'll come see you. She liked you."

Baba grinned. "She did? I've still got it. That old Saifi charm. You have it too, even if your father doesn't. It skips a generation sometimes."

"Will you step out, please? You've made enough of a scene."

Baba licked his lips, clearly considering the offer. "I also want a subscription to a porn site of my choosing. No matter what the cost. And no judgment."

I sighed. "Fine."

"And I want it charged on the mosque's credit card. That'd be funny, hmm?"

"Baba."

"Okay. Not that then. At the very least get your mother to write a prescription for Viagra so I can properly enjoy it."

"She's not going to do that for you."

"Then tell her it's for you. Tell her Madi sprained your cobra commander because she went too hard doing the ottoman. That happened to me once. I was drooping like a wilted flower stalk for—"

I sighed. "No. Just . . . no. You've got my best offer."

He looked out the windshield at unit two. "Saqi is right next door?"

"Yeah."

"How thin are the walls?"

"Pretty thin."

Baba grinned. "Then I'm going to find the loudest pornos ever made."

Shaking my head, I started to step away from him, but Baba's hand shot out and caught my arm with surprising speed. "One more thing. You have to come sit with me every once in a while."

"I thought you didn't want to waste what little was left of your life getting to know me."

"Well," Baba said, "it turns out I have more time than I thought."

"That was well done," Jibreel said, stepping up next to me as we watched Baba being helped—wheezing, stumbling, and cursing—into what had been the apartment assigned to me. "What did you tell him?"

"I . . . uh, just reminded him that there are things still worth living for in the world."

"Yes," he agreed solemnly, "we should always count our blessings. Listen, there are a couple of things I really need to discuss with you. Walk with me."

I nodded and followed as he led me toward the mosque itself. "We had your bags put in unit three. It is upstairs and your grandfather can't climb—"

"I get it. Thanks."

"Here are the keys. You can give the ones you had before to your baba."

"Sure."

"You must be careful," Jibreel went on, "climbing those stairs. Some of the treads weren't installed properly and are slipping. We don't want you to fall."

"What's a tread?" I asked.

"The part where you put your foot, man."

"That makes sense."

Jibreel took a deep breath. "What doesn't make sense is something I've heard about you."

I raised my eyebrows. What fresh hell was this?

"Is it true, brother, that you told Nusrat's daughter to move away from home?"

"Who are you talking about—oh." I realized what this was. I had figured there'd be blowback for what I'd said to Badr, the girl who wasn't allowed to play Monopoly, but I hadn't expected it to happen this fast. "I'm guessing this Nusrat is Badr's mom."

Jibreel nodded.

"Yeah, I did that."

"Why?"

I was not in the right mental space for this conversation. I could barely bring myself to care. "It was good advice."

"Telling a young Muslim girl to leave her home—"

"Not now," I pointed out. "When she's eighteen."

"That is still unacceptable." His voice started to rise, carrying indignation within it. "What were you thinking? Nusrat is so mad I wasn't able to calm her down. She is going to complain to your father."

"Don't worry. I'll deal with him."

"But why would you—"

"Because it's enough, Jibreel. All right?" I snapped. "It's enough. We're suffocating our children. I know a lot of Muslim kids live perfectly normal lives. Most of them, in fact. But there are people like this Nusrat person who take things too far."

"She is a little extreme," he granted.

"Imams tell us we can't listen to music because it's the devil's instrument. They say we can't be friends with anyone who isn't our own gender. You know what? Forget that. I've heard them say we can't go to weddings where men and women aren't in segregated sections. We can't have 'free mixing,' can we?"

"Brother, what you are saying is—"

"We can't shake hands with women. I've heard imams say we can't watch movies or television because they have soundtracks and there might be people in them who aren't covered properly. Now we can't play chess or video games or Dungeons and Dragons? Men can't wear silk ties or gold watches and no rings on the index or middle finger and no necklaces."

"There is no reason for men to wear those things," Jibreel said.

"That's not the point. Think about the minute level of

control we live under. We can't shave our beards or have pants that fall below our ankles. Women aren't supposed to sing in public or travel far without certain family members. We are even taught which foot to put shoes on first, which foot to use to step into a building. And the people constantly preaching these things? They're not angels. I know people like this Nusrat. She's probably a hypocrite. These people become religious and they forget everything they ever did before that, they forget they were ever young—"

"You should not talk like this about a good Muslim woman, Azaan."

"Do you know what's going to happen? Next thing you know she'll be beating and whipping her children. That's how this ends. I'll bet she already yells and screams at them all the time. A teenager in this situation comes to me and asks for help. What am I supposed to say?"

Jibreel held up a calming hand. "You refer them to the Quran and the way of the Prophet—"

"They don't want to hear that. That's the answer they get from someone who doesn't know what they're going through. I know exactly what their experience is. I have to let them know there is a way out. People need freedom. Human beings chafe against chains. It's our nature. It always has been, from the very first of us. Have you ever thought about why Adam ate the apple? I think, ultimately, it was not because he was curious, not because he was disobedient, not because he wanted to sin, but because it was a restriction he couldn't make sense of. No reason was ever given to him. The mind can't bear that. It's too much. It shouldn't have to be endured."

I stopped, finally out of things to say. I hadn't spoken this much in one go ever in my life, except of course professionally.

To my surprise, my fists were clenched and I was breathing hard. My heart was racing.

"Azaan," Jibreel asked quietly. "What happened to you?"

I exhaled. "I'm sorry. That . . . that wasn't meant for you."

"Was Imam Saifi really that strict?"

I shrugged and looked away.

"I'm sorry," he said. "I'm not sure how to help you."

I snorted. It was too late for me. But . . . "He would have killed me," I told him, "if he'd had that app you're trying to make, where everybody's sins are known to everyone else. I'd be dead. I swear."

Jibreel frowned, maybe thrown off by the change in topic, maybe disturbed by the thought.

"Don't build it. Please. There must be a reason God made it so that people's thoughts, people's mistakes, people's faults are hidden from us. Maybe it's a sign of His grace that only He gets to know everything. Don't take that away."

"I . . . hadn't thought about it like that," Jibreel admitted. "I have to tell you, though, that I never suffered because everyone knew what I was doing."

"What do you want me to say? That you're better than me? Yeah. You are better than me. Congratulations. But those who have already been given guidance don't need this veil of His. Mercy is for those who struggle. Forgiveness is for those who sin. Don't deprive the wretched of what God has given us."

I was feeling pretty bad about biting Jibreel's head off when my father came to find me, so I wasn't in the mood to lash out anymore.

"Welcome to the new studio," I said as I let him in. "Same as the old studio."

He looked around at the emptiness, nodded though I wasn't sure why, and said, "We need to talk."

"I don't know if I have anything to say."

"Then listen, Azaan."

I leaned against the wall nearest to me and gestured for him to go on.

"It's a difficult relationship, the one between a father and son."

"I think maybe it's just us."

"It's not," Dad said. "Remember that disgusting Greek myth and the sick psychology that came out of it? What was it called? *Oedipus*."

"Well, sure, in comparison we look all right."

He didn't find that amusing. Maybe we would have gotten along better if I'd been funnier or if he'd had a sense of humor. "My point was that from ancient times people have seen this is not a simple bond. I think maybe we see too much of ourselves in each other. That's the problem."

"We're nothing alike," I said.

"No? I cannot agree with that. There is in all Saifi men a tendency to rebel against the will of God. We are weak, aren't we, to the whispers of the devil? We are too ready to believe what Shaitan says, to follow him. You had this flaw, too, when you were growing up."

"Mom told me you were determined to get it out of me, that you'd beat it out of me if you had to."

He nodded. "I wanted you to submit to the will of God, this is true. But also, as you now know, I was frustrated and disappointed that I had failed to do so myself. In that sense, when I disciplined you, I was really hurting myself."

"Yeah? That's amazing. Because I could have sworn you were hurting me."

Dad ignored the jab. "I was often angry with you, but the times I lost control . . . looking back at them now, maybe that was me being furious with myself because, despite all the spiritual work I'd done, I was no better than Baba. Did I not give into my lusts? Had I not compromised my holy mission? Was I not too weak, too pathetic to save myself? If I could save you, I thought maybe that'd be enough to redeem me. And it worked, Azaan. That's what matters in the end, right? Look at what you became. It worked."

I wanted to tell him that it hadn't, to tell him the entire truth about who I was and what my life had been and what I believed and how I lived, but I couldn't bring myself to do it. For the first time ever, my father was giving me an explanation as to why he'd made my life miserable. I needed him to finish it.

Also, as petty as it might be, I had the high ground for once. I didn't want to yield that to him. Not yet.

"I may have not always liked you." I rubbed the center of my chest as I said it, urging the muscles to stay relaxed, to let me get through this. "But I always thought you were . . . moral. How could you abandon Ilham and Kashaf like that?"

"I provided for them. I paid their mother off even though she couldn't prove they were mine. That—"

"That's an excuse. You could've taken a paternity test. You didn't want to because it wasn't the convenient, easy thing to do."

Imam Saifi stood up straighter, speaking with his whole chest for the first time since the conversation had started. "I did what was necessary. I was trying to build a mosque. This entire project, this divine task, would have ended in disaster if anyone had even suspected I was their father. My marriage to Reysham would have come out, and polygamy is a crime here. And even if it weren't, the community would look down on me like they look down on Tiger, especially because Iqra didn't know. The old ways are no longer accepted by people. I would have lost all our funding."

"Right," I said. "And the mosque is the most important thing in the world to you, isn't it?"

"It is."

"You say that like it's true," I whispered, "but you know it's not. You wouldn't have stolen from this 'divine' project of yours just to protect your reputation if that were really the case."

He bowed his head.

My throat was constricting. It felt like my heart hurt. It was becoming difficult to breathe, and talking felt like it would make me cry. "When I found out about the missing money, I thought that if you had taken it, it'd have to be for someone you valued more than God and more than this place. I thought to myself there's nothing like that. But there is, isn't there? It's you. That is who you care about most in this world. Yourself."

Without looking at me, he said, "Everybody is like this, Azaan. It is human nature. It's not possible for us to value someone else more than ourselves. People always choose themselves first."

In a sermon my father had given long ago, he'd taught me the right response to that sentiment. It came to my mind now, in a flash, and the words poured out of me, thick and merciless like lava from a mountain.

"You told me that Prophet Muhammad said, 'No one of you truly believes until I am dearer to him than his father, his son, his own self, and all the people.' In other words, Dad, there is no faith where there is no love. If you aren't able to love anyone more than yourself, what has all your religion been for?"

Chapter Twenty

Four days passed without my father saying another word to me. I was used to worse than the silent treatment from him, so I was fine with it. At least it looked like the mosque's problems would soon be under control.

According to Tiger, Dad was going to meet with Ilham the next day to agree on what portion of the proceeds from our home's sale would go to the twins.

Jibreel—who seemed to have decided to ignore my outburst about the Badr situation—was ecstatic. He reported that Tiger Uncle had agreed to sit down with him soon and explain the books to him. Tiger promised that he would clear up everything and make sure the mosque was not out any money. I had no doubt that the old cat would find a way to spin all this to Jibreel's satisfaction.

This, combined with the fact that the grand opening of the new mosque had been set for next week, had Jibreel positively giddy.

As far as my real job was concerned, I had a second audition the next day, this one online. I figured my best bet was to do it at Madi's house.

I was on my way to her place right then as well. From there, we were planning on going to my mother's for that high tea she had extorted out of me, and to which Madi had surprisingly agreed. I had no idea how it would go, but I was determined not to worry about it.

Most people, when they bring a girl home, do so because they are in a relationship they think is serious. My . . . whatever it was with Mads . . . well, it wasn't unserious, but we knew we would drop out of each other's lives again soon. This made taking her to meet my mother feel really strange.

"Hello, Mother, this is Madison. She and I have spent all our nights together copulating passionately\, but it's all casual and we'll be going our separate ways soon."

It just didn't feel like the kind of thing normal people did, though I suppose "normal" hadn't ever been an adjective that could honestly be applied to my family.

When I got to Madi's, I found her dressed in a pale-blue mock neck full-sleeve shirt over a pair of dark jeans. As soon as she saw me, she asked, "What do you think?"

"About . . ."

"What I'm wearing, Azaan."

"It's fine."

She raised her eyebrows. "Fine?"

"I'm sorry. Let me try again. You look like the sky on a cloudless—"

"Oh, shut up. Seriously, tell me, this is conservative enough, right?"

"Well," I said, "every inch of you is covered, which I can't say I like—"

Madi rolled her eyes.

"—so what exactly would you do if I said it wasn't?"

"I don't know. I could find a looser top. The material is a little clingy . . ."

I bent down to kiss her forehead. "It'll be fine."

"There's that word again," she grumbled as she hurried away, back toward her bedroom. "Hang on. I'm almost done with my makeup."

I followed her, shaking my head, and watched as she stood in front of a mirror and applied a light pink lipstick that I could barely tell was even there.

After a moment, I walked up behind her and wrapped my arms around her waist. I was about to tell her that she looked great when our reflection caught my eye and I realized that was only part of the truth.

The whole truth was that *we* looked great.

Together.

Just like that, lightning, as it apparently has a habit of doing, struck me as it had once before.

I knew then that if I ever stood with any other woman like this, if anyone but Madi were in my arms, it wouldn't feel right. It would be less than what this was, less than this picture, less than perfect.

I held her tighter and buried my face in her black hair and breathed in vanilla and jasmine and relished the warmth of her, which would only be mine for a little while longer, because we had agreed we were temporary and fleeting and there were supposed to be no strings. But this was Madison Porter, and I'd been tangled up with her always, and now it felt more unlikely than ever that I'd be able to extricate myself completely from her being.

Decades ago, I'd prayed for her to be my Juliet, and I'd gotten just that, a woman I was bound to love and lose. I couldn't say that fate had been cruel. I'd gotten exactly what I had wanted, except now I wanted more. It reminded me of a story my father had told me once, the story of the last man to enter Paradise.

I tried to be grateful for what I had now, in that moment, when I felt whole, and not look forward to the future, where I knew I'd feel broken.

I sighed, let her go, and stepped away from her. Mads turned around with a question in her bewitching eyes. "What is it?"

I cleared my throat. "Nothing. It's just . . . you. You're so beautiful, I can't even take it sometimes."

She considered my words for a moment, then declared, "That cheese is so fake it's Cheez Whiz."

I didn't tell her she was wrong.

She didn't ask me for the truth, though, so I didn't tell her that either.

Instead, I asked, "Are you ready?"

"You're very quiet," Madi noted as she drove us to my mother's place.

"Oh. It's nothing. I'm just thinking."

"About?"

"A story," I said. "Do you want to hear it?"

Madi glanced over at me. "Is it a long one? Or a sad one?"

"Neither. It's one of my favorites, though."

She smiled. "Let me guess. We're going to talk about Shakespeare."

I shook my head. "Actually, my father told it to me."

Madi blinked. "I didn't think you listened to him."

"I desperately try not to. Sometimes I fail."

She chuckled.

"It's the Day of Judgment. Everyone's deeds have been weighed. Good people have been sent to the Garden. Evil people have been sent to hell. There is one man left, though. He will be the last man to enter Paradise."

"Who is he?" Madi asked.

I shrugged. "I have no idea. The point is that he'll initially get sent to hell, but God will take him out of there and put him just outside heaven, near a tree and some water he can't get to. Obviously, he'll be super grateful to be out of the fire—"

"You would think," Madi said.

"Eventually, however, he'll start looking at the tree that's near him, and he'll ask God to let him be closer to it so he might shelter in its shade and drink the water. And God will tell him, 'O son of Adam, perhaps if I give you that, you will ask Me for something else.' But the man will swear that he won't ask for anything else and he will be content. He'll be allowed to come closer to Eden."

"Do Muslims call it Eden too?"

"Doesn't matter. So, listen, this man, right, he'll get to the tree and water like he wanted, but after a while he'll notice another tree, a bigger tree, more beautiful than the first one, and he'll start wanting to go to it. So, he'll ask God to let him make his way to that second tree, and he will assure God he won't ask for anything else."

"And God will say no this time because the man is breaking his word?" Madi guessed.

"Actually, God will say, 'O son of Adam, did you not promise Me that you would not ask Me for anything else? Perhaps if I bring you near to this, you will ask Me for something else.' Again, the man will promise he won't ask for anything else, and so he'll be permitted to inch closer to heaven still. Except—"

"Human beings are never satisfied."

"Exactly," I said. "Now this guy, he'll be near the walls of heaven, and from where he is, he'll hear joyous voices coming from there and he'll ask God to let him in. And his Lord will say: 'O son of Adam, what will make you stop asking? Will it please you if I give you the world and as much again?' And this man, who was miserable and in hell just a little while ago, won't be able to believe that getting such untold blessings is possible for him. He'll ask God if God is making fun of him, and God will smile and say, 'I am not making fun of you. I am able to do whatever I will.' And so the man will get more than he ever hoped to and become the last person to enter Paradise."

Madi looked over at me. "You always told me your father was all about brimstone."

"He usually is. Maybe that's why I remembered this lecture of his. It involved mercy. Things would be better if people focused on that more than wrath."

She nodded, was silent for a while, then asked, "What made you think of it?"

The fact that you are the first tree.

And the second tree.

And Paradise.

And I am the man who had no hope and then had hope and now begins to dare to hope for more.

You, however, are not God and all things are not within your power, and if I ask you for more than you have given me, I'm afraid you won't be generous.

"I don't know," I said. "It just came to me."

My mom had gone completely overboard with this business of a high tea, for which she had apparently raided several local bakeries and patisseries. The result was a truly astonishing amount of food. She had pretty much forgone the savory in favor of the sweet, with the exception of cucumber sandwiches, which were, of course, compulsory. Her living room coffee table was overflowing with cakes, éclairs, macarons, lemon and chocolate tarts, cookies, and cupcakes.

The teas on offer included a necessary Earl Grey, a Ceylon, a mint, and a delicate, refined, floral rose, which I had always adored. It was calming and soothing, which were both useful qualities just then because I was rather nervous about my worlds colliding in this fashion.

It was going well so far. I was feeling, in fact, a little like a third wheel, as they discussed a bunch of subjects about which I had nothing much to say.

These included my mother's decor choices—which, I suspect, a designer had made but Mom was taking credit for—the color of Madi's outfit, Iqra Saifi's large, bold earrings, how there was too much food, the fact that the smoke from the latest fire was finally dissipating, the chances of the mayor being reelected, and the breaking news about influencers Astiazh Haqiqi and her fiancé, Amir Mohammad Ahmadi, who were in their twenties and had been arrested in Iran for a viral video of them dancing together in public, for which they had been sentenced to ten years in prison each.

When my mother was done castigating the mullahs for this outrage, Madi said, "I thought you'd be a lot more religious."

"What would make you think that?"

Mads looked pointedly over to me.

"Azaan, did you tell this darling young woman that I was religious? Why would you say such a horrible thing about me?"

"Oh, he didn't say that, exactly. It's just . . . well, he said he had a very strict upbringing."

"I wasn't responsible for that, my dear. That was my ex-husband. That man is practically a fanatic."

"You didn't—"

"Say anything? No, I couldn't. You see," my mother explained, "when Azaan was conceived, I was rather distressed."

"Aw thanks, Mom," I muttered.

"I didn't want a child. I believe I have been rather up front about that with you, young man."

"Yeah."

"Why are you engaging in your typical histrionics then? Honestly, Madison, I'm not sure how you put up with him."

Madi smiled.

"Saqi was insistent that I carry the baby to term. We reached an agreement. I would perform the necessary biological functions, but I was to be absolved of any actual childrearing duties. Saqi would raise the boy as he wished, and he wished for Azaan to be a good Muslim. Did it always go perfectly? Well, you know what they say about the best laid plans . . ."

Madi gave her a sympathetic look. "That must have been hard for you."

"Hard for her?" I demanded. "Wait a second—"

"Yes, Azaan," my mother snapped. "Hard for me. To let that fool damage you was very uncomfortable. Even now, you are rather . . . what do the kids say these days? Messed up. Eventually, it got to be too much for me to take. Do you remember that day when your father tried to whip you eighty times?"

Madi choked on the tea she'd just sipped. Coughing, she asked, "What?"

"Oh yes, dear. It was horrible. Azaan got his hands on alcohol somehow and the punishment for drinking in the Sharia is to be lashed, so . . . well, you must have seen the scars on his back."

Madi nodded.

"That's when he got them. It was awful. Can you imagine coming home from work to find your child fainted on the ground, welts all over his back? He'd been beaten senseless. I had to practically carry him to his room and nearly threw my back out. How old were you, Azaan?"

"Fifteen," I said.

"He could barely stand the next day. I had to call his school and tell them he was sick."

Madi looked over at me. "How did I not know about this?"

I shrugged.

"When exactly did it happen?" she pressed.

"A long time ago," I said. "It doesn't matter."

"I believe," Mom told her, "it was right before you moved in across the street."

"So right before my parents' plane crash?" Madi furrowed her brow as she went chasing after memories. "That's right. You weren't at school the day before. You were supposed to come over and couldn't."

I nodded.

"But the next day, when my parents died, you did come."

"Of course," I said.

Tears were shining in Madi's eyes now, threatening to fall. "You must have been in so much pain."

"That didn't matter. You needed me."

Mads shook her head, blinked rapidly, then, wiping at her eyes, got to her feet. "Mrs. Saifi, where's the powder room?"

"Down the corridor to the left, dear. It is the first door on your right."

We watched her go, then Mom beamed at me. "There are no secrets as beautiful, are there, as the secrets of love?"

The way Madi and I made love that night when she took me to her bed was dangerous. We were slow, tender, and reverent. Her blue-gray eyes were locked on mine throughout, except when her neck arched back and her lips parted and I watched and caused her little deaths, but gasping for breath she returned, always, to meet my gaze.

"You really loved me," she whispered in my ear as she moved on top of me. She said it with absolute certainty, as if it were a fact undeniable, which is exactly what it was.

"I really did."

Later, when she was lying beside me, I tucked some of her hair back behind her ear and said, "No one makes me feel like you do."

"I could say the same thing."

I ran a hand over her shoulder, down her arm to her fingertips, which she interlaced with mine. "Maybe we should talk about that."

"No. We shouldn't."

"But—"

"Let's not ruin this." She brought our hands up to her lips and kissed mine. "We agreed to keep it casual."

"And that's really all you want?"

"That's all there is," she said.

"We could—"

Madi sighed. "We couldn't. Have you wondered what it would look like if we tried to make this—to make us—happen? How would it work? Our lives aren't compatible. You're in London. I'm here. What is that? Eleven or twelve hours one way? How often would we make it over? How would we afford it? How long would it go on? Is it just a matter of losing you now or losing you later? Because in that case, I'd rather just lose you now. It'll be harder the longer this goes. And I've got Julie. I can't leave. I can't ask you to leave. You're building a career there. It's something you've fought for, something that's important to you, something you want. I'm not going to ask you to give that up."

"Wow. You have thought about this."

"Of course I have. I'm not . . . I'm . . . we're not meant to be. That's all there is to it."

I touched her chin and made her look at me. "If we could make it work, would you want to?"

With her eyes shining, she nodded.

"Okay," I said.

"It wasn't supposed to go like this," Madi told me.

"I know."

"I thought this would be a good way, a safe way, to get back to seeing people, to dating again. I didn't want to get hurt. I know you. I trust you. I figured this could be harmless and fun."

"It is fun."

"There is just . . . going to be a lot more pain than I bargained for when it's over."

"Yeah," I said. "For me too."

"I'm sorry. I know I started this. I—"

"It's okay, Mads. You can hurt me anytime you want."

She chuckled.

"I'll stay for as long as I can."

Mads buried her face in my chest. "I know you will."

I held her for a long while, my mind, my heart, my soul all restless, completely at odds with my body, which was still and satisfied even if they weren't. Eventually, when I wasn't sure if she was still awake, I whispered, "Madison?"

"Hmm?"

"If we didn't have all these impossibilities between us, do you think you could fall in love with me?"

"No. Azaan. There's nowhere left to fall."

Chapter Twenty-One

Breakfast was a subdued affair. We'd said too much to each other last night and were left with the uncomfortable enormity of it that morning.

I drank coffee while Madi ate. I'd explained—and returned to—my single meal a day routine. Even so, I eyed her eggs and toast with some regret. It is easy to give up a thing entirely. Once you've had a taste of it again, however, temptation gets harder to resist.

Her phone was pinging relentlessly, until eventually I felt compelled to ask if everything was okay.

Madi shook her head and put it on silent. "It's emails from work. I did a review of a YA book by a Muslim author for the paper and—"

"YA?"

"Young Adult."

I made a face. "Right."

"Don't be a snob. It's the golden age of YA."

"If you say so," I said. "It's not for me."

"Then maybe shut up about it."

I held up my hands. "Sorry."

"Don't . . . don't apologize. I'm the one who . . . I'm just annoyed. I've been getting all these complaints about my review because I didn't mention how bad the 'representation' in the book allegedly was. I swear I hate that as a metric. It's like audiences are being trained to think the highest form of art is a perfectly painted fruit bowl."

"Who are they?" I asked. "These critics of my critic?"

She sighed. "I don't know. Just random guys. A lot of them have the same domain name, though: jibreelsarmy.com. Have you heard of them?"

I struggled to keep a straight face. "I'd ignore them, Mads. You're not going to be able to reason with these people."

"Oh, I don't intend to. It's just so frustrating, you know? This idea of representation, it started out as shorthand for giving minorities opportunities in the arts, but now people seem to think it means that art must reflect life."

"That would gross Wilde out."

"Probably. It definitely grosses *me* out. It's, like, mutated into an ideological purity test that only people who look a certain way or believe certain things have to meet. It's a bigoted standard."

I was about to respond when my phone started buzzing too, over and over again, and then Madi's lit up as well. She already had hers in hand and shouted, "Grab the TV remote. Put on Channel 7."

When I did, I was immediately rewarded by a picture of the new Redding mosque on the screen, with the somber voice of a news anchor speaking in the background.

"—bring you more information about this tragic incident as it unfolds. The police have not yet released an official statement, but we know that as of right now, Imam Saqlain Saifi, the spiritual guide of the Redding Muslim community for decades, is in custody. It remains to be seen whether or not charges will be brought against the preacher for the tragic death of an unidentified young man he was having an argument with. We will be showing you shocking footage of the incident, but before we do so, please be advised that it is graphic in nature and may not be appropriate for all viewers."

The mosque faded away, and the scene cut to a shot of Ilham and Dad standing by what looked like a bus stop near a park. They were in the middle of a heated argument, which is likely why someone had pulled their phone out to start filming them. The picture was shaky and not of very good quality, but it showed that at one point, while my father was shouting at Ilham, the younger man pushed him.

Dad staggered back, screamed something that was carried away by the wind, recovered his balance, and responded with a shove of his own. Ilham stumbled, his ankle twisted, and his momentum carried him off the curb and into oncoming traffic.

Ilham's head spun around as a massive Ram pickup truck barreled toward him at high speed. The driver tried to brake. Dad tried to reach out to grab Ilham and grasped only air.

Ilham was nearly parallel to the ground when the truck crashed into him, snapping his neck at an odd angle. It was clear at the moment of impact that he could not have survived.

There was shouting, and whoever was holding the camera started to run forward. The recording became a blur of motion. When it stabilized again, we were left with an image of Dad leaning over Ilham's lifeless, broken form, trying to bring back to life a boy he'd always wished never existed.

For the second time since I had gotten to Redding, there was media outside the new mosque. The energy this time was very different than it had been when the mayor had visited. Instead of being calm and bored, the reporters now were like piranhas frantic to feed. There was a story here, a big one, and all of them desperately wanted to get it.

When Madi dropped me off at the gate, I was worried that they'd ask me for a comment, either as Saqlain Saifi's son or as someone who was supposed to be an imam. None of them, however, seemed to know who I was yet, and since I'd ditched the costume for my role already, they probably assumed I was just another worshipper.

I found the board of directors gathered in the prayer hall. Tiger Uncle, who looked pale and humorless, as if drained not just of his blood but also his personality, hurried over to me. "What is happening, Azaan? Have you heard anything?"

"I called the police station. They're still questioning Dad."

"I will get him a lawyer," Tiger declared, pushing past me and making for the exit.

"What should we do?" Jibreel called after him, but Tiger just waved him off dismissively. So, the mosque's treasurer posed the same earnest question to me.

I frowned. "I think we just wait. We'll have more answers soon."

"Who was that man Imam Saifi was arguing with? Who is dead?" Uncle Karar, the liberal with the yoga-loving daughter, asked.

"What does that matter? What matters are the affairs of the Muslims," Uncle Nadeem, the conservative who was poised to give Friday's sermon here tomorrow, said. "Imam Saifi will be fine. He was clearly defending himself. We, on the other hand, find ourselves short an imam."

"Well," Jibreel said, hesitating a little before nodding in my direction. "Do we?"

"I . . . uh . . . honestly, I don't think I should get involved."

Both Uncle Nadeem and Uncle Karar protested.

"Look, someone has to speak for the community," I told them, "and address the media. It shouldn't be someone named Saifi. It'll just create confusion and complicate the story. Jibreel should do it."

My old schoolmate seemed taken aback by the idea, "Me?"

"You are the only one everybody will agree on," I said.

Uncle Karar grumbled, which was understandable because Jibreel was sort of a hardliner, but he seemed to realize I was right. "It is okay to have Jibreel speak to outsiders. When it comes to the community, though, why should they not turn to you for guidance while you are here? Why? We can call you Imam Azaan instead of Imam Saifi if it makes you feel better."

I sighed and tried to think of a way out of this. I couldn't find one.

When no one spoke, Karar clapped his hands together. "Then it is decided."

"What about the grand opening of this mosque?" Uncle Nadeem asked. "Are we going to postpone it?"

"Yeah," I said. "I think that'd be smart. It'd look terrible if we did it now."

"Not to mention," Jibreel pointed out, "that your father would miss it."

"He'd get over it. Look, I really have to go."

"Are you going to the police station?" Jibreel asked. "I can come with you."

I was, in fact, going to go there. Not right away, though. I'd already been told there was no chance I'd be allowed to see

Dad until they were finished with their interrogation, so it was pointless just then.

As cold as it sounded, the truth was I had an audition, and there's this famous thing people say about the show going on.

If I had more time, I would have canceled. That was not really an option at this point, and I couldn't just flake on it. Otherwise, Brayden would have several very large cows.

"No," I said firmly, "you're needed here."

Jibreel hesitated, then nodded. "Okay. If you need anything, man, like money, let me know."

"Why would I need money?"

"To post bail, of course."

I had missed calls from Mom, Madi, and Tiger Uncle by the time my online audition wrapped up. I was confident I'd landed the part. The director had praised me profusely for capturing the anxiety and anguish of someone going through a great and terrible inner turmoil he was completely unequipped to handle. It would have been a compliment, really, if I had been at all focused on actually trying.

My mind, however, kept asking all kinds of unanswerable questions.

My first concern was what Dad's statement to the police would be. Surely they would want to know who Ilham was and what they had been arguing about. I wasn't sure my father would tell them the truth. It would expose the secret of his second marriage, which he'd kept for decades. Dad was more likely to perjure himself, which was both a major sin and a major crime, than admit that the man . . . the boy, really, since Ilham had been nineteen, was his son.

Of course, the cops wouldn't just rely on what he said. They'd speak to witnesses. They'd ask around in the community about Ilham too. There were, to the best of my knowledge, only three people in town outside of police custody who could tell them his true identity—Tiger, Kashaf, and me.

Would they interview me? Could I just claim ignorance because of how little time I'd spent in town? But lying to law enforcement wasn't like lying to your parents to sneak off to a country you weren't supposed to be in so you could pursue a career they didn't approve of. There could be actual consequences this time.

And what would Kashaf say when they found her? Where was she? How was she? She had to be a wreck. She was alone now in a way that she hadn't ever been before. It was impossible she was handling this well.

I'd been able to channel all this confusion, this angst, into my audition when I'd been playing someone else, but now that I was myself again, I required real answers.

That is why I called Tiger back first.

My mother would want to know what was happening.

Madi would want to know how I was.

The man who no longer called himself Sher Dil, however, might have information.

"My lawyer just met with him," Tiger said as soon as he picked up the phone. "Saqi is telling everyone he doesn't know who Ilham was. Now we are going to have to support him, which makes us criminals as well. Bhai, I make it a point to always stay in the bounds of the law. How many times have I told people this? Now—"

"You could just tell the truth."

"Is that what you are going to do? Your father will end up

in prison for a long time if you do that, beta. That would be wrong. You must confirm what he is saying."

"How is it wrong?"

Tiger tried to come up with a response, stuttered, then gave up. "We all saw it. It was an accident. He didn't do it on purpose."

"Which would have still been true if he hadn't lied. He did that just to protect his reputation."

"Well, it's done now," Tiger said. "Meri jaan, we can't let them send someone we love off to prison."

Did I love Imam Saqlain Saifi?

I wasn't sure I knew the answer to that.

"Where is Kashaf?" I asked.

Tiger cursed under his breath. "Right you are. That little bitch has to be found. We have to figure out what she is going to do and say before we make any plans. She knows everything. If she tells the police what really happened, then the game, as they say, will be up."

"She's probably at the hospital," I said. "They must have taken Ilham there. I'll go and see if I can—"

"Stay where you are," Tiger said. "She will come to you."

"How do you know that?"

"Ilham will need final rites. You will have to do his ghusl. As your grandfather recently found out, in the end, every Muslim comes to the mosque. Kashaf will come with him."

"Shit," I said. "Baba."

"What about him?"

"I forgot to check on him," I said. "He must be so worried. I'll go see him now."

I made my way, carefully, down the unstable stairs that led from my new studio to the one I'd inhabited before. I knocked on the door but got no response. Worried, I tried the door handle. It turned and I walked in.

I was hit immediately with sounds of people loudly and theatrically copulating. Baba had one of his hands stuffed in his pants. I grimaced and turned away.

"Oh, Azaan. One second." He found, thankfully, the volume button and turned it down. I don't know why he didn't just hit pause. "You really should knock, hmm? I was just trying to wake up my oldest and best friend. He has died before me, I'm afraid, and there appears to be little hope of resuscitation. Wait. Why do you look so worried? Did something happen?"

Tiger was right. The ghusl would have to be performed for Ilham. He was also wrong, though. I didn't have to wait till then to see Kashaf.

A quick call to the coroner's office revealed that they planned on releasing Ilham's body tomorrow morning, Friday, which meant that his funeral would take place then too.

Friday was also considered an auspicious day to be returned to the embrace of the earth. I wasn't sure if that would be any consolation to Kashaf. I doubted it, and when I saw her a few hours later, when she showed up at my door, I didn't ask her.

Her strangely dark eyes were swollen and red with grief, but she was all cried out by that point. When she came to find me, she spoke in a completely flat, matter-of-fact way, like her brain could not find the right emotions to attach to the words she was saying.

"You will lie for me," she said, without bothering to offer the greeting of peace she'd made a point to extract from me when I'd visited her and her brother to have dinner. That seemed now like a lifetime ago. I suppose, in a terrible way, it was.

"Kashaf," I said, stepping back to let her into my studio. "Come in."

She didn't move. Instead, she stood where she was and repeated herself without any change in inflection. "You will lie for me."

I was about to tell her that I was sorry about her twin, about to offer my condolences, or ask her if there was anything she needed, all the usual things people say when someone passes. But they all seemed hollow and useless, and I was sure she didn't want to hear them. So, I asked, "About what?"

"The police asked me if Ilham knew Imam Saifi. I told them that to the best of my knowledge he didn't. You will say the same."

"Giving false testimony is a crime."

Her lips twisted in an ugly way that could not be called a smile. "I don't care. I want your father out, where I can get to him, where I can hurt him, where I can punish him. God's law says I'm entitled to an eye for an eye."

"That leaves everyone blind," I told her almost automatically, repeating what had once been sage words and had now become an overused, trite platitude.

"Good," Kashaf said.

"Tiger wants me to do the same thing. But—"

"You have no choice," my half sister told me. "I am going to hurt someone for what happened to Ilham. I want it to be the man who killed him. But if I can't get to him, I will go after your Madison Porter."

"Leave her out of this."

"Make sure I do," Kashaf countered. "Lie or your lover will

suffer. Don't look at me like that, brother. You are an imam. You should be used to submission. That is what the word 'Islam' means, yes?"

"It means submission to Allah's will. Not yours."

"I will decide who lives and who dies. So, if it helps you, think of me as a little bit of a god."

"God is forgiving," I reminded her, trying to calm her down a little, "and merciful."

"In my life, I have not seen anything to make me think that is true," she said. "Do not cross me, Azaan. I don't want to destroy you or your woman, but if I have to, I will."

"And if he gets out, what are you going to do to Dad?"

"I am going to show him hell."

Chapter Twenty-Two

Ilham's ghusl felt different than the one I'd performed for Uncle Tariq. He was a young man, extinguished at the beginning of his life by a senseless tragedy. There were no sons to help me prepare his body, no life lived full of joy and happiness, no loved ones giving each other consolation and comfort. Ilham was just . . . over.

It didn't help that the corpse was in bad shape. Jibreel, who had seen it, reported that Ilham's face had caved in. He had put a cloth on it, like the private parts of the body were traditionally covered, because washing it was impossible without damaging it further and he worried people would find it distressing. He asked if I agreed that this was okay to do, and I said yes, not because I knew the Islamic ruling on the issue, but because I didn't think I could bear the sight.

His neck was also broken and had to be propped up so that it would stay in place. It was all horrible and gruesome.

I had memorized the rules of doing the ghusl this time and I was able to perform it without any mistakes, but the serenity I'd felt in it before eluded me.

My peace, however, was unimportant. What mattered was that Ilham found it, wherever he was, and I hoped he would.

Jibreel wanted us to offer the Friday prayer first, before doing the funeral, because this would mean many more people would be gathered to pray for Ilham. While this was true, there was another consideration.

Dad was being arraigned on the charge of voluntary manslaughter, and it was possible he might get out on bail. In fact, the lawyer Tiger had hired for him was fairly confident he would. Imam Saifi had very deep ties to Redding and was widely known and respected. He was not a flight risk.

If Dad was released, it was possible the media would follow him here. A picture of Imam Saifi next to the body of the boy he had killed was something I felt we should avoid.

Also, my father—our father—might try to be part of the funeral prayer. He might even try to lead it, and I had no idea how Kashaf would react to that.

So, I insisted that the funeral be done right away, the burial completed, and then we return—not to this mosque, but to the old one, in the business park—for the Friday service. This would give Dad the opportunity to go back to his apartment without being mobbed by those wanting to wish him well or condemn him.

"You're managing this well," Jibreel said.

"Someday you're going to pay me a compliment and not sound surprised."

He smiled. "I don't see that happening."

"Yeah . . . well, anyway, thank you for today, for helping with the body and—"

"I am always at the service of my Muslim brothers and sisters."

"You are," I agreed.

"Don't say that now. Say it before God on the Day of Judgment. It could help me."

I chuckled. "What are you worried about? You've done all the math. Your good deeds outweigh your bad deeds. You're golden."

Jibreel shook his head. "No, brother, that's not true. I know they must have taught you at Al-Azhar that we cannot save ourselves. Only God's grace can do that."

I frowned, trying to figure out what that meant.

He seemed to understand that he needed to explain himself. "They say you can live your life being the best person possible, but you might do one thing so horrible that it wipes all your good away and gets you thrown into the fire. Or you can live your life sinning all the time, but it's possible that you might do something great that lands you in Paradise."

I nodded, as if I understood, but I couldn't help wonder what the point of all his recordkeeping was then. I didn't ask because it seemed like the kind of thing a real imam would know.

"I heard someone say that Umar ibn al-Khattab was beloved to Allah even when he was bowing to idols in Mecca," Jibreel said, referring to the man who went from being a sworn enemy of Islam to one of its exemplars and eventually the second caliph. "These matters are beyond our understanding."

"Yeah."

"I have been thinking about this a lot," he told me, "after what you said to me a few days ago, about how you thought I shouldn't make my AI. I have come to the conclusion that you're right. It might end up causing pain to a sinner Allah loves more than me, and I can't risk that."

I stared at him. "You're serious? You're giving it up?"

He nodded. "All this technology keeps coming into this world, man, and sometimes those of us who are making it . . . we get so focused on the benefits it can provide, we don't think enough about the harm it can cause. With social media and all, Muslims already have enough ways to judge each other. We don't need more."

"Yeah. I agree. Wow. Um . . . honestly, Jibreel, I don't know what to say. I didn't think I could change your mind."

"You didn't, Azaan. Allah did. You are just the tool he used to make it happen."

When a baby is born into a Muslim family, the father whispers the call to prayer in its ear. That call goes unanswered for a while—hopefully, for many, many decades—until the community gathers to offer funeral prayers.

Dad had not been there to do that for Ilham and Kashaf. I wondered, as I prepared to lead the small group of people gathered before the Friday service, if someone else had done it for them, who that had been, if that person was still alive, and whether they would even hear of Ilham's passing.

It was a reminder that I did not know the twins at all. They had been cryptic about what their lives had been, and I hadn't really tried to find out anything. If I had learned of their existence in different circumstances, if they hadn't threatened to hurt Madi, I suspect I would have been more curious, more interested.

As it was, I had treated them the same way my father had

treated them, as a problem to be overcome. At least in my case, that was how I'd found them. Dad—his absence, actually—had contributed, at least in some part, to making them who they were.

It was funny really. I'd always imagined that my life would have been better if Imam Saifi hadn't been around. Now I was about to bury someone who had experienced what I had sometimes wished for, and his life had been worse.

If there is a God, he does not tire of irony.

I nodded at everyone assembled and said, "Let us pray."

And then, "Allahu Akbar."

God is Great.

My recitation of the Quran wouldn't have been great, even though I had practiced a little by now. It ended up not being an issue. No verses had to be recited out loud. The prayer for the dead was a silent one.

After we were done, I looked for Kashaf, but she was already gone. I wasn't sure if she was coming to the cemetery or not. Some Muslims claim that women are not allowed to visit graveyards, while others say it is permitted. I wasn't sure what Kashaf believed, but it seemed like she wasn't going.

Where had she gone off to? What was she planning?

Jibreel came up to me and asked, "Are you going to ride with the hearse?"

"Sure."

"Where is his family?" he asked.

Right here.

I didn't say that, of course. "His sister just left."

Jibreel frowned. "Can you get in touch with her?"

"Why?"

"Money. She has to come up with the burial costs."

I sighed. "What does dying cost in Redding these days?"

"Around seven thousand dollars."

"That much?"

He shrugged. "Do you think she can afford it?"

I figured Kashaf, despite her objections to Ilham blackmailing Dad, would be all right with using that money to help put him in the ground. "Yeah. Probably. If not, we can talk to Tiger Uncle—"

Jibreel made a face. "We rely too much on him."

"It isn't fair," I agreed.

"It is not just that. It's . . . I worry about how much influence he has over people here."

"I know you don't like him."

Jibreel gave me a tight-lipped smile. "He is like a developer who is very skilled with the programming language he is working in but has no idea what the end user actually wants. You know what? Never mind. We shouldn't be talking like this. It's backbiting. I'll just say that I've been disliked by better men. Like you."

I laughed. "Me?"

"You have to admit you didn't think much of me in high school."

"Yeah, well, you were so . . ."

"Perfect?" he suggested.

"Annoying," I said.

"And you were a punk."

I shrugged. "You still wanted to be my friend, though."

"I was desperate."

"Anyway, I'm not better than Tiger Uncle. He's helped a lot of people out. Including me."

"He has, but I saw how you did the ghusl for this young man, what's his name?"

"Ilham," I said.

"And you did the same for Uncle Tariq. You take serious things seriously, Azaan, and you feel deeply for others. Tiger Uncle doesn't. He treats everything like a game, always looking to bend the rules and find ways out of doing what is hard. It's difficult to respect someone like that."

"I don't know. I'm not special."

Jibreel snorted. "I never said you were special. Just that you are adequate."

I watched as the hearse pulled up. "I guess that'll have to do."

I found the police were waiting for me in the cemetery's parking lot after Ilham was buried. They nodded respectfully, held out their hands for me to shake and gave me their names, which I promptly forgot.

"Heard someone calling you Imam Saifi," one of the officers asked. "Family business?"

"It appears that way," I said.

"Tragic what happened to this young man."

"Absolutely. How can I help you two?"

"We just have some questions. From what we've heard, you live in England and are just visiting."

"Yeah," I confirmed.

"Then you didn't know the victim?"

There it was. The first lie my dad and Tiger and Kashaf all wanted me to tell.

I don't know what I would have done if Kashaf hadn't threatened Madi. Maybe I would have perjured myself to protect my father, maybe I wouldn't have. As it was, I felt like I had no choice. "I didn't know him."

"You hesitated, sir. Why?"

"I may have seen him around the mosque or maybe somewhere else, but I can't say that I knew who he was."

"I see. And to the best of your knowledge, did you father know him?"

I shook my head.

"Do you have any other information that might be useful?"

"I'm afraid I don't."

The cops exchanged glances, then thanked me for my time.

As soon as they were gone, I felt someone grab my arm. I spun around, half expecting Kashaf to have appeared from somewhere. She would, after all, have been very interested in seeing how I performed in front of the police.

It was only Jibreel.

"We have a problem," he said.

I chuckled. "Only one?"

"Uncle Nadeem and Uncle Karar are fighting each other over the Friday sermon."

"Okay, well, I told Nadeem he could do it. If Karar wants to present a liberal point of view, he can do the next one. That'll even things out."

"No, man. You don't understand. It got physical. Uncle Karar hit Uncle Nadeem. We have to go."

"What the fu—" A disapproving look from Jibreel made me change the direction of my sentence. "What happened?"

On the way to the business park, which my father had been trying to escape for decades, in Jibreel's Tesla, he told me what he knew.

"From what I can tell, Uncle Nadeem started his sermon, and it was about the way a proper Muslim woman should conduct herself in public."

I resisted the urge to roll my eyes.

"Specifically, he started talking about khalwa."

"Uh-huh," I said, trying to sound like I knew what that word meant even as I pulled out my phone and, facing the screen away from Jibreel, started looking it up.

"Apparently, Uncle Nadeem saw Uncle Karar's daughter, Abeer—the yoga instructor—at the mall getting into an elevator with some White man and tried to use this as an example of what not to do."

I frowned as I read what khalwa was. It was apparently when an unrelated man and woman were alone together, a condition they were required to try to avoid and, should it happen, try to cure as soon as possible.

"Uncle Nadeem was correct. As a Muslima, Abeer should have stayed where she was and waited for the next one. However, it was wrong of him to—"

"Hold on." I said. "Do you really think that she should have just stood there waiting for an empty lift to come along?"

Jibreel looked over at me and frowned. "Isn't that the best way to protect her chastity and reputation?"

"What if it's busy and every time the doors open, there is someone inside? And what are we afraid of? That's she's going to jump him in the thirty seconds they're in there together?"

He shrugged. "At most she would have to wait a few minutes. Eventually, she would be the only one on there or, perhaps, there would be more than just one man inside, in which case it would be permissible for her to enter."

"Uh-huh. So what happens if, let's say, she's trying to get to the fourteenth floor and she's alone, but the lift stops on the fifth floor and a man gets on?"

"Then she has to step out and wait again."

I buried my face in my hands.

"Or she could take the stairs," he added. "No one said that

the laws of Allah were convenient to follow, man, but they must be obeyed."

The Prophet was reported to have said that Islam was easy, that no one who burdened himself with too much religion did so without being overwhelmed by it, or something of that sort. Dad used to tell me that—the first part of it, anyway—when I struggled with all the rules he imposed on me as a teenager.

Since I didn't know the exact quote, I didn't volunteer it. Even if I could remember it word for word, I was sure that Jibreel would have some perfectly reasonable explanation as to why it did not apply in this woman's situation.

"As I was saying," he went on, "it doesn't matter what Abeer did. It was very wrong of Uncle Nadeem to name her in his sermon. He should not have called her character into question like that in public."

I wanted to scream "She just stepped into an elevator" at the top of my lungs but managed not to do so.

"I am not surprised Uncle Karar defended his daughter, but striking him was also bad. I just . . . I wish none of this had happened."

"What are we going to do?" I asked.

"I will go speak to them," Jibreel said. "You have a sermon to deliver."

It's just another performance, I told myself as I walked up to the minbar—the pulpit on which my father had held court for most of my life—and the restless, agitated, excited congregation gathered at the old mosque began to quiet down.

I'd delivered a thousand soliloquies. This was no different. Well, okay, so it was slightly different. I had never had to come up with something to say during those. The words were already written. I just had to recite them.

This was more like improv, which I'd never enjoyed. It'd be fine, though. I'd just thread together some religious stuff I had absorbed over the years and it would make sense. Hopefully. I could do this. It wasn't a problem.

I took a deep breath and smiled at the Muslim community of Redding, as they sat before me, looking up expectantly in my direction, legs folded underneath themselves, ready and willing to receive spiritual guidance, something I was completely unqualified to give them.

I started the sermon the way my father started every single one he'd ever delivered. "My brothers and sisters in Islam, I greet you with the greeting of peace, as-salamu alaykum."

A few voices murmured "wa ʿalaykum salam" in response.

"As you have seen, we're having some technical difficulties."

A couple of people laughed, more of them smiled.

"But I am happy to announce that we're returning to your regularly scheduled programming. I am Imam Saifi 2.0, which means that I'm the new and improved version. Don't tell my father I said that."

More restrained chuckles.

"Anyway . . . uh, well . . ."

I had no idea what to say next. I should have at least tried to think of a topic to lecture them on. The problem was, of course, that I didn't know enough about anything Islamic to actually teach it. I decided to keep stalling while I tried to come up with something profound to tell everyone.

"Like anything new, I have flaws and bugs. It's a little unbelievable standing here today, in front of this group of people. More than a few of you, I'm sure, remember that I was not exactly a compliant teenager. I know over the years my dad has told you all about me and how difficult I was to raise."

There was a lot of grinning and shaking of heads, as they recalled my many offenses and how they had been listed out for them in prior Friday services in this very room.

"So . . . yeah, it's weird to be back here and to be speaking to you from the spot from which my faults were broadcast. And I guess that's what happened today as well, right? I mean, someone did something that a member of the community disagreed with, and they got up here and announced it to you all. That's how you ended up with me babbling at you."

I ran a hand through my hair. It was impossible to think, to try to come up with a proper lecture, while talking at the same time. I glanced at the clock near me. If I could speak for three or four more minutes, even if I didn't say anything of value, I could credibly say I'd done my job.

"I guess I just want to say . . . I just want to remind you that the Prophet Muhammad, Peace Be Upon Him, said that he was sent as a mercy to humankind. If we're supposed to emulate him, we should try and be the same. We should start by being merciful to each other. We can start by not judging each other and advertising each other's sins."

I paused as the door opened and my father and Tiger Uncle walked in. Even from where I was standing, I could see Dad looked worn down, haggard, and stricken with grief. He bowed his head a little to acknowledge me when our eyes met.

"I think I was twelve when my father told me about the Battle of Uhud. I mean, he probably tried to tell me about it earlier too, but I wasn't big on listening. Anyway, um, yeah, so Uhud. That was the second war the Prophet fought in, and it was the only one that the Muslims lost. And the reason they lost was that a group of them ignored his orders and abandoned their posts, which caused their army to get flanked. Everyone knows this story, right?"

Nods all around. This was expected. We were all taught the history of the Prophet and the three major battles he had fought in—Badr, Uhud, and Khandaq—were always covered.

"Who were these soldiers who disobeyed the Prophet and because of whom hundreds of other Muslims were slain and a campaign lost? How many were there? Thirty or forty? You all know what happened. You know their story. Tell me their names. Tell me who they were. You can't. I can't either. I don't know. Maybe there's some book out there somewhere that has this information, but we aren't taught it. When I asked my father about it, he said I didn't need to know, that I should leave what doesn't concern me alone."

I paused and took a breath. I wasn't sure, but it seemed like I hadn't been totally incoherent. There was no point in pushing my luck, though. It was time to wrap this up.

"This is the grace of Islam. It's the etiquette of your religion. It's the quality of mercy, which you'll remember was the mission of your Prophet. So, try to be better to each other and to all people. I'll do the same. After all, that's the point of all this, isn't it?"

No one, it appeared, disagreed.

I stood there, silent, wondering what to say next, then realized they were waiting to hear one more thing from me. "Please, rise for prayer."

Chapter Twenty-Three

I didn't speak to my father at the mosque. As soon as prayers were over, he was mobbed by his well-wishers and supporters, and I didn't want to be counted among their number. I went back to my apartment and called the one person whose voice I had any interest in hearing.

"How are you?" Madi asked.

"I'd be better if I were with you."

"I can come over after work."

"Oh, yeah, that'd go down really well with the khalwa police."

"What's that?" she asked.

"It's a—"

"Long story. I should have guessed. Hey, at least you got some good news. Some of the other reporters here were saying they let your father out on bail."

"Yeah."

"You could sound more thrilled about it," Madi said.

"I know. I'm just . . . drained. Not to mention the fact that I lost track of Kashaf. She was being all crazy before. She might try to do something stupid."

"Your sister?"

That was something I wasn't at all used to hearing. "Yeah."

I was in the process of telling Mads about Kashaf's latest threats and the promise she had made to exact revenge on Dad, when another call came in. I frowned, checked the caller ID, and asked, "Can you hold on?"

"Sure."

"It'll just be a second. It's my agent."

A moment later, I was talking to Brayden.

"Guess what?" he shouted as soon as I picked up. "Somebody's going to be a star."

"I got the part?"

"You got the part. Congratulations."

"That's great."

"Jesus Christ, mate," Brayden complained. "Show some enthusiasm. You should be on cloud nine. You're going to be in a blockbuster. I'm telling you, Azaan, this is going to be your big break. I can feel it."

"How's Sonya taking it?"

"Not great. She's a little crushed, poor thing. I promised her I'd find her something else. She's a tough bird. She'll rebound. If she couldn't get it, she is glad you were the one who did."

"Right."

"Why aren't you more excited?" My friend demanded, sounding properly put out.

"No, I am. It's just . . . it's been difficult here."

"Has your grandad not croaked yet?"

I shook my head. "He's out of the hospital. It seems like he's sort of okay."

"Well then, come back. Atherton was asking about you. Something about a Shaw play. What was it?"

"*Arms and the Man*," I said.

"That's the one. Let's get you out of all those beaches and away from all those women in bikinis—"

I chuckled. "We don't have those in Redding."

"It's California, isn't it?"

"Only technically. Look, Brayden, I have to go. I have a—"

"Listen, I know you. You're ready to come back. You're probably sick of all that sunshine by now."

"We haven't had much of that either. I'm going to run, okay? I've got a call waiting."

"Fine. Let me know when you're flying back. We need to put you to work."

I switched back over to Madi.

"Sorry about that—"

"Did you get it?" she demanded.

"Yeah."

"That's amazing. I'm so happy for you."

"Thanks, Mads."

"What's wrong?" she asked.

"Nothing."

"Don't lie."

I sighed. "It's just . . . it's a lot right now, that's all."

"Come over tonight. I know things are grim right now, but we can celebrate at least a little."

"I'd love to. I just need to see how things are here before I commit to anything. I want to see if we can find Kashaf. I wish I knew what she was planning."

"Well," Madi said, "you know where to find me."

So does Kashaf.

I didn't say that though. I'd warned Madi. There was no

reason to scare her. Besides, I had followed Kashaf's directions. There was no logical reason for her to go after Mads. It made a lot more sense for her to go after my dad, which is what she'd said she intended to do.

That thought would have made me feel better if I'd thought my half sister were in a rational state of mind.

"Hey," Madi said.

"Yeah?"

"Are you sure you're okay?"

"I will be when I see you."

"Ugh." I knew that Madi was rolling her eyes just then. I could imagine it perfectly. "That was terrible cheese."

"Maybe," I conceded. "But it was also true."

I found my father once he was back in his own studio, sitting at the edge of his bed, a copy of the Quran in his hand. I could tell from the traces of grief on his face that he had been weeping. I hadn't ever seen that before. I hadn't known Imam Saifi cried.

"Are you all right?" I asked him, which I knew was an inane question as soon as it was out of my mouth.

He made a despairing gesture with his hand and set the holy book aside. "It's all gone wrong. None of this was supposed happen, was it? I did not want this. I spent my life building this dream, this mosque. Then, just when the fruit of my patience was in my hands, it turned sour. Because of Ilham, I am unable to enjoy it. Tell me, Azaan, is this fair?"

I thought about Kashaf and Ilham and their mother, Reysham, and my own mother and how she'd been betrayed, and I said, cruelly perhaps, "Yeah. I think maybe it is."

Dad gave me a smile laced with bitterness. "You are a

hypocrite. How can you say that to me after lecturing the entire community about mercy? Is all your goodness for strangers? Is there nothing left for your family?"

I didn't answer him.

I couldn't.

I mean, he wasn't wrong. I was a literal hypocrite. I wasn't who I claimed to be. I hadn't been for years.

I had deceived people just like my father and Tiger had. My intentions hadn't been as malicious as theirs or driven by lust like theirs. I'd just wanted a little freedom. The means I had used weren't noble or righteous, though. I had done what they had done, just for different reasons.

That wasn't nothing, which was some consolation. Actions are judged, as the Prophet said and my father had always told me, by their intentions.

So while I could tell myself I was a little better than they were, it was undeniable that I was like them.

Tiger had told me as much, when he'd revealed the truth about my father to me.

"You and I are the same. We both use lies to make life easier."

I'd denied it then, instinctively, but I could see now that in a way he was right.

Eleven years ago, I'd taken his advice and started using his tools for my own purposes.

What would have happened if I hadn't?

Things would have been difficult, at least for a while.

I would've had to find somewhere to sleep. Maybe I would have had to take a job I didn't want and live somewhere uncomfortable. It's possible my relationship with Dad would be worse than it was now. For a while, at least, I would have lost the company of my family.

But how different was all of that than what had come to pass on the path I'd chosen? All that suffering I imagined, I'd endured some portion of it in London. My life had been easier than it would have been if I hadn't changed my nature and abandoned the truth, but not by much.

Had it been worth it?

It had cost me all those years with Madi.

Maybe she wouldn't have married someone else.

Maybe she would have married me.

Maybe our paths wouldn't be as divergent as they were now.

Wouldn't that have been better than what I had?

My chest seized up hard as I wondered what I had truly gained because of all these falsehoods on which I'd built my life. It felt like my heart, or something near it, was cramping, twisting, threatening to snap and break beyond repair.

I realized my father was on his feet, looking at me with concern now. "Azaan? What's wrong?"

"I made a mistake," I managed to tell him.

"What are you talking about?" Dad asked, clearly confused. "Your past? Why are you bringing it up now? We all have a past, don't we? Look at me. Even I have one. Just breathe. Sit down, relax. It's okay. Everything will be okay. Remember what the Mevlana said: 'Ours is not a caravan of despair.'"

His words were useless. The knot wouldn't loosen. My mind was racing and was unwilling to slow.

Brayden had asked, when I'd been leaving London, when he'd seen me packing my imam costume, *"Do you really need to do all this?"*

I had thought I did because, for some reason, I'd still wanted my father to love me.

I'd craved the approval of this man, who had turned out to

be small and cruel and flawed worse than I was, who had so little that was true about him. I had built my life trying to placate him, this hollow person who had beat me and hurt me and threatened to kick me out of his life, who after having caused one of his sons to die could only complain that his moment of glory had been ruined.

Why?

What had made me think he was worth it?

Were the bonds of blood really this strong, and, if so, why did they have no pull on Ilham or Kashaf?

Maybe they did.

Maybe that is why the twins had come here in the first place.

I pushed away my father's hand as he was reaching out to me and walked out of his apartment, the knot still overpoweringly strong, and struggled up the poorly constructed stairs to my new studio and lay down, alone, on the floor with my knees against my chest, regret falling from my eyes.

A smell woke me. I couldn't immediately place it, even though it was very familiar.

Rubbing sleep out of my eyes, I reached over and checked my phone. It was ten o'clock at night. It should have been dark. However, the bright orange light hitting my window made me believe, for a moment, that I could look outside and see a pretty sunset.

Then, all of a sudden, I recognized that smell.

It was acrid.

I jumped to my feet, jogged to the studio's door, and opened it. Nearly choking on smoke, I looked down at the source of the light. It was my father's mosque. It was engulfed in an inferno.

I started to run downstairs, but in my hurry forgot Jibreel's warning to be careful. A piece of wood slid under my feet, a sharp pain flared in my left leg and I pitched forward, tumbling down.

I grabbed at the handrail. My fingers closed around it. With a grimace I tried to pull myself up, but my damaged ankle would not support me.

I forced myself to stand, putting almost all my weight on my right leg and using the railing for support, I hobbled my way, slowly, painfully, to the ground floor and then to the parking lot beyond.

The entire building was ablaze, all twenty thousand square feet of it. Dark smoke billowed all around. The flames were shooting high in the night, red and hungry and furious, like the fires of . . .

"I am going to show him hell."

"Kashaf," I whispered.

This was revenge. Revenge for Ilham. Revenge for the life she and her brother should have had, and as horrible as it was, I knew, it was also perfect. It was a sight that would cut Imam Saifi deep.

I heard rapid footsteps behind me, and a moment later my father ran past shouting something incoherent, heading straight for his evaporating dream, all the long years of his life that would soon be ashes.

"Dad. Stop."

"I can save it," I heard him say. "I have to save it."

"No! Shit," I yelled, following as best I could on my hurt leg. "Dad. Come back. Don't go in there. Dad!"

I watched as he reached the wooden door and yanked it open before plunging inside.

"Dad!"

I tried to run after him.

My ankle gave, I stumbled and fell, breaking my fall with my hands. They slapped against concrete and came away raw, bloody, and skinned.

Gritting my teeth, I managed to get up and limp forward, still calling out to my father, but whether he heard me through the crackle and roar of the inferno and the pained groans of the collapsing building, I'll never know.

I was close enough to the mosque now that the heat stung my eyes and made it difficult to draw breath.

"Dad!"

Did he really have a chance to put all this out? That seemed impossible, at least without help. I reached into my pocket to call 9-1-1 but realized that I'd left my phone upstairs.

I stared at the mosque and took a deep breath. The air felt like it would melt my lungs. It was obvious what I had to do. I had to go in there to get him out.

I took a moment to gather my courage and yes, a moment to pray, and then forced my body to move, trying to hurry, trying not to wonder if I would make it out.

I'd staggered up past the mosque's Roman columns, and, coughing violently, was reaching for the door, when someone grabbed my shirt and pulled me back. I cried out as I fell, the sharp, unexpected movement sending a fresh wave of pain up my leg. Through the haze and the smoke, I saw who had stopped me from marching into the fire.

Kashaf.

I was about to ask her why she'd done that, to let her know that our father was inside, when the howling started.

It was coming from inside the building. Scream after scream of agony, wild and tormented and barely recognizable as belonging to a human, much less Saqlain Saifi, as he and all his demons burned.

I can hear him still, truth be told. I fear I always will.

The conflagration before us made Kashaf's dark eyes seem incandescent somehow, and I saw that tears were running down her face. She seemed to not register them at all. She stood where she was, staring and transfixed, at what she had done, until we couldn't hear our father anymore.

Then she looked down at me and said, "You would have died."

"I know."

Kashaf shook her head, her voice full of awe, like she had seen a marvel. "Then why were you going in there? Did you really love him?"

"I guess so."

"Why?" she demanded.

"I'm not sure."

Kashaf smiled, not a lot, but a little. It was a small, sad thing. Then she turned and walked away, off the mosque's grounds and somewhere into the vast world that lay beyond it.

Chapter Twenty-Four

I SAT IN THE BACK OF AN AMBULANCE AND WATCHED firefighters douse the flames that were still eating the mosque, gnawing away at what was left of its bones. Most of the structure had crumbled. I couldn't imagine they'd find Dad in there anytime soon. There'd be no speedy burial for him, no ghusl, no last rites, except for the funeral prayer, of course.

Madi, who was sitting next to me, put her arm around my shoulder and gave me a quick squeeze. Her presence beside me had drawn some curious looks, but everyone was too preoccupied with what was happening to ask questions.

My mom had come, but she was standing by herself, as close to the building as they would let her go, grief etched on her face for a man she had probably never loved, but to whom her knot had been tied and with whom she had spent the majority of her life.

Tiger was there too, looking broken. He'd tried to speak to me but, just then, I couldn't bring myself to say anything to him. He had kept to himself after that and was, for once in his life, silent.

Jibreel, who had gotten there first, had gone to check on Baba and found him still asleep with a "filthy movie" playing on his tablet. I was sure that the sirens and the din around us, flashing and wailing, must have woken him up by now.

I wanted to go tell him what had happened myself, but paramedics were examining my leg and would not let me leave. I was told that someone would check on him, though Jibreel made it clear he would not be the one to do so.

The paramedics' verdict was that I had to be taken to the hospital. It was possible I had a fracture. They had immobilized it for now, but they said that my ankle would need an X-ray.

I didn't want to leave yet and, more important, the police still needed to speak to me, so I was told I could stay a little while longer if I remained off my feet.

"This needs to be investigated as a hate crime," I heard Jibreel say to an officer nearby. "The mosque was clearly the target."

"Sir, I promise you we will look into it. As of right now, we don't know what happened. Until more evidence is in, it is useless to speculate. This could have been an accident."

Jibreel scoffed, as if the notion were completely ridiculous.

"It is possible. We can't rule anything out. So, yes, maybe it was Islamophobia, but—"

"It wasn't Islamophobia," I called out.

Everyone turned to look at me.

Breaking away from Jibreel, gratefully it seemed, the officer walked over to me. "Mr. Saifi, right?"

I nodded.

"What makes you say it wasn't Islamophobia, sir?"

"I just don't think anyone's this afraid of us."

That earned me a frown. "Excuse me?"

"A phobia is a fear. Isn't it more likely for someone to commit a crime out of enmity than fright?"

Madi gripped my bicep and murmured, "Maybe this isn't the best time for semantics."

The officer seemed a little put out at this explanation. "Ah. I thought you might have seen something. You were the only one on the scene after all."

"My father was here too."

"Right. Of course, but . . ."

I glanced over at Tiger, who had his gaze fixed on the ruins of the structure he'd helped his friend build, and sighed. Earlier that night, before I'd fallen asleep, I had realized that perhaps lying under his tutelage had saved me a little trouble at great cost. It was enough to make a man swear off that practice entirely.

If I did so now, that is to say, if I spoke the truth now, the cops would start to hunt for Kashaf. They would probably find her sooner or later and then . . . what? They would get her for arson for sure. Would they charge her with murder? They might.

Except she hadn't killed Dad.

Love had done that.

Had he chosen to do so, my father could have done what I ended up doing. He could have watched his mosque burn. He'd decided not to because it was *his* mosque. At some point, I don't know when, in Dad's mind it had stopped being something that belonged to God and existed for God's sake alone. Instead, it had become a manifestation of Imam Saifi's hard work, his ego, his vanity, and his purpose.

It's the best thing I've done in my life, he'd told me.

You know, Baba had said, *that is Saqi's baby*.

It was his desire to preserve this brick-and-mortar child of his that had killed him.

Besides, hadn't Kashaf already suffered enough?

Not to mention the fact that she knew both Tiger and I had misled the authorities in their investigation into Ilham's death. How long would she keep that secret once she was arrested?

For all these reasons, merciful and selfish, I decided to tell one last lie.

"Mr. Saifi?" The officer prompted.

"Yeah?"

"Did you see anything? Do you know anything?"

"No," I said. "I am afraid I don't."

If there is such a thing as a great funeral, my father got one. The crowd gathered for his last rites was massive. People drove from Sacramento and the Bay Area and even Stockton to attend. They thought they knew him. He'd been visiting their places of worship for decades, asking for donations for the very mosque that had, in the end, killed him. They wanted to pay their respects.

The mayor came. So did her opponent in the upcoming election. They shook hands with me and the rest of the board and the press took pictures. It was in the paper and on the news, and everyone talked about the great religious leader who had been lost in a senseless tragedy.

Major scholars who lived in the area, some YouTube sensations, some who had built schools and given lectures that influenced a generation of Muslims, attended as well. They were all very solemn and looked very wise.

The most famous among them asked if I was leading the

last prayer, and I invited him to do it. I told him it was because he was more pious than I was, which caused him to act all modest, but he agreed to do it. The truth was that I asked him to lead because I figured that's what Dad would have wanted.

The service was grander, I think, than he could have ever imagined it would be. It would have made him happy to see the legion that had shown up. After everything, finally, Imam Saifi had what he'd long aspired to possess—the unconditional admiration of complete strangers.

For my part, even as I lined up to pray for him, I couldn't help but think of who was absent.

Baba had refused to come. The old man had gone quiet. His tablet lay discarded in a corner of his studio. Every time I'd gone to check on him, I'd found him staring at either a wall or the ceiling intently, like he was watching a show only he could see.

Maybe he was thinking about everything that had happened between him and his son, Saqlain, who had to have been a baby once, then a toddler, a child, a teenager, before becoming an adult who had then become ash.

There had to have been moments of love and amity and closeness between them in that time, which resentments and misunderstandings and disappointments in each other had shrouded and made obscure. I hoped he was remembering those good times. I hoped he found some solace in them.

Mom had also decided not to be there. She told me she did not need to grieve in public, especially not around people she'd never much liked. Whatever regrets, whatever sorrows she had, she wanted to keep to herself. As for the final prayer, she said her work was her worship, as it always had been.

Kashaf wasn't there either, obviously. I hadn't seen her since the fire, and I probably never would again. Of what remained of Imam Saifi's family, I was the only one present. Well, of his living family, anyway, because Ilham was there, buried in the same graveyard, destined to spend eternity a stone's throw away from the man whose absence had defined so much of his life.

"Allahu Akbar," the acclaimed imam now leading proclaimed, starting the service, and I, sitting in the first row while everyone else stood, raised my hands to my ears like Saqlain Saifi had taught me when I was just a child.

I went to check on Baba afterward. He was how I'd left him, his eyes fixed on nothing at all. Setting aside the crutch I was currently reliant on, I sat on his bed next to him and called him out of his reverie. "Baba?"

"Hmm?" His hand went to cover the stoma on his throat so he could speak. "Azaan. I thought you'd left."

"My flight is tomorrow. I wouldn't leave without saying goodbye."

"Why not? It's what people seem to do."

"I guess it is," I said.

Baba let out a deep sigh. "Your father was a fool."

"He'd say the same thing about you."

"No, he wouldn't. He would think it, but that religion of his, it would rein in his tongue. He would pretend to love me more than he did. What do they call it in their sermons, hmm? Filial piety. That's what he would show if I had gone first. The truth, however, is that boy did not like me and I did not like him."

"I had the same relationship with him, I think."

"A nice circle we make, we Saifi men."

"It's not a circle," I told him. "I like you fine."

Baba reached over and patted my hand. "Yes, yes. You're also . . . tolerable."

I smiled.

"I get jealous of devout people," he said. "It would be comforting to be religious, to be sure you'd see the people you loved, even badly, again so you could make things right. To me, it seems unlikely that the truth is that pretty. Probably this life is all there is, and by the time you get to the end of it, when you look back, all you see is an ugly, jangled mess, like a knot no one can make sense of or undo, or one of those terrible modern paintings that everyone interprets differently."

"Abstract art."

"Yes. Exactly. That is what your life is when you look back on it. It's what other people's lives are too. Chaotic. Difficult to understand. Not at all organized. Without form. Without structure. Just paint on canvas that could mean anything. What are we to do with that?"

Two weeks ago, before I'd reignited with Madi, before everything that had happened had happened, I wouldn't have known how to answer that question. Now, with some confidence, I said, "We're supposed to look for beauty and hope that we find it."

Baba glanced over at me and smiled. It was the first time I'd seen him do that since the fire. Well, the second fire. Around these parts, in these days, one had to be specific. "That is a nice thought, but heaven would be better."

"Sure," I agreed.

"'Hum ko maloom hai jannat ki haqiqat lekin,'" he quoted, "'dil ke khush rakhne ko Ghalib yeh khayal achcha hai.'"

"What does that mean?"

"'I know the reality of this thing people call Paradise,'" he explained, "'but believing in it anyway is good, it keeps one's heart mollified.'"

I nodded.

"Though I have to say," he went on, "if all this God stuff does end up being real and I miss out on seventy-two hundred virgins, I am going to be very upset."

"I think it's just seventy-two, Baba."

"Maybe that would be enough for you, hmm? Not for me. I would go through seventy-two in the first month. Then I would ask for more. I would get them too, I think. After all, what kind of heaven has limits?"

Jibreel was all abuzz about some kind of interfaith outreach shindig he had organized at the business park where my father had occupied the pulpit for so many years. He begged me to promise I'd attend.

It wasn't how I'd wanted to spend my last evening in California, but Madi said she was busy, so I had nothing better to do. Besides, it was a convenient way to say goodbye to everyone. They'd all be gathered in one place, after all.

When I got to the mosque, I found it packed. The turnout was like nothing I'd seen before. There were people everywhere. The lot where Mads had first kissed me was overflowing, and more than one person had double parked. That's how you knew it was a Muslim event.

I limped my way through the crowd, looking for familiar faces, and saw Tiger Uncle first. He gave me a cool nod when I drew close.

"Azaan. Are you going to talk to me or pretend you didn't see me and walk by?"

"I am sorry, Uncle. I have been avoiding you, that's true. I shouldn't have done that."

Tiger started to speak but seemed overcome by emotion. He took a moment to compose himself, during which he spun around some of the rings on his fingers. "Beta, it is not my fault what happened to Saqi. I didn't make him run into the fire."

"I know. It's what he chose. It was just hard, right then, to not think that if he hadn't met you things would have turned out differently in this life."

Tiger made a grand gesture with his arms, sweeping them to encompass everything around us and almost hit Uncle Nadeem, who was walking by, in the face. "Look at all these people. Do you know what they have in common?"

"Redding?" I asked.

"Yes. But also Adam, no? That is what the Quran calls us all. The Children of Adam."

"Sure."

"How would the human story have unfolded if that first father of ours had never met the serpent? Would he have not eaten the apple?"

I shrugged.

"Nothing would have changed," Tiger claimed. "With or without the devil, Adam was meant to take that fruit, because all of this was meant to happen. You and I were meant to be here. This is fate, no?"

"So," I couldn't help smiling as I asked, "in your mind, Satan is blameless?"

"Meri jaan, the existence of Shaitan is a mercy in a way. It allows us to forgive ourselves by making everything we do not entirely our fault. As the song goes, have a little sympathy for the devil."

"I don't think many people would agree with your theology, Uncle."

"I am right regardless. Anyway, listen, I know he was your father, but he was also my best friend. You should know you are not hurting alone."

"Right," I said. "I am sorry for your loss."

"I am supposed to go abroad soon again, to get married once more. After all these years of traveling with Saqi, I don't like the idea of going alone. You should come with me."

I laughed, then caught sight of someone waving at me. It was Jibreel and next to him . . . "Is that Madison?"

Tiger Uncle turned to look at them. "That's the reporter, the Jewish girl, the one who came up with the idea for this event."

I raised my eyebrows. "Really?"

"Jibreel says she spoke to a rabbi at their temple here and told them about what happened to the mosque. The rabbi spoke to some people he knows at the Diocese of Sacramento, and it grew from there. Sikhs are here, Hindus, Buddhists, they're all helping raise money to rebuild Saqi's dream. That's what tonight is about."

"You're kidding."

"I'm not," Tiger assured me. "As you know, I always speak the truth."

I chuckled.

"Uff. Just look at that Porter woman. She's a red Ferrari, no?"

"A what now?"

"A hot car. Imagine being lucky enough to take her for a ride."

"Imagine," I said dryly.

"Come with me and I'll find you girls who will make you forget you ever even saw her."

"That's not possible, Uncle, and even if it were, why would I want that?"

After I finally managed to shed Tiger, I made my way over to Jibreel and Madi, pausing to accept the condolences of several people along the way. When I finally got to them, Jibreel said, "as-salamu alaykum" at the same time as Madi said, "hey you." I nodded at them, then leaning on my crutch, turned in the direction they were facing, so we could look at what they had put together.

"This is amazing," I told them.

"Your father would have been very happy if he'd seen this," Jibreel said.

"Yeah."

"We owe Madison a debt," he added. "She made this all happen."

"I heard. I'll thank her properly later."

They both looked at me. Madi exasperated, Jibreel curious.

"Follow me," he demanded. "I need to talk to you."

I glanced at Mads, who shrugged as Jibreel started to walk away.

Instead of following immediately, I reached down and took her hand. "Seriously, Madi. Thank you."

"Anything for you," she said.

I found Jibreel outside, looking up at the sky, where the moon was finally visible. He didn't look at me as I came to stand next to him.

"You're flying out tomorrow?" he asked.

"Yeah."

"My wife wanted to have you over for a farewell dinner."

"That's not necessary," I told him.

"She was very impressed with the sermon you gave."

"Oh. Well—"

He folded his arms across his chest. "I thought it was very interesting too. Are there many graduates of Al-Azhar, do you think, who don't know how many archers abandoned their post in the Battle of Uhud?"

I shrugged.

"And to do an entire sermon without quoting a single line of the Quran? That's some achievement, man."

"Okay," I said. "The truth is—"

"You were never trained to be an imam."

"I was going to tell you."

"When?"

"Just now."

Jibreel threw his hands up in the air. "Unbelievable. I had my suspicions after the advice you gave Badr and how you reacted afterward, but I got pretty sure when instead of using the proper Arabic, you said 'let us pray' at Ilham's funeral."

"Hold on. That was before the Friday service. You made me give a sermon even though you thought I had no business doing it?"

"I figured you would come clean," he snapped.

"Oh."

"And then," Jibreel admitted, more calmly, "I thought you'd fall flat on your face, which is what you deserved for mocking us. You didn't, though. My wife is not wrong. You did a good job."

"Look, I'm sorry, really. I didn't mean to take on any imam

duties. I was just pretending because I wanted to make my dad happy. It got a little out of hand."

"You think?"

"And," I added, "for what it's worth, I wasn't trying to mock anyone. I just—"

"You're not really Muslim," he said, "so you don't understand our ways. They seem strange to you. I get it."

"I *am* Muslim. It's a huge part of my identity."

"It's not supposed to be an identity, Azaan. It's a religion. It's a specific set of rules that only make sense if you really believe they come from God. That's why it doesn't matter if you think listening to music or drinking alcohol or going out with women or playing dice are okay things to do. Allah and His Messenger said they weren't, so they aren't. It's about submission. Except you don't want that. You want to do what you want to do. You want to use your judgment, which is not based in our tradition to define our tradition. Your gaze is an external one. You're not really one of us."

I ran my hand through my hair. "I get that you're angry—"

"I'm not," he assured me, and it sounded true. "You think you are Muslim because that is what you were raised to think. Except the way you were raised . . . I wish you could have come over for dinner. You could have met my wife, who is happy in her role and with her life, even if all the Western world tells her she shouldn't be. You would have met my children, who I've never hit. You would have met my father and my mother, who never hit me. What you experienced, my brother, how you grew up, that wasn't what this religion is about."

"I never said my experience was universal."

"No? You assumed that Badr's mom, who didn't want her playing Monopoly, would beat her like Imam Saifi beat you, because deep inside you think that's what Muslim parents do.

It isn't. That's just what one Muslim did. And, man, I'm sorry that happened to you. If our places had been switched when we were young, maybe our places would be switched now."

"I'd be the one giving a self-righteous lecture and you'd be the one listening to it?"

Jibreel smiled. "You're getting off easy. I could ask you to go in there and tell everyone the truth."

"Why don't you?"

"It won't help the community. I mean, what good would it do? They like you. Besides, do you know what the word 'imam' means?"

"Isn't it just a title?"

"It means 'leader,'" Jibreel explained, "and . . . well, you weren't terrible at being one."

"That's not a great compliment."

"I suggest you take it."

"All right," I agreed. "I will."

He nodded, was quiet for a while, then said, "So, you and Madison Porter, after all these years."

"Yeah."

"I swear," Jibreel muttered, "God favors who He will."

"Is that your way of saying I don't deserve her?"

"Yes."

"You're probably right."

"How is it going to work between you two if you're leaving tomorrow?"

"It won't. Madi and I . . . it's just . . . complicated."

Jibreel considered this for a moment, then asked, "Can I give you some advice? I am, after all, happily married and you are . . . doing whatever you are doing."

"Sure."

"If you think she's worth it, then figure it out."

I waited for him to go on.

He didn't.

"That's it?"

"That's it," Jibreel confirmed. "Love is like religion. It's an if-then function."

"I don't know what that means."

"It's just 'if A, then B.' For example, if God is real, then I must obey him. Right? Similarly, if love is real, then I must preserve it. I don't understand how this stuff confuses people. It's really very simple."

Chapter Twenty-Five

"How's your ankle?" Madi asked as we walked back, slowly, to her car later that night. The business park was almost entirely deserted now, except for some volunteers helping Jibreel clean up the place.

The event, which had combined interfaith outreach with fundraising, had gone really well. The generosity and sympathy of the other religious communities in the area was astonishing, moving, and unexpected. It wouldn't be enough to rebuild the massive structure that had burned down, not exactly like it had been, but with the proceeds from the night and the insurance money the board would get, someday soon Redding would have a proper mosque again.

"It's not so bad."

"Are you sure you're okay to fly?"

I looked over at her. "Are you asking me to stay?"

Mads shook her head.

"Ask me and I will."

She nodded. "I know. I just can't. I've spent my whole life

wishing people had stayed with me instead of going away. I'm not doing that anymore. The girl who breaks when she's left behind, who lives in fear of being alone . . . I need her to grow up now. It's time, I think."

We walked in silence for a while after that.

Then Madi went on. "Anyway, I can't ask you to choose between Redding and London. Who would choose this place?"

"There are people who would," I said.

"Not you, though."

"No. Not me. Hey. Wait a second. This way."

Mads frowned as I started leading her to the right.

"That's not where I parked."

"Come on."

With a shrug, she followed.

I led her toward the center of the parking lot, searching for the spot where my life had changed. She caught on to what I was doing and, when we got there, said, "Here, I think."

"Yeah."

Madi smiled. "What are you planning?"

Instead of answering, I asked, "What are you going to say to me tomorrow, when I'm leaving?"

She grew serious. "I . . . don't know."

"I don't know what I'll say to you either, Mads. I've been thinking about it. I don't know if I have the words for it."

"Then you'll use someone else's. Shakespeare has always been your real crutch."

I winced.

"Sorry. Too much honesty?" Madi asked.

"Just a little. Listen, the only thing I can think to say to you is . . . well, it's cruel, in our circumstances, and it's not what you want to hear, so it may upset you. That's why I want to say it now, while I'm still around. That way I'm with you tonight, in case you need me, in case you don't want to be alone."

"You're going to hurt me and then heal me?"

"I guess so."

Madi took a deep breath. "Go ahead."

Putting all my weight on one foot, I let my crutch clatter to the ground.

"What are you doing?" Madi asked.

I held out a hand to her and she took it. I pulled her close and smelled that mix of bergamot, vanilla, and jasmine with which I'd gotten so familiar. I tilted her head up so that her spellbinding eyes met mine.

"Madison. I'm sorry to tell you this—" I paused, waiting for and expecting my curse, that knot that lived in my chest, to act up again like it always did when I let myself be vulnerable and talk about my emotions.

Somehow, for reasons I don't understand, it didn't.

"Just say it," she prompted.

"I love you, Madi. I'm just . . . in ridiculous amounts of love with you."

"I know."

"I realize that we said no strings, but . . . wait. That's . . . it? You know?"

"What?" Madi teased. "Was there something you wanted me to say too?"

"You're making jokes. I'm trying to do this emotional thing here and you're—"

"I love you too, you idiot. You know that."

I did.

"Kiss me," I asked her. "Like you did the first time."

Madi stood on her tiptoes, grabbed the front of my shirt,

and pulled my mouth down to hers, just like she'd done eleven years ago.

I kissed her back.

Like I'd never kissed anyone before.

Like I'd never kiss anyone again.

The next morning, I met Mom for breakfast. She had volunteered to take a day off to drive me to the airport in Sacramento. That was a first. Iqra Saifi had never missed work on my account. Well, at least not that I could remember. I mean, she must have taken some maternity leave, right?

She took me to the home I'd grown up in, which Dad had been in the process of selling. On the way there, I told her about my life in London, what I really did for a living, and admitted to the lie I'd started telling her and my dad when I'd been seventeen.

"Well, my dear," she said as we walked into the empty house, her voice echoing eerily off the walls we had once known so well, "I'm happy for you. I think it's fabulous."

"That I've been deceiving you for a decade?"

"It isn't the kind of thing a parent wants to hear, I suppose. But I understand people will do crazy things to get out of dire circumstances. My father was also . . . extreme. He made Saqi, especially when Saqi was young and more liberal, seem reasonable."

I raised my eyebrows.

My mom smiled. "It's true. Honestly, Saqi wasn't all that bad when you were young. He wasn't great, but I think it was only after he got married to that other woman and hid it from me that he got really out of control. Maybe he was somehow compensating for what he knew was wrong or maybe he was just venting his self-loathing. Maybe that's why he got increasingly obsessed with that mosque of his. He figured it'd be his salvation."

I hadn't thought of it that way.

"Anyway, what was I saying? Ah, yes, darling, so you see, I understand that sometimes, to escape desperate circumstances, we have to do unpleasant things. I mean, I married your father. We do what we must."

"You're taking this really well," I said.

"Not everyone has your talent for being dramatic, Azaan. At least you've found a use for it."

I chuckled and, changing the topic, asked, "Why are we here?"

"We need to decide what to do with this place."

"Isn't that a question for your financial adviser?"

Mom frowned. "You do realize that you own half of this, yes?"

"I do?"

"Well, I wasn't married to Saqi, thank God, so I don't inherit from him. His will leaves everything to you. I suppose he must have figured your Baba would pass first. Anyway, like I said, we need to make a decision about the fate of this property, which we are partners in."

"I . . . don't know what to say, Mom."

"Well, we could keep it and rent it out. Or we could sell it, as your father planned, and that will get you some cash now. Given the fact that you're living on a couch, that should improve your quality of life quite a bit."

I was having some trouble processing what she was saying. All of a sudden, I apparently had several hundred thousand dollars. It was more than I'd ever had before or, frankly, ever expected to have. "What do you think we should do?"

"I think you should wed Madi and move in here. Other mothers would say have lots of children, but you know I don't like those. Though, given how you two look at each other, I fear that in the absence of diligent birth control, such little tragedies will be inevitable."

I laughed. "Let's be serious."

"I am serious. Why not? The girl loves you. I know you love her. What's the problem?"

"Mom, it won't work. My career is in London. Her daughter is here. She can't leave."

"I see. You're right. How silly of me. I had forgotten that no acting is ever done in the great State of California. For some reason I thought we were famous for it, but I must have been thinking of someplace else."

I rolled my eyes. "Redding is not LA. It's a thousand-mile round trip."

"Find a middle ground. My God, Azaan, you've seen all your life what it's like when someone marries a person they don't love. You've seen what it's like when a marriage is unhappy. If you think this woman is your woman, your person, then you can't let something small like the width of the world get between you."

"Moving to the States from England—"

"Which I would never recommend," Iqra Saifi told me, "in any other circumstances."

"—would mean giving up everything. All the relationships I've built, the connections, the friendships, all of it."

Mom nodded. "That's true."

"Would you do it? Your career is important to you. It always has been. Would you give up your practice for someone? Move to a new place? Get a new medical license? Start over?"

"No," she admitted. "But I've never been in love for even fifteen minutes, let alone for nearly fifteen years. So don't think about what I would do. Decide for yourself what you want. You must choose between Madi and your work. That's the . . ." She broke off when her phone buzzed. Glancing at it, she frowned. "Sorry, I have to take this. I told the hospital to only call me if there is an emergency."

"Okay. I'm going to walk around a little," I said.

"While you do, think about what Shakespeare said."

"And what was that?"

"'To thine own self be true.' Or something to that effect, right?"

"I seriously wish people would stop quoting that line. That advice didn't come from some wise character. Everyone repeats it, but no one mentions that Polonius was not only a buffoon, he was also a villain."

"How can you possibly remember his name?"

"It's my job."

"Well," Mom said, before she turned away to take her call, "just because a fool says something doesn't mean it isn't true."

I had to concede that point because I knew Shakespeare would have.

As my mother talked medicine on her mobile, I limped through the house. It didn't feel any different than it had when I'd done the same thing two weeks ago, when it hadn't been mine even in part.

I couldn't imagine living here with Madi. Not because I couldn't see a future with Mads—I saw that clearly—but because I'd been so unhappy in this place that I couldn't imagine trying to be happy here.

That reminded me of Kashaf. Even if Dad had left everything to me, surely she ought to have some of this inheritance. If we sold the place, I could give her half my share, if I could find her, which seemed unlikely.

There was also Tiger, who had the right to expect two hundred thousand dollars from the proceeds of this place. It wouldn't be right not to reimburse him for the money he had given to the mosque to hide Dad's indiscretion, which meant that the small fortune my mom had said I'd get if we sold the house was probably actually a rather modest sum.

Shaking my head, I walked into my old room, which my father had been using during his last days here. I gathered up his books in one neat stack and started to put away the last of his belongings.

As I was doing so, my eyes fell on the old poster of Andre Agassi sitting on a motorcycle, with the words "Image is Everything" written on it in bold.

I walked up to it, pulled it down from its place, and tore it to shreds.

Iqra Saifi was silent as we drove out of Redding's city limits. She seemed upset. I think she had been hoping I wouldn't leave, that the prospect of a future with Madi in my childhood home would convince me to stay here and abandon London. She'd apparently read more than her share of romance novels.

I wanted to tell her that we don't all get happily ever afters. Not everyone gets to be with the people they love. Life is about more than who you end up with. Sometimes it's just too complicated to be with someone.

"Figure it out," Jibreel had said.

His words came to my mind unbidden and made me smile, even as my chest constricted a bit.

"Anything for you, Mads."

I tried to push the memory of my own words away.

Madi had made sure I knew this wasn't meant to last. She had laid out ground rules for our relationship at the very beginning. I had to respect those. If she'd changed her mind, she would have asked me to stay, but she hadn't even after I'd told her she could. That meant something.

I mean, the woman had balked when I'd called her "babe." I wasn't sure what she'd do if I missed my flight for her and showed up at her door.

No. I was doing the right thing. I had to leave.

My life was waiting.

Though maybe I should have insisted we talk about us more, to see if there was a way to make a relationship work. Maybe I should have actually said that I'd changed my mind about what I wanted.

Then again, I'd told her I loved her. That was the same thing. Wasn't it?

I grunted as the knot in my chest got worse.

Mom looked over at me. "Are you all right?"

I nodded.

Brayden had warned me this would happen. *"That seems like a deep wound, mate. It'll hurt like hell if it opens up again."*

I'd be fine. I just needed to relax.

I told myself that it was possible this wasn't the end. Maybe I'd see her again someday. I wouldn't have to stay away from Redding like I had before. I could come back more often.

"Do you think you will always be young and beautiful?" Baba had asked. *"Or that you are guaranteed tomorrow? What if*

it never comes? What if tonight is all the time you two have together and there is nothing more?"

"Damn it," I whispered as I doubled over, clutching my breast.

"Azaan?" Mom asked. "What's wrong?"

Madi's question from a decade ago echoed in my mind. *"So, kissing me is something you've thought about?"*

"Yeah." I'd admitted. *"Kind of a lot."*

"What were you waiting for?"

"You."

I shouldn't have waited then.

We could have been more to each other than we had been if I hadn't, but I had, and now, all these years later, was I needlessly waiting for her again?

I realized my mother had turned on her car's hazard lights and was pulling over.

"I'm fine," I managed to tell her. "I'm okay."

"I can't ask you to choose," Mads had said.

"You're the one I choose first."

"I haven't broken anyone's heart," I'd told Tiger.

"Not yet," he'd warned.

I felt Mom's hand on my back. "Tell me what's happening."

"Nothing. It's just the knot."

She let out a relieved breath. "It doesn't want to leave Madison?"

"Yeah. It's my curse."

"Or maybe it's a blessing," she countered. "It won't let you lie to yourself. It knows what you really want."

"She didn't ask me to stay," I told her. "She said she needs to learn how to be alone."

"That's not the same as *wanting* to be alone. Tell me, did you ask her to come with you?"

"No."

"Why?"

"Because," I said, "that would be unfair."

"I would bet, darling, that's what she's thinking too. By trying to be selfless, you two are throwing away a great gift. Take it from someone who never found it, love is rare. Don't forget that just because you were lucky enough to stumble upon it twice."

"A man who lives by a river doesn't often think of the desert, does he, Ilham?" Kashaf had asked.

"Don't waste it, Azaan," Mom urged.

What was it my dad had said?

"God loves not the wasteful."

The sun was high and bright when I got to Madi's place. I took a deep breath, prayed harder than I ever had before, wiped my hands on my jeans, and rang the bell.

A moment later, Madi opened the door and stared at me.

"Honey," I said. "I'm home."

"You are such an ass," she told me, even as she moved to pull me into an embrace, her voice breaking as it was pulled between tears and laughter. "You . . . you complete idiot. I fucking hate you. I can't believe you almost left me. What's wrong with you? I've been crying for hours."

"I'm sorry," I said. "Really, Mads, I won't do it again."

"You better not."

"But in my defense, you said you didn't want a serious relationship."

"An eternity has passed since then."

"It was two weeks ago," I reminded.

"'Lovers ever run before the clock,'" she quoted the Bard as she pulled away from me.

"Damn, that's hot."

"Seriously, Azaan, jokes aside . . . are you sure about this? If you stay here, what are you going to tell everyone at the mosque?"

"I think I'm going to try the truth."

"That's going to be hard."

"Yeah," I agreed.

"And you'd be giving up a lot."

"We'll do what Jibreel said."

Madi raised her eyebrows. "What's that?"

"We'll figure it out. Look, I can go back for this movie when they start shooting. It's not a big deal. As for the rest of my career—"

"And your agent. Your city. The home you've made. Your friends."

"Right. As for everything else . . . I love you more than all of it. I want you more than all of it. I wasn't lying, Mads, when I told you all those years ago that I'd always choose you first."

She bit her lip and shook her head. "You have to know I can't promise you the same thing. I have Julie. But I swear, Azaan, I'll always choose you second."

I leaned down and kissed her forehead. "I'll take it."

Photo credit: Samantha May Photography

AUTHOR BIOGRAPHY

Syed M. Masood grew up in Karachi, Pakistan. A first-generation immigrant twice over, he has been a citizen of three different countries and nine different cities. He is the author of *The Bad Muslim Discount,* a Book of the Month add-on pick and an Indiebound Bestseller, and two YA novels, *More Than Just a Pretty Face* and *Sway with Me*. He currently lives in Sacramento, CA.